TIMESHIFT

by
Phillip Ellis Jackson

AmErica House
Baltimore

First printing

ISBN: 1-58851-433-1
PUBLISHED BY AMERICA HOUSE BOOK PUBLISHERS
www.publishamerica.com
Baltimore

Printed in the United States of America

To Dawn—who believed in me.

PROLOGUE

For all of mankind's hopes for a bountiful future, fueled by spectacular, almost-unimaginable leaps in technology, the world still reeled under the heavy threat of the killing ash.

Centuries earlier a world-wide thermonuclear war wreaked havoc on an already divided society segmented into two cooperative but separate nations, the East and West United States. With the conflagration came a rapidly-multiplying mysterious new life form, the deadly ash, that forced the surviving population beneath the earth's surface in a desperate attempt to stave off its lethal touch. Mankind struggled to rebuild its institutions in a twilight world of its own making where despair replaced hope and suicide became rampant. The social order was collapsing amid the corruption and inefficiency of their elected leaders. It seemed as if humanity itself might go the way of other dominant species that once walked the planet's surface—to live and rule for a brief reign, only to die off in a forgotten ignominious way.

Turning again to technology, mankind began a long, slow, fight for survival. Washington D.C., now "The District", became the focal point of this effort, where the discovery of Beta Light had inspired the people with a new hope for a better life. Scientists discovered that after leaving the sun, *Alpha Light*—the spectrum ranging from infrared to ultraviolet—split off and continued on into space while a new, hitherto unknown companion particle, *Beta Light*, was trapped in a sediment-like swirl by the earth's magnetic field. Because of its unique properties, Beta Light acted like a recording film capturing the images of the past exactly as they happened—sights, sounds, everything just as it was. Man could view the past, but not interact with it. Still, it was enough to replay the 3-D holographic images they retrieved, allowing the people of the present to share in a life that once was, and might never again be.

The discovery of Beta Light drove man into a frenzy of exploration in a realm never before accessible. Mysteries were explained, acts of heroism that had gone unrecognized were now revealed and acclaimed, and the crime rate plummeted as the ability to hide social wrongdoing vanished in the wake of a single Beta Light jump. With this also came an interest in the more personal benefits of Beta Light technology. Everyone had their own favorite period of time. Some people had ancestors they wished to see, others wanted to witness great moments in history, or just visit pristine lands unspoiled by man's presence or the ravages of his wars.

Massive resources from the public and private sectors were poured into exploiting Beta Light's properties for the benefit of all mankind. Three companies were created—B.E.T.A., T.I.M.E., and P.A.S.T.—that worked together to control what amounted to a "time viewing" process. But viewing Beta light images was more than a source of amusement and entertainment. The new technology was also a tool in mankind's liberation. With the wonders of this discovery came a glimmer of hope that they might uncover the true origin of the deadly and enigmatic ash and, ultimately, find a way to eliminate it.

Time viewing was unbelievably expensive, each year commanding a greater share of society's limited resources, but it gave people hope on many different levels. And hope was what the last of mankind needed.

Man would fight to survive, and his weapon would be the past.

"LITTLE SECRETS"
Monday, September 23, 2416 AD
09:32 HOURS

There are no secrets... except
the secrets that keep themselves.
-George Bernard Shaw

The Transmission Center was housed in an underground complex carved out of solid rock three hundred meters beneath the surface of what used to be Pennsylvania Avenue. Reinforced with tons of concrete, steel, and radiation shielding, it was used by the government as a command and control center in the years before the nuclear wars of the twenty-first century. Isolated, impenetrable to attack, the bunker-like fortress was a monument to the failed policies which had brought humankind to the brink of disaster. Now, centuries later, the same dark, foreboding, grey concrete walls surrounded and protected the *time viewing machine*, humanity's great hope and last chance to save itself from what had become increasingly apparent to the leadership of the United States East and West—the slow, strangulating end to all human life on the planet.

An armed guard stood at his post in front of the main access way, his holstered pistol more a symbol of his authority than an instrument of expected use. Weaponry of all kinds still existed, leftovers from the early twenty-second century when the manufacture of new armaments largely ceased. As the problem of the ash grew to worldwide proportions, mankind devoted more and more of its dwindling resources to fighting the spreading plague, instead of fighting among itself. The vintage weapons were reserved exclusively for the authorities and there were severe penalties for private possession, but some citizens held them secretly, nevertheless. Like the District Police Officers, who guarded key government installations, and their Tunnel Police Officer counterparts, who patrolled the byways and juncture points of the multi-layered passage ways radiating beneath the surface, they had little real need for the protection a weapon might offer. Respect for human life was ingrained enough into the public psyche that crime against people—or any crime at all—was as rare as the sight of a bird in flight or a free roaming animal of any kind. Having weapons was simply a way to give the people who held them some small sense of control over their own destiny at a time when shaping the future seemed increasingly beyond their reach.

The guard looked down the long walkway as a young man approached, his slow and relaxed gate giving him no cause for alarm. He adjusted his gunbelt while the solitary figure drew closer, maintaining a stern demeanor in spite of the young man's easy smile.

"I'm sorry, sir," the guard said. "This is a restricted area."

"I'm, er, supposed to be here," the young man answered apologetically. Not quite twenty, handsome, dark-haired, he fished through his pocket and withdrew a small oval disk, then handed it to the guard, who slipped it inside a reader. "Director Hollock couldn't make it. I was told to come instead."

"Thorndyke. You're new?"

"Yes sir. I just started a couple of weeks ago."

"I'm going to let you through this time. But next time use the access portal on E corridor, level 5. That's the one reserved for B.E.T.A. personnel."

"Okay, thanks," Thorndyke mumbled. Easing past the guard he headed into the interior of the complex. A nervous thrill coursed through his body as the immense building swallowed him up. While a graduate student at the Time Research Institute he had seen holo-clips of hundreds of jumps, read about the great men and women who created the complex—Knoble, Escobar, Sherwood—even toured its public areas as a school child on one of his many Kinderblock outings. Now he was inside, walking the halls and brushing lives with the hundreds of scientists and technicians who kept the massive time viewing machine in perfect operating order.

The click of his heels off the smoothly polished floor was the only sound Paul Thorndyke heard while he made his way down the corridor. Ahead lay another double door opening automatically when he approached. The noise and bustle of personnel on the other side caught him by surprise as he emerged into an open area cordoned off into room-sized squares housing dozens of men and women huddled around banks of humming, buzzing equipment.

"You look a little lost," a soft, feminine voice finally broke through the muddled workplace clatter.

"I am," Thorndyke turned, registering embarrassed surprise when he faced into a beautiful young woman. Her round, mesmerizing eyes searched his face as he stared back at her, completely captivated by her beauty. "I mean, er, I came through the wrong entry point. I'm a little turned around."

"Where are you trying to get to, Mr.—"

"Thorndyke. Paul Thorndyke. I'm supposed to observe the Haley jump."

"You must be a very important person," she teased playfully. "That jump is high security."

Thorndyke blushed and his eyes sought the ground, not sure how to respond. "I'm filling in for Director Hollock," he said, looking up to find her eyes fixed unwaveringly on his. "Something came up at the last minute and, er—"

"You don't have to explain," the woman smiled pleasantly. "It's just, we don't get many visitors here. At least not in this section."

"Oh? Where am I?"

"Archival Records. We download the images, process them, archive them in the proper files, and match them to other existing historical records. Things are pretty quiet around here until there's a jump, then everybody's on full alert."

"Sounds interesting."

"Really?" Her face became serious. "Most people want to be on the jump support teams, like you. But we can't all start out as 'very important people,' now can we?"

He caught the twinkle in her eye and returned her thin, self-effacing smile. For a long, silent moment they stood facing each other, their eyes locked, saying everything and nothing while others in the room scurried around them, until the young woman finally spoke.

"You're going to be late."

"Huh?"

"For the jump?"

9

"Oh, yeah," Thorndyke suddenly remembered with a start.

"Down that hall, three doors to the left. Next time, you might want to use the access portal on E corridor, on level 5. It's easier."

"Thanks, I'll remember that," he sprinted away, then suddenly stopped—almost slipping on the slick polished floor. "Wait!" he called as he turned to watch the woman's long, slow strides take her in the opposite direction. "What's your name?"

With a coquettish smile, she paused and looked back his way.

"You'll find me if you want to."

"At least, give me a clue!"

"Sharla," she said softly before rounding the corner and disappearing from view.

"What? Did you say... *Sharla?*"

For a moment it seemed as if he might follow after her, much to the amusement of two people in a cubicle to his right, but their muffled laughter caught his attention and snapped him back to reality. Spinning on his heels, he dashed toward the entrance way to the main control room.

The Transmission Center, the focal point of a jump with its massive power generators and rows upon rows of support staff and equipment, was alive with activity. Launch Director Abraham Held, a gruff-looking man in his late fifties, sat in a big, black, overstuffed chair surrounded by a dozen screens monitoring the upcoming jump. Margaret Zhow, a tall, thin attractive oriental with a quiet demeanor but commanding presence, was already dressed in her bright red jump suit, her helmet affixed over jet black hair streaked with strands of grey. A jump pack recorder was strapped to her chest, activated and blinking.

"Signal's five-by-five," Jerry Greene, Senior Flight Controller announced from his console. "Backup channels' on line and operating. We're ready to launch."

"Give me another second," Zhow called over the open link. "I want to run through one more check with my research support."

"Take all the time you want, Dr. Zhow," Held replied blandly. "Launch team, give me a status check."

"Power level is at three and holding," one voice cut through the hiss and crackle of kinetic energy bleeding into the room. "We can begin the energy spiral at any time,"

"Shielding's at ten. Energy boosters are on-line," another station reported.

"Telemetry's a go. Primary and backup systems functioning normally."

"Medical reports all readings nominal."

"All right, team," Held responded. "Hold where you are. Standby to go on my command."

Thorndyke stood to the left of the entrance way just inside the main launch area. As he watched the unfolding jump preparations, a member of the ground support team in a hooded, silver-blue suit walked over to him and stood, hands on hips, looking at him with a puzzled frown.

"Lose your way on the tour?"

"No. I'm supposed to be here."

The man's eyes narrowed in a disturbing focus. Thorndyke immediately fished the oval-shaped disk out of his pocket and handed it to him.

"What am I supposed to do with this?" the man said gruffly, staring at the disk but making no effort to take it.

"I'm from B.E.T.A. Director Hollock couldn't be here, so I'm here."

"Not *here,* you're not. You should be up there, in the observation lounge. You'll get fried down here when the vortex snaps on if you're not wearing a protective suit. The energy spiral throws out twenty trillion gigabytes of power."

"I'm sorry. I wasn't sure where—"

"Who's that civilian down on the floor?" Held's voice boomed over the external loudspeaker.

"Uh, I'm Paul Thorndyke," he replied, looking up toward a small bank of equipment jutting out of a second story overhang on the other side of the room where Held was seated.

"Get that guy out of there," Held bellowed, then focused on Thorndyke. "Don't you know you'll get fried if you're not wearing protective gear!"

"He's from B.E.T.A.," the grey haired man said over his communications link.

"All right—get him to the observation lounge. And lock those doors! I don't want anyone else wandering in. We're going critical as soon as Dr. Zhow finishes her prep."

"Er, how do I get there?" Thorndyke asked as the loudspeaker snapped off.

The support tech sighed and walked to a nearby door, silently pointing to the words **OBSERVATION LOUNGE** stenciled onto it.

"Sorry," Thorndyke mumbled. He quickly pushed through the door and climbed the steps two at a time, whispering to himself disgustedly. "Man, this is a *great* start!"

Everywhere on the ground floor technicians readied themselves for the jump into the Beta Light images of the twenty-first century. Margaret Zhow walked along a long, narrow ramp to the center of the ball shaped room and it was as if the world held its breath. All movement ceased, all eyes were on her.

"We've got enough power in the transmitter core to create a spiral warp," the loudspeaker cracked over the electrical din, the deep whine of a dynamo now filling the air. The room twinkled with lights as launch team members throughout the Transmission Center huddled over their stations.

Still looking completely out-of-place, Thorndyke entered the VIP lounge and walked over to the observation deck window. A seat front and center had been reserved for him.

"Mr. Thorndyke, glad you could make it," a slightly built man in his forties said, shaking his hand. "I'm Jerry Greene, Senior Flight Controller."

"Er—I don't mean to take you away from your station, sir. I think I've caused enough confusion already."

"My job's over," Greene laughed easily. "Held runs the final countdown. I get to watch. This your first jump?"

"Yes, sir."

"Zhow's one of the best. Researches the hell out of her subject so there's no wasted time. We can usually get her down to within two minutes of the event. You can't believe the energy it saves when you don't have to shift the jumper back and forth through the Beta Light strata until you find your mark."

The whine of the dynamos grew deafening and a crackle of electric blue energy built around Zhow. The clear glass-like window shook slightly with a low, even rumble.

"What's happening now?"

"We're creating a sub-vortex—locating the right layer of Beta Light and punching in the longitudinal and latitudinal coordinates. Feel your skin tingle?"

"Yes!"

"We're close to launch. Henry Sherwood's been working on some baffles to dampen the escaping energy so the ground techs won't need to suit up. These windows will protect you from any serious damage, but it's going to get a little uncomfortable when we hit full power. I just wanted to warn you."

"Thanks," Thorndyke mumbled, rubbing the annoying prickles from his arms.

"It's almost time. Look at Zhow."

On the platform below, the red suited figure began to glow with sparkling light as if a thousand iridescent bees were buzzing angrily about. The light burst into blinding brilliance and the noise rose to a thunderous roar. A tornado of bluish-white energy swirled around the slowly moving figure, her exaggerated motions becoming increasingly difficult to discern through the vortex of energy and pulsating light engulfing and compressing her.

"The core's at mass," the loudspeaker blasted above the hellstorm.

"Fire the switch to the pulse generator," Held commanded.

A huge, spiral warp sprung up and swept the barely visible figure down into the core of the Time Machine. Zhow's shimmering image disappeared into a black void like water spiraling down a drain. With a loud **POP** the room went stone silent.

"Good grief!" Thorndyke shouted, embarrassed by how loud his voice was and at the same time relieved he could hear at all. "Now what?"

"Come on," Greene said. "I'll take you to the telemetry console and we can watch her do her work."

"Are they coming?" Thorndyke motioned toward the dignitaries in the room who had turned away from the observation window and begun conversing among themselves.

"They can see it on the big screen," Greene whispered

conspiratorially. "They're just here for the show—friends of friends in high places. You B.E.T.A. guys get to see the real stuff."

Slipping past the smiling, gushing men and women, Greene took Thorndyke to a restricted lift. They emerged at the entranceway to a room where Held was already ensconced at a central console surrounded by an array of monitors.

"We're getting the first pictures, Mr. Held," a young support tech said. The oval office of the President of the United States struggled into view, wavy patches of distortion breaking up and obscuring part of the picture.

"Give me more power to the relay transfers."

The picture sharpened. Black and white images took on color while a miniature two-dimensional schematic slowly began to take shape.

"Where's the sound?" Held snapped.

Garbled voices broke through the static as ground technicians fine-tuned the frequency, rendering their speech and other sounds audible.

"Don't get your hopes up too much," Greene smiled. "This is real-time data. It's noisy and hard to see at times. Dr. Zhow is capturing the full-sized 3-D holograms on her suit recorder. When she comes back we'll download them in the data bank and play out a life-sized version of everything she sees."

"Can you talk to her?" Thorndyke wondered. Though familiar with the end product of a successful jump, the mechanics of capturing the images and bringing them back for viewing was a complete mystery to him.

"Yes, with difficulty. If we see something she's missing, we can get her to focus on it by sending a pulse wave signal to the wrist band molded into her suit. Just data, no voice. It takes a lot of energy and sometimes degrades the image, so we only do it as a last resort. That's why it's so important the jumper be thoroughly prepared before we send them out. See?"

On the screen in front of him, Thorndyke watched the image of a well-dressed black man, Peter Haley, 48th President of the old United States, sit behind his desk, reading from a small laptop computer. Zhow was nowhere to be seen, the eye of the camera her eyes, her steps its movement and direction. She moved closer until Haley's image filled the screen.

A door opened and Haley looked up. Gaila, his thirteen-year-old daughter, swept into the room in a fit of teenage pique.

"Daddy," she moaned theatrically.

An embarrassed secret service agent appeared in the doorway, stepping tentatively inside.

"I'm sorry, sir," he mumbled. His eyes darted between the bemused Haley and the young girl laying prostrate on the couch, one arm draped over her forehead, the other hand dangling toward the floor.

"It's all right, William, she gets by me too," Haley smiled. Rising and walking around his desk, he spoke softly to his daughter. "Are we're having a difficult time being the President's daughter... again?"

"It just isn't fair," Gaila moaned. "Why do they have to go *everywhere* I go? Why can't I just be with my friends by myself without some tall, overbearing, gun-toting *adult* always hanging around?"

"Because, you're the President's daughter," Haley soothed. "One thing goes with the other. They're there to keep you safe." He sat on the couch and stroked her hair gently.

"Well, I want you to know I'm so safe, I may never get to grow up!"

Haley laughed and allowed the little girl to snuggle closer, putting her head in his lap. "Oh, you'll grow up," he said wistfully. "Time will cause you to grow up before you know it."

Also chuckling softly, the secret service agent closed the door. Instead of continuing to focus on Haley, Zhow now moved closer to his desk where she directed her gaze to the computer screen and read a message that Haley had been reviewing when he was interrupted. Back in the control center the entire room erupted in applause.

"That's it!" Greene shouted. "By God, she did it!"

Thorndyke read the message, understanding now why it had been so important for him to attend. There, in the lower quadrant of the screen, was a reference to the location of the Shibboleth Project, a secret government research center experimenting with a new bio-genetic process to clean the air of poisonous toxins. The research was based on experiments conducted by Dr. Alicia York at the turn of the century that ended with her abrupt, untimely death in 1999. Using her work, scientists had succeeded in creating an entirely new species of hybrid plant-animal life that cleansed the air as a by-product of their own respiration.

It was hoped that the same process might be used now to help reclaim the planet's surface, if only the basic scientific principles behind it could be understood. Almost all of York's original research was lost in the conflagration of two atomic wars. Efforts to access the Beta Light recording of her actual work at the Fermilab outside Chicago were blocked by ambient nuclear energy, which blotted out segments of the sedimentary swirl. Now an expedition would be mounted to the Shibboleth site to see if any new insights could be gained. It was humanity's best chance to turn the tide before the every-growing ash swept everyone from the surface, forever forcing man to live under a protective outer covering or deep within the ground.

"Zhow's incredible," Greene shook his head with admiration. "Most of the records of that era were destroyed in the Little War and its aftermath. She pieced the puzzle together and figured out that Haley would be reviewing an 'eyes-only' briefing report on Shibboleth on this day and time. We've known from other records of that era the exact date of the first successful trials, but until now we had no idea *where* the center was located. Now we can go back and actually see what they were doing, maybe find a way to stop the ash before there's nothing left to go back too."

"Well, it looks like we've got our work cut out for us," Thorndyke smiled.

"You guys at Betalight Electromagnetic Technology Applications are the best," Greene offered sincerely. "We can research the hell out of a subject, but you need to configure the coordinates to get us in the right strata. Miller's Crossing, Pearl River New York—January 17, 2035. Hope this gives you enough to work with."

The sound of President Haley talking with his daughter flittered in the background, the compassion and understanding in his voice overtaking everyone's attention one-by-one. Soon Thorndyke found himself drawn back to the monitor. Zhow had moved away from his desk, her attention also directed toward the couch as she, too, became caught up in the moment.

"Want us to bring her back?" an assistant launch controller asked Held, who was watching the exchange on his screen. "We've got the data we wanted."

"Give her a few more minutes," Held said softly.

Gaila, now sitting, cradled her head against her father's shoulder. His words were a warm comfort to the young girl whose fingers entwined with his while he patiently explained the need to assure her security—and how deadly the world had become.

"How much longer does he have?" Thorndyke asked.

"We're at June 10, 2034. He'll be assassinated on the first of August when a separatist missile takes out his plane... one of the splinter groups that sewed the seeds of the second Civil War," Greene said, almost without emotion. "Then Witherspoone will take over. The son of a bitch will fuck things up pretty soon after that. Before Haley's death, the country was threatening to subdivide into different economic federations. A few had even begun claiming sovereignty from old Washington and were trying to set up their own governments. Haley was managing to isolate the real kooks and keep the country together when someone took him out. We don't know who—probably doesn't even matter. Witherspoone tried to cut a secret deal with the two strongest breakaway groups but that only emboldened them, and they seized Port Manhattan. When word got out about what he did, there was a national outcry. The SOB launched a surgical strike against some old Soviet state that was making noises against U.S. possessions in Italy and Greece."

"He thought the Little War would divert attention enough to ride out the political crisis at home."

"Yeah. But a few months later, they retaliated by detonating a thirty megaton thermonuclear bomb stowed in the hull of a ship in Boston Harbor, and then the missiles started to fly. Back then everyone thought we'd escaped pretty well unscathed. Just a few low yield nuclear strikes at some SAC bases in the Midwest and along the Eastern seaboard. But then the ash began to emerge. No one knew what it was at first or where it really came from. It was killing people everywhere, but nobody was connecting the deaths to it. The country was focused on repairing the damage to its cities and trying to hold itself together. It wasn't until a few decades later that the ash had multiplied enough to become a real problem, and the connection was made. But by then it was too late to do anything about it. People just tried to stay away from it."

"And then the Big War fed the flames."

"I guess it was inevitable. All Witherspoone succeeded in doing was stirring things up overseas. The people thought the hostilities ended with the armistice and Witherspoone's impeachment, but our enemies just used the time to build up their strength while we continued to tear ourselves apart. When the New Federation Agreement was signed in 2065 ending the Second Civil War and giving the country two national governments, our enemies were strong enough to attack. The ink on the agreement was hardly dry when the U.S. West refused to honor its treaty obligations to the East, not joining the war until its own economic interests were threatened. But by then, the whole world was involved in a full scale thermonuclear conflict."

"The fallout was like throwing gas on an open fire," Thorndyke sighed. "The ash fed on high levels of airborne pollution and began growing at a phenomenal rate, becoming more toxic to plant and animal life with each new mutation."

"Which is why Zhow's jump is so important. York's research, the fallout from the nuclear war, and the emergence of the ash—they're all linked. We don't understand exactly how the ash was created, but maybe using the results that came thirty-five years later from York's research we can find a way to destroy it. Put the genie back in the bottle so to speak." Greene's gaze drifted to the screen where Haley and his daughter were finishing their conversation. "There are times I wish we could actually go back and change things, not just watch them."

Haley's daughter, smiling in spite of herself, kissed her father's cheek and rose from the couch. Prancing out of the oval office she closed the door with a gentle click. Haley shook his head and chuckled to himself, returning to his desk and shutting off his computer. He leaned back in the soft, high back leather chair, turned and looked out the window.

"Okay, bring Dr. Zhow back," Held said quietly. Like everyone in the room his eyes were fixed on the clear blue sky outside Haley's window holding a brilliant white sun delicately in its grasp.

The picture began to fade, and as Haley turned again in the camera's direction, it winked out with sudden finality. Technicians held their stations as a growing whine pierced the silence and the vortex reappeared with a roar. With a snap of crackling energy, Zhow materialized on the edge of the platform, her red suit tinged with crusty flakes of carbon that shed like dust once the spiral warp collapsed and returned the room to normal.

"Recovery team, check her out," Held's voice boomed over the internal communications link.

"Abraham, I'm all right," she replied blandly, brushing the dust from her shoulders.

"Looks like we've got more of a burn than normal. Check the suit for surface degradation."

"Just a little carbon flaking," Zhow said while her helmet was lifted from its neck brace. "Nothing out of the normal. It's always a rough trip back."

"You seen enough?" Greene asked Thorndyke who was still looking at a replay of the Haley jump mission on a monitor to his right.

"Yes, thank you, Mr. Greene. We'll begin a Beta Light search right away for the right coordinates once we cross reference *Miller's Crossing* with topographical maps of that era. Sounds like it might be a small town or other out-of-the-way place, like they used to have in twentieth century Arizona and New Mexico when they hid the germ warfare manufacturing and storage sites from the public. Probably some kind of sub-surface complex with a sham building on top, like a farmhouse or grain silo. Since it's a bio-genetic research facility, they'll need access to plants and livestock without arousing suspicion. Anyway, it's just a first guess."

"Yeah, well, like I said," Greene smiled. "You B.E.T.A. guys just need to get us close enough to put a jumper in the vicinity. We'll do the rest."

"How far back do you want to go?"

"A week or two before the Boston detonation. We know Shibboleth succeeded in creating a new hybrid life form just before the Little War escalated. The project was abandoned shortly after that when all non-military resources were diverted to rebuilding the country."

"It's a narrow window to hope for," Thorndyke's eyes lifted while he went over the calculations in his mind. "If your timeline is correct, we'll have to be there literally at the moment of discovery to see how they did it. After that they'll undoubtedly lock the records away in electronic storage. Unless someone pulls the data up to look at it, we won't be able to access any of it."

"Well, that's not going to happen. The shutdown was complete. We know they abandoned the site and moved all the records to Atlanta, which, coincidentally, became the new capital of the Eastern United States. The city—and everything in it—was completely destroyed in 2066 when the Eastern Block of the Soviet Alliance launched their first strike, which started the Big War."

"Any chance they might have field tested the organism or put it in production somewhere else in the country? Most of the national reconstruction from the Little War was finished by 2055, if I remember my history correctly. With pollution becoming as bad as it was by that time, surely they would have used the discovery to begin reversing its effects."

"No. There's nothing after 2035. The truly virulent pollution didn't reach North America until just before the Big War began. Africa, Asia, Eastern Europe—they were all pushing their economies without any regard for the environment. For the most part, they were poisoning their own water and air, so it didn't impact us. Besides, the old U.S. wasn't in any mood to spend trillions of dollars, which was a lot of money at that time, to clean up foreign factories while ours were still being rebuilt. There was some debate about using the new technology once the trade winds began to bring the really bad stuff across the sea, but by then the country had all but divided in two. Neither the East nor West wanted to foot the bill, so the technology stayed where it was—in storage. No, Mr. Thorndyke, 2035 is our best hope of re-discovering the secret. I only wish Alicia York hadn't died. She was close to a breakthrough on her own. If she'd succeeded, by 2035 the technology would have been available everywhere throughout the world. Little War... Big War... none of it would have mattered. There would have been no pollution for the ash to feed upon."

"We'll get on it right away."

His attention again drawn to Margaret Zhow, Thorndyke watched her strip off her red jump suit and hand it to a technician. The body-conforming undergarment she wore was drenched with perspiration. She toweled her face and arms dry with a small hand cloth before slipping into a loose-fitting sarong.

"Everyone dreams of being a jumper," Greene laughed, noticing Thorndyke's apparent interest.

"Not me!" he raised his hands in mock horror. "Scrambling my atoms, shooting me into an energy spiral, no sir. I get terribly bothered by static electricity off a rug! I'm quite happy to be a numbers cruncher."

"Well, you're an exception, then," Greene laughed easily. "Come on, I'll show you how to get out of here."

"Any chance we could leave through Archival Records?" Thorndyke asked.

"Sure. Are you looking for something in particular?"

"Yes, Sharla."

"Pardon me?"

"Yeah—something in particular," Thorndyke smiled, following Greene toward the exit.

11:15 HOURS

Jim Robenalt sat at his desk, puzzling over the information on a small circular disk he held in his fingers. Thin and wiry, with deep, dark eyes and a finely chiseled face, he was one of the more popular teaching assistants at the Time Research Institute. Only one semester away from receiving his Ph.D., he was debating whether to stay at the Institute or accept an offer to join B.E.T.A. like so many of his fellow students. Whichever course he took, his future seemed assured until he stumbled across a confusing fragment of coded data. The mathematical language was unlike anything he'd ever seen, and he wasn't quite sure what to make of it. For several weeks he played with the data, more out of curiosity than concern, viewing it as an intellectual challenge to decipher its meaning. Tantalizing bits of knowledge emerged, but never enough to reveal its secrets.

Finally, he put the mystery aside to get through a busy week of grading exams. But then Ben Mitchell—a former student and brilliant archivist—was found murdered at his desk, and he looked at it again with renewed concern. Mitchell had called him the day before he died with a puzzle of his own, something he had encountered while archiving a Beta Light file. There didn't seem to be any connection between the two, at least in Robenalt's mind, but he wanted to make sure. A call to B.E.T.A. Director Scott Hollock, who Robenalt knew to be a decent, honest man, had gone unanswered. Hoping to bring the perplexing data to Hollock's attention, but receiving no response, he wanted another one of his students to have a look at what he had, someone who had an uncanny ability to piece things together from even the most disjointed information.

"Vid-phone, I want to make a call to Paul Thorndyke. Pull up his number from my call list."

"A link has been established with his office. Mr. Thorndyke is not available. Do you wish to leave a message?"

"Is it a private line?"

"The Vid-link is a department-wide communications terminal. Individual calls are routed to a specific cubicle, but messages can be retrieved through multiple access points."

"No," Robenalt pondered. "Get me his apartment. I'll leave it there."

"Accessing. I have Mr. Thorndyke's personal Vid-phone ready."

"Paul, it's Jim," he began. "I've found something... curious. I need to talk to you, but not over the phone. If you're back by five, meet me at Mickey's—third floor. I'll wait about a half an hour. See you. Transmission off."

A few seconds passed while Robenalt continued to mull the baffling scenario over in his mind when Betty, the portly, middle-aged departmental secretary, called him on the inter-office screen.

"Excuse me, Jim. There's, er, someone here to see you."

"Not now, Betty. Tell them to come back tomorrow."

"It's, er, the police," she said nervously.

"Police! What do they want?"

"I don't know."

"James Robenalt, this is Chief Investigator Kenneth Grimes," another face appeared on the view screen. "My partner and I would like to ask you some questions. Will you please disengage your security protocol and open your door."

"What kind of questions?"

"If you don't disengage your security protocol, we'll break the door down," Grimes said impatiently.

"I've—sure, no problem," Robenalt stuttered. As he keyed in the release code, he slipped the small disk into a slot in his console and downloaded its contents into an encrypted file. Removing the empty disk, he placed it back on his desk.

"Mr. Robenalt," Grimes said, entering the room with his partner behind him. "We'd like you to accompany us to the station."

"Why can't we talk here?"

"Look, you can make this easy, or do it the hard way."

"What's this about?" Robenalt swallowed.

"Come with us now and we'll avoid any public displays. If you resist, you'll be handcuffed and restrained."

Standing, Robenalt allowed himself to be sandwiched between the two men, whose grim demeanor only added to the heightened tension. A small crowd had already begun to gather outside his office as he was led away. Amid a buzz of excited, overlapping conversation, another call came into Betty's station.

"I have a call for James Robenalt from Director Scott Hollock of B.E.T.A.," the face on the screen announced.

"Mr. Robenalt isn't here," she stammered, unsure what to say.

"Mr. Hollock is returning a call from Mr. Robenalt from yesterday. He would like to see him as soon as possible."

"I don't think that's going to happen," Betty said, watching Robenalt and the two men get into a waiting car and drive away.

13:15 HOURS

Scott Hollock was a big man, with wavy hair and a neatly trimmed beard that made him look quite a bit older than thirty-five, his actual age. The Director of Betalight Electromagnetic Technology Applications, he was one of three individuals who controlled the time viewing process.

B.E.T.A. was a thirty-year-old company founded by Constantine Knoble and Michael Escobar, discoverers of the Beta Light principles, which made time viewing possible. Hollock was the person who oversaw the management of the company, allowing Knoble and Escobar, now in their sixties, the freedom to continue their research into the scientific underpinnings of the Beta Light phenomena.

Increasingly, though, both men had come to withdraw from the

23

scientific discussions spawned by the new field of physics they created, content to bask in the endless interviews and public limelight which followed their every movement. The closest things to true national celebrities in an otherwise anonymous society, they had little time to pursue new practical applications of their discovery. Nor did they have the patience to rebuff the challenges of a small, but increasingly vocal group of scientists convinced that the Beta Light images were more robust—and interactive—than the passive hologram-like effigies would seem to suggest. Rather than dignify the ludicrous notion of these maverick theorists that the past could actually be entered and changed, Escobar and Knoble at first dismissed their ideas with humor, then with derision, finally trying to silence the debate by completely ignoring them. However, the questions persisted, and the two great men left it to others to argue the fundamental truths of physics while they retreated to a loftier plane of public relations tours and extended vacations.

Henry Sherwood, an eccentric eighty-year-old industrialist, built the device which enabled a human being to be projected into the swirl of Beta Light particles endlessly circling the earth in a sedimentary-like swirl. His company, Particle Accelerator Shuttle Transmission, P.A.S.T., constructed the giant, hermetically-sealed above surface building that was also used to anchor one side of the giant dome covering The District. Its towering exhaust vents billowed heat and smoke into the outside environment, venting the searing gasses which formed as a byproduct of the enormous energy discharge accompanying each jump.

Although advancing age had begun to exact its toll on him physically, Sherwood remained a strong, forceful presence among younger engineers, who looked to his wisdom and leadership to guide their actions. So much of the machine was a reflection of the brilliant, innovative, constantly-changing modifications he made to its ever-evolving design that many worried it could never be rebuilt should it become damaged or dismantled following his passing.

The last company, T.I.M.E.—Transitional Insertion Management Enterprise—was a huge bureaucracy charged with managing the enormous power and personnel needs of the time viewing process. It controlled the assignments of all jumps into the past and was run by Abraham Held with tight-fisted authority. Rumors abounded that one day he would take over the entire time viewing complex, fed by the controversial decision to house all three companies in the same general complex. The close, physical proximity resulted in a blurring of lines of authority, which many feared was a first step in selecting a single individual to be in charge. Had it not been for the strong, dominating presence of Henry Sherwood, for whom Presidents would routinely sit and wait until he had time to see them, the indifference of Escobar and Knoble would, in the minds of many, have allowed this to happen long ago.

"Robert, get me Henry Sherwood on the secure line," Hollock called to his secretary over the office Vid-phone.

Robert stopped what he was doing and reached for a yellow tap-switch to the left of his horseshoe-shaped console. A ringing pulse sounded twice before the irritated face of Henry Sherwood popped into view on the center monitor.

"What?"

"Director Hollock calling, sir. I'm going to patch you through."

In the blink of an eye the screen blanked out, sending the call directly to Hollock. Moments later the polished brass door to the Director's office sealed with a hiss, blocking all entrance until the security measure was released.

"That's the third time today," Carla, another administrative aide whispered from her station across the room.

"Haven't a clue. Don't need to know," Robert shrugged, returning to his tasks.

* * *

Approaching the front of the ugly, sixty-story building, Thorndyke looked up. The words BETA TIME PAST in bold, iridescent letters protruded from a section of wall that was now outside the newly-constructed dome, visible through the protective covering as if a beacon to anyone still outside that there was sanctuary within The District.

The dome itself was less than ten years old. Built over a dozen years, it encompassed a fifty square block area of the old capital. Ash clung to the rounded surface of the outer dome like snow on a street lamp, blocking out portions of the sky here and there, but not enough to completely cut out the light of the sun. Still, with each passing month, the ever-present ash blew in greater concentrations across the pallid blue sky, building up in drifts where the base of the dome burrowed deep into the ground. The day would soon come, Thorndyke knew, when the ash would multiply to such an extent that the sun itself would become a memory. For now, though, he and the others who came out occasionally to walk the streets of the old surface city could still look up and see the burning white sphere that once gave life to an almost unimaginable menagerie of plants and animals, but now shown down on a planet too sick and deformed to heal itself of the infirmity caused by its inhabitants' own misdeeds.

The enviromask Thorndyke wore filtered the inner dome air, which allowed him to use the surface entrance instead of the underground accessway. Even though the visible deposits of ash that once soiled the streets of old Washington D.C. had long been removed, smaller, almost microscopic particles remained. Great vacuum pumps constantly stirred the dust and debris floating in the air or clinging to the sides of buildings, sucking them into enormous filters, which deposited them outside the dome. Hundreds of robot sweepers were also set loose on The District to scrub and clean, purify and sterilize, working without stop until the buildings and land upon which they stood could be reclaimed. Grass grew on the great mall, flowers bloomed here and there in beds of carefully tended soil, and small, newly-planted trees dotted the gentle slopes of Capitol Hill—many encased in protective bubbles of their own. The District had become a giant oasis of life in an otherwise forbidden environment, thanks to these tireless, mechanized brigades.

Arriving at the top of a long row of steps leading into the building, Thorndyke entered a featureless room and waited until the outer door sealed. He turned to face a pattern of blinking lights on the opposite wall, legs apart, arms away from his sides, hands open and fingers outstretched.

"Thorndyke, Paul Richard."

"Beginning decontamination sweep... now," a hollow voice returned. He stood still while a beam of light criss-crossed his body, searching every crevice of clothing and flesh. "Scan complete. There is no evidence of any ash on your clothing, skin, or enviromask filter."

"Great!"

He slipped off the mask and deposited it in an open vent, which quickly sealed shut. An interior door opened and he stepped into a busy walkway, immediately spotting a blond-haired friend, who rushed over to greet him.

"Paul! I heard you got to witness the Haley jump! How was it?" Quentin Cottle gushed.

"Incredible! I'll tell you all about it at the pub tonight. Right now I've got to report to Hollock."

"Tonight? No can do, *amigo*. Ruth's got the night off, and we've already made plans. They've restored more artifacts from the old Smithsonian, and tonight they're going on exhibit. Nahuatl culture, pre-Cortes Mexico. You know, Aztecs. I love that stuff. What about tomorrow?"

"Sure. You know, Quentin," Thorndyke smiled impishly. "You've been seeing Ruth since, well, our first year at The Institute. It's been four years. You ought to marry that poor girl soon and make an honest woman out of her. Unless you two just plan on partnering instead."

"Despicable practice," Quentin exhaled noisily. "What's the world coming to? If you love someone enough to commit, it ought to be through marriage, not a five year contract like renting a Vid-phone."

"I agree, but for some people having a contract companion makes more sense. Things were different when marriages produced a lot of children. It won't be long before we just harvest the essentials from healthy bodies, pull everything together in a birthing chamber and raise the child in a Kinderblock. Remember when we were kids? Kinderblocks were school, then we'd come home to Mom and Dad. Only orphans lived there permanently. Today, with the birthrate so low, real families are starting to be a thing of the past. I'll bet no one even tries to get pregnant anymore."

"You sound like you've given up on the world."

"No, just reconciled myself to certain things," Thorndyke sighed. "We can't change the way the world is, so I think it's best to adapt."

"What we do as a society to perpetuate ourselves is one thing, Paul. I'm talking about what we do as individuals! If you love somebody, truly love them, then it's more than a legal issue. It's a lifelong commitment that takes you through the good times, and bad. Marriage isn't just a temporary alliance, it's a communion of souls."

"Quentin Cottle, for a mathematician you're quite a poet," Thorndyke laughed easily. "You really are serious about Ruth, aren't you?"

"Yeah," he grinned sheepishly.

"You want babies and everything! You are a goner!"

"Okay... yeah."

The bustle of the passing crowd had, by now, drawn them away from the center of the hallway toward one of its pristine white walls. Quentin rested against it with his arms folded, cocking his head toward the accessway that Thorndyke had used to enter the building.

"Say, you come in from outside?"

"Yeah. I took 'The Walk'."

"Tunnel corridors and lifts would have been faster, you know."

"I know. I just wanted to see the sun."

"Can't say I blame you," Quentin replied philosophically. "I hear it's getting harder to see all the time—or anything else for that matter. Pretty soon everything above ground will be completely buried by the ash."

"Thank God, we've been able to reclaim at least a little bit of the surface, even if it is under a dome."

"I just hope they can *really* clean it all up," Quentin worried.

"There's been no trace of ash anywhere inside the dome for six months now," Thorndyke replied casually. "Longer, if you eliminate everything below three angstrom units. That stuff's too small anyway to get in the lungs and stay. It flushes right out before it has a chance to stick. Just think of it, Quentin. Before long we'll be able to go outside without a mask. Like a hologram of the years before the Little War—only this one you can touch and smell."

"No masks? You sure it's safe?"

"They're going to remove all cautions by the end of the week. Adler in Visual Records says there's going to be a big ceremony with both Presidents of the United States to celebrate the occasion. They've even got a Beta Light recording of the Washington monument and rigged a device to project the missing upper half that was toppled in the war. It almost looks like it's there again. You should go above, see for yourself."

"I'll think about it."

"Well," Thorndyke chuckled, "I've got to get going. Give my best to Ruth."

"I will. You know, Paul," Quentin grinned mischievously, clasping him affectionately on the shoulder. "You ought to find somebody and settle down, too."

"See you tomorrow, around six," Thorndyke smiled without acknowledging the remark, then headed toward the lift that would take him to the Director's office.

13:59 HOURS

"Mr. Thorndyke is here to see you," Robert announced over the office Vid-phone.

"Thorn-what?"

"He's here with his report, sir. On today's jump."

"I don't have time for—"

"The Haley jump, sir."

"Oh, hell."

There was a long pause while Thorndyke glanced awkwardly around the room, Hollock's voice and image clearly audible and visible on the desktop view screen. The other four administrative assistants stole quick looks in his direction, then returned to work with practiced efficiency. After what seemed like minutes—but could only have been a few seconds—Hollock barked a terse reply.

"Send him in."

"The Director will see you now," Robert said.

"Thank you," Thorndyke mumbled, moving forward in a daze.

The double doors opened to reveal a giant room with the Director's work station nestled at the opposite end. Thorndyke walked past walls laden with art and other priceless relics, giving the room a museum-like quality. A huge oak table carved into the shape of an eagle sat imposingly near a window that looked out onto the old capital mall. Hollock, almost swallowed by a wing-tipped chair matching the architecture of the table, leaned back as the young man approached nervously.

"Paul Thorndyke, sir," he said as calmly and professionally as his voice would allow.

"Yes."

"The jump was a complete success. We discovered the approximate location of the Shibboleth Project, in upstate New York. T.I.M.E. wants to configure for a follow-up jump as soon as we can pull the numbers together. Sir?"

Hollock sat with his eyes closed, his fingers pressed slightly against his lower lip. Thorndyke wasn't sure if he'd heard anything he'd said. His face remained passive and emotionless as if the extraordinary news had absolutely no meaning.

"Should I, er, inform B.E.T.A. targeting support staff, sir?"

"Yes, by all means," Hollock responded quietly. "Thank you for your report, Mr. Thorndyke."

The monitor screen on the edge of his desk snapped to life and Robert's face came into view.

"Mr. Sherwood is here, sir."

"Send him in. Mr. Thorndyke, thank you for coming."

An echo rumbled slowly through the immense room as the heavy brass doors popped open and Henry Sherwood entered. He was not at all what Thorndyke had expected, the youthful vibrance of his step giving lie to the rumors of his ill health and old age infirmities.

"This the one you called me about—Robenalt?" Sherwood spoke past Thorndyke as if he wasn't even in the room.

"No. This is Mr. Thorndyke who works in our targeting support area. He was just leaving."

"Robenalt?" Thorndyke replied absently. "Jim Robenalt?"

"You know him?" Hollock asked suspiciously.

"Yes, sir. He was my TA—teaching assistant at the Institute while I worked on my Masters Certificate."

"What kind of man is he?" Sherwood's words were instant and probing.

"Well, he's a brilliant mathematician, and a skilled computer programmer. One of the smartest, most decent people I know."

"I've heard he's a *social interventionist,*" Hollock said.

"Well, Jim has, er, strong opinions about things, but he doesn't force them on other people."

"Is it true or not that he wants to use the time viewing process to change our society?"

"Well, yes—he does," Thorndyke conceded, unsure of where Hollock was taking the conversation. "But lots of others do, too. It's a hot topic of debate back at the Institute." He paused momentarily, looking both Hollock and Sherwood directly in the eyes. "Surely Jim's not in trouble for expressing his ideas?"

"Depends on what he does about them, don't you think?" Sherwood grunted.

"Does about them? I've known Jim Robenalt since I entered The Institute. I mean, he's passionate about the things he believes, but he also respects other people's opinions. That's what made him such a great instructor, and friend. And I'm not the only one who feels that way. All the students like and respect him. Is, er, something wrong? Is Jim in some kind of trouble?"

"Thank you, Mr. Thorndyke," Hollock said. "You've been very helpful."

The two men turned and began another conversation that he was clearly not part of. Unsure whether to offer his hand or leave silently, Thorndyke mumbled his appreciation at having the opportunity to be in Henry Sherwood's presence, and then left as awkwardly as he entered.

15:29 HOURS

Brightly colored lights twinkled like tiny beacons, lighting the way for an endless stream of humanity moving back and forth in front of the brown-trimmed window. The cool night air was filled with random noises—honking horns, the distinctive clatter of internal combustion engines, a hand-held bell jangling in the distance—overlapping the quiet conversations of several passers-by. Most people, however, walked along the busy city street with stony resolve, their eyes riveted on a distant point and faces little more than an expressionless mask. Despite the festive, holiday trappings that dotted storefronts up and down the street, many people seemed oblivious to their surroundings. For them it was simply another workday coming to an end, and another cold December night creeping in to take its place.

Outside an upscale restaurant, two men in light colored coats and fur hats loitered in the crisp night air. Light from a nearby street lamp cast an eerie shadow across the sidewalk, hiding their faces while they shifted nervously on their feet. Another similarly-dressed pair stood a few feet away, one man smoking casually, the other's eyes fixed on the slowly moving traffic that wound its way along the asphalt channels running throughout the city.

Across the street, three other men watched the restaurant entrance with cool dispatch. One of them signaled to the others when a dark colored Lincoln pulled into a No Parking space in front of the Steak House. A well-dressed man emerged from the driver's side to scurry around and open the door for the car's lone passenger, a middle-aged man in wire frame glasses and a thin winter coat. Before he could reach the door, the impatient man opened it himself and stepped on to the sidewalk where two of the waiting men had already begun approaching him, their arms extended, the glint of polished metal reflecting off the bright city lights.

"No, God, no!"

The muffled crack of a discharging weapon sent Paul Castellano back against the car. Blood spilled from wounds to his face and chest while the driver, hunching behind the front of the car the moment the shooting began, was shot in the back by the other two men who circled around behind him. Across the street the three back up shooters holstered their weapons and watched the screaming people who witnessed the attack fall to the ground or begin running away.

As quickly as it began, the barrage of gunfire stopped. One of the assassins stood over Castellano's body and dropped to one knee, placing his revolver directly against the dying man's head. The single shot exploded his skull in a shower of flesh and bone. The gunman quickly rose and raced down the street, leaving two dead men lying on the ground as the wail of police sirens were heard in the distant background. Then, the picture winked out.

"It's hard to believe," Claudia sighed, returning the bright red holodisk to a dime-sized slot in one of the storage units lining the walls of the catalogue room. "Such a violent era."

"It's difficult to think someone could take a life as, well, so callously as that," Sharla shook her head. "But I've seen too many of these to know differently."

"There's another jump to Chicago this week, circa 1929."

"Al Capone, I heard. More gangsters."

"And pirates, cowboys, gladiators. We can't catalogue this stuff fast enough before they send it off to the Theaters."

Each holographic recording was carefully indexed and cross-referenced with similar material, giving researchers, government officials and the public-at-large instant access to the data bank of images retrieved from the past. When combined with the historical documents and other artifacts that survived the Little War and its deadly aftermath, they provided as complete a picture as possible of life in the past. In a world driven underground, relying on artificial light to see and synthetic food to eat, the years before the great calamity were wondrously mysterious. As Beta Light images became increasingly accessible to the public, a clamor arose for more and more of these pictures from the past. Jumps, once a monthly event planned with all the detail and preparation of a late 20th century space launch, were now an almost daily occurrence.

"Oh, would you look at this?" Claudia reached for a small holodisk left at one of the empty workstations. She placed it in the correct container and turned again to her friend. "I'll be glad when that new library is finished. We're running out of room here. Say Sharla—?"

"Yes."

"Who was that tall guy I say you talking with today? He new?"

"No. He's from B.E.T.A."

"B.E.T.A., really?

"Yes," Sharla met her mischievous smile with an indifferent shrug. "Lost his way trying to find the Transmission Center."

"He was cute."

"I suppose so."

"You can't fool me, Sharla Russell. I know you liked him."

"Oh?" she let an eyebrow rise. "And just *how* would you know that?"

"Because I know you."

The smile on Claudia's face had widened to a self-satisfied smirk. Sharla's own lips curled into a bemused grin, her changing expression conceding everything and nothing.

"His name is Paul Thorndyke."

"When are you going to see him again?"

"I don't even know if he noticed who I was."

"Oh, he noticed," Claudia grinned. "He left the Transmission Center through the north entranceway—you'd think he'd have used the access portal on E corridor. It's easier."

"Maybe he got lost again." Sharla fought to suppress a smile.

"Mr. Greene was escorting him. The poor man, I thought he was going to sprain his neck the way he was looking all around. You'd think he'd never seen a data storage center before. Or, maybe he was looking for something or... someone else?"

"Why didn't you tell me he came back?"

"I thought you didn't care."

"You are so wicked!" Sharla laughed as Claudia reached out to hug her.

"He asked me who you were, if you were seeing anybody."

"What did you tell him?"

"I said 'Sharla Russell can break any man's heart, and you'd better just forget about her because she'll add you to her list.'"

"No—you didn't! What did he say?"

"He said, 'well, you tell Sharla Russell that Paul Thorndyke is a man who knows what he wants, and isn't afraid to go after it'."

"Really?" Sharla eyed her friend suspiciously. "You're making this all up."

"You *do* like him," Claudia exclaimed.

"I didn't say that... but I do."

"Well," Claudia sighed theatrically. "I never thought I'd see the day that Sharla Russell would get all worked up over some man she hardly even knows."

"Oh, he's not just 'some man'," Sharla said under her breath. Closing the file she was working on she shut down the data bank. "He's the man I'm going to marry."

17:12 HOURS

"Dr. Emory? There are two District Police Officers here to see you."

"Yes," the white haired man replied softly from behind a cluttered desk piled high with research material spanning several centuries. "Send them in."

34

The image on the videoscreen went blank. Dr. Charles Winston Emory, Supervisor of Archival Studies at the Time Research Institute, slowly rose from his chair to greet the grim-faced detectives who entered from a small foyer on the other side of his office.

"Please, Doctor," Chief Investigator Kenneth Grimes waved for him to remain seated. "No need to stand."

Frail and elderly, Emory exhaled softly and returned to his chair. His skin was pasty yellow, hands hiding a slight tremble, eyes alert but fatigued. The cancer that was slowly destroying his liver had begun to spread to other parts of his body. He had, at most, another month or two before the drugs he took to fight the disease would no longer have any effect and his body would begin a slow, painful deterioration. The great strides that medicine had made in the last twenty years to eliminate disease through genetic manipulations had come too late for the men and women of his generation. Soon, disease and humanly imperfections would be little more than a distant memory—but all that seemed like a distant dream as Charles Winston Emory counted the days until death overtook him.

"Dr. Emory," Grimes began while his partner Ed Webber, a short, slightly overweight man with a receding hairline, stood beside him. "I have to ask you a few questions."

"I know why you're here."

"What can you tell us about Jim Robenalt? Why would he break into the Central Archives? What was he looking for?"

"I blame myself," Emory's voice was barely audible.

"You, sir?" Webber replied, puzzled.

"Yes, I should have known. I should have done something to stop him."

"Known what?" Grimes asked.

"Mr. Robenalt was an exceptional student. And, like most brilliant men, he was impatient. He was convinced that the time viewing technology should be used for more than bringing back 'pretty pictures' as he called them. He wanted more time devoted to serious research. Jumps that could help mankind address its problems, bring back discoveries to benefit humanity, not simply amuse it."

"Forgive me, Doctor," Grimes interrupted. "But Webber and I spent the morning reviewing the Central Files. In the last three years, seventy percent of the jumps have been to bring back information lost over the past two centuries—Medicines, surgical techniques, industrial science. I don't understand Robenalt's criticism."

"Well, that's just it. Mr. Robenalt wanted the technology used for more than mechanical forays into the past. He thought it was a useful social tool to police the actions of those who hold power or control the distribution of resources throughout society."

"Privacy laws prohibit jumps after 2379 when the technology to access Beta Light was developed. We don't want to use this technology to spy on our citizens. Only a DPO directive can authorize the collection of Beta Light images after that date."

"Precisely," Emory nodded.

"So our boy Robenalt was a social interventionist," Webber grunted.

"I'm afraid he was more than that." Emory took a deep, painful breath and looked away. "I believe he had been making unauthorized jumps into the recent past."

"How could that be?" Grimes was almost too stunned to asked. "It takes a team of thirty people to do something like that."

"No. It can be done with fewer. Much fewer."

"Are you telling me Jim Robenalt and some others were breaking into the Transmission Center and using the machine to do... what?"

"To be precise, only one other person would be necessary to execute a jump, if all the calculations were completed in advance. Robenalt was more than capable of managing all the calculations himself, particularly if the coordinates were for a recent event. All he would need was someone at the controls to insure that he be brought back before the degradation of the electro-chemical bonds holding his atomic structure together reached a point of no return. A human being can only survive in a de-atomized state for so long before reconstitution to a flesh and blood form becomes compromised."

"But what about the power demands for a jump? Even if he could pull it off with only one other accomplice, the energy requirements to make a jump would be so great that he'd be found out immediately after he returned."

"There is only a significant power demand for prolonged jumps into the distant past, where the exact timing of an event is uncertain,"

Emory explained. "A launch director may have to move the jumper days, weeks, even months through the time strata before the proper coordinates are reached. But something in the recent past, on the uppermost layers of the sedimentary swirl where a precise time can be easily acquired, requires only a fraction of the power for a normal jump. And if the individual is clever enough, that small power drain can be hidden in the record of the previous jump, or the one following after."

"You have any evidence Robenalt was actually doing this, Professor?" Grimes prodded.

"Evidence? No, it's just my suspicion. I wouldn't have any way to know for sure.

"Ed, make a note to interview the Launch Director at T.I.M.E., see if there are any unexplained energy drains in the power record for the last few month's jumps. Now tell me Professor, if Robenalt was pulling a stunt like this, what do you think he was looking for on these jumps? Was he trying to blackmail someone? Was he jealous of someone or something? What was he doing? This guy Mitchell was just an Archivist. What was so important about him?"

Emory folded his hands across his lap and closed his eyes, as if searching for an explanation.

"I don't know."

"Is there anything else you can tell us, Dr. Emory? Anything that might help us understand why Robenalt killed that man?"

"No, nothing. I'm sorry, you have everything I can tell you."

"Well," Grimes rose as Webber followed. "I think we got more than we came for. Thank you for your cooperation, Dr. Emory."

"What will happen to Mr. Robenalt?" Emory asked. "Are you going to arrest him?"

"He's already been taken into custody."

"And then?"

"He'll be tried, convicted and sentenced for the death of Benjamin Mitchell."

"Such a waste of a promising life," Emory said, shaking his head.

"Any life, Doctor."

"Yes. I agree."

19:03 HOURS

The door to the holding cell opened and a small, needle-nosed man stepped inside. He waited for the solid metal barrier to slide closed and lock him inside. Sitting anxiously at a short, narrow table—the only piece of furniture in the otherwise barren room—Jim Robenalt stared nervously at the solitary figure, who nodded awkwardly and forced a brief, fleeting smile.

"Mr. Robenalt. My name is Elgin Long, esquire. I've been appointed your counsel."

"Why am I being held? Why was I arrested?" Robenalt was instantly on his feet, facing the man, who placed his briefcase on the table separating them.

"Haven't you been made aware of the charges?" the man replied, puzzled. "I was told that the particulars of the warrant had already been explained—"

"I know what the charge is!" Robenalt said, exasperated. "What I want to know is, why was I arrested!"

"Well, the evidence, I presume. It's rather overwhelming."

"I did not murder Ben Mitchell! He was my friend!"

"You settle down in there!" a burley guard yelled through an oval-shaped vent that snapped open at the sound of Robenalt's shouts, only to have Elgin wave him away with a sympathetic flick of his hand. The guard's eyes darted between the little man and Robenalt, piercing the silence with their intense scrutiny before sliding the view port closed and resuming his post outside the cell.

"Now, I need to ask you a few questions," Elgin began, arranging the contents of his briefcase on the table while he prepared to take Robenalt's statement.

"I didn't kill Ben," Robenalt repeated in a defeated voice, before sinking back into his chair.

Elgin stared at his client, studying him and saying nothing as the anguish and confusion of his arrest and incarceration played itself out on his face. He had seen this same thing happen many times before. In a world where Beta Light technology made it virtually impossible to hide one's complicity in a crime, there were still a few people ignorant or deluded enough to think they could conceal evidence of their guilt. In the end, when presented with the actual images of their misdeeds, the accused usually consigned themselves to accepting whatever punishment the State meted out. But every once and a while they would continue to profess their innocence in spite of overwhelming proof to the contrary. These sad cases were made even more disheartening when the accused had as promising a future as Jim Robenalt, and when the crime was as heinous the one he was charged with.

"Within forty-eight hours you will be brought before a magistrate for sentencing, Mr. Robenalt," Elgin began patiently. "I need to prepare your defense. Will you help me?" Robenalt's eyes were fixed on a distant point, his mind racing, but his gaze a vacant stare. When he did not respond to the question, Elgin put his hand on his wrist to draw his attention back to him. "Mr. Robenalt, please. If I am to help you prepare for the hearing, I need your cooperation. Are there any extenuating circumstances that I can use to explain your behavior? We do not have a great deal of time to plan a strategy for your defense. You do realize the seriousness of these charges, Mr. Robenalt?" he tried to hide his impatience. "You took the life of another human being. In all probability, the court will sentence you to the maximum penalty. After that, well, except for a brief moment to settle your affairs, there is no 'after that.' I'm not trying to be unsympathetic, Mr. Robenalt. I could have turned the court's request down to become your counsel, but I feel everyone deserves competent representation. Even those accused of the most brutal crimes."

"I don't care what you think... or what you think you *know*," Robenalt finally replied. His words were devoid of emotion, but the intensity of their delivery punctuated the air like crisp, stinging darts. "I did not kill Ben Mitchell."

"Yes, well," Elgin cleared his throat. "Is there someone you want to have present at your sentencing? Someone who can speak for your character? A loved one, associate, close friend?"

"No," Robenalt sagged. "What's the point anyway? I've already been convicted."

"No one?" Elgin furrowed his brow. "I must tell you, in all candor, you face the gravest situation, Mr. Robenalt. Benjamin Mitchell, by all accounts, was a fine archivist, a man with a brilliant career ahead of him. Society will exact justice for his killing. My only hope in saving you from the ultimate penalty is to find someone of importance who will speak on your behalf. If not, we need to plumb the depths of your relationship with Mr. Mitchell and find a reason to help rationalize your actions, horrible as they were. In either case I need your help. I cannot present an adequate defense if you just sit there passively."

"My relationship with Ben?" Robenalt repeated, letting the thought mull around in his mind. "Yes—maybe that's it after all."

"Perhaps you could share some of this 'understanding' with me?" Elgin said, confused by the lingering silence.

"I appreciate your efforts, Mr. Long," Robenalt said sincerely. "I don't know who did this to me. But I may know *why*. I'm sorry, there's nothing you can do to help me."

"Not insofar as the charges are concerned, but let me at least offer the Court some kind of justification to keep them from imposing the maximum penalty. Help me, please. Tell me about Ben Mitchell. Why would someone want to kill him?"

"We have nothing further to discuss, Mr. Long," Robenalt said quietly. "Good bye."

"As your counsel, I can argue against this ill-advised course of action, which I have," the little man exhaled noisily, rising from his chair. "But I cannot *force* you to cooperate. I'm afraid my value to you is at its end. Guard."

The metal door slid open and the little man departed unceremoniously, leaving Robenalt somber-faced and alone in the cell. Outside Elgin's assistant, Janice Ackerman, waited for him with an armful of computer disks and printouts. Together they walked down a dimly-lit corridor toward the exit to the holding area.

"Did you discover anything useful?" she asked as they pushed through the double glass doors and entered the main tunnel.

"Very little, I'm afraid," Elgin shrugged. "He's still in complete denial. So, have you finished your review?"

"Yes, sir. His normal routine appears to have been the same for the past few days. Teaching, research, spending social time with some of his acquaintances. I've compiled a list of names of his closest associates."

Elgin took one of the print-outs and scanned it while they walked. "Nothing here. It would be better if he had someone of importance to speak for him at his sentencing. These are all students and academics." Flipping the page, his eyes focused on another name. "Who is this fellow?"

"Um, er... Paul Thorndyke," Janice said, leaning over to see what he was glancing at. "He works at B.E.T.A., in targeting support. He's one of Robenalt's former students. In fact," she continued, searching through another file, "—yes, here it is. The communications record we subpoenaed from Robenalt's office indicates that he left a Vid-phone message for Thorndyke earlier in the day, before he was arrested."

"Is he anyone important?"

"He's only been on the job two weeks."

"What was the message?"

"Nothing consequential. Just to meet him at the Microtech Library."

"Did he say why?"

"No. But from what I've gathered, they were personal friends as well as professionally acquainted."

"Well, whatever it was about, Mr. Thorndyke isn't going to do our client any good, unless he can pull a few strings in high places. Otherwise, I'm afraid Mr. Robenalt's days in this world are numbered."

22:15 HOURS

The cramped, single-room apartment sprang to life when Paul Thorndyke entered through the corridor door, sealing it closed with a touch of his hand. Three-D images of landscapes and open spaces framed its walls giving deceptive depth to the twenty-by-thirty foot room. To one side, the rolling hills of an Alpine view, snow-capped peaks rising in the distance, brought a sense of openness and wonder. Across from it densely packed trees of a primeval forest butted against a windswept prairie alive with tall grass and flowers. The captured Beta Light images played through a twenty-four hour cycle, dimming and brightening with the setting and rising sun. Even now, during the night, a bright full moon illuminated the surroundings, allowing him to see small animals and birds that occasionally passed into view as they searched for food, a mate, or simply took survey of the magnificence of their world.

"Good to have you home, sir," the pleasant voice of his Interactive Home Security Unit called from somewhere above him. "How was your day?"

"Exciting," Thorndyke said. He dropped to the edge of his bed and took off his shoes.

"Would you like to tell me about it?"

"Maybe later. I'm more tired than I thought. Any calls while I was out?"

"Just one."

"Going to let me in on it?" Thorndyke paused, glancing toward a spot on the ceiling.

"Certainly, sir."

A flat, egg-shaped monitor rose from a slit in the corner table and unfolded into a three-foot wide screen. Thorndyke slipped off his trousers and unbuttoned his shirt while the screen flickered and resettled, coalescing into the image of Jim Robenalt's face.

"Paul, it's Jim. I've found something... curious. I need to talk to you, but not over the phone. If you're back by five, meet me at Mickey's—third floor. I'll wait about a half an hour. See you."

The image snapped off leaving a blank screen that slowly began to sink back into the slot from which it emerged.

"What? Dial him up. Damn, I wish I knew Jim called."

"I took the liberty of doing that the moment you returned," the empty voice replied while the screen continued to descend. "I know Mr. Robenalt is a special friend of yours and that you'd be very disappointed to miss his call. He isn't home, and his apartment IHSU doesn't know where he is, or when he'll be back. Most unusual."

"Did his IHSU say anything about why he called?"

"No, sir, we had just the usual chit-chat. It's a 500 series model. They don't like to give out personal information. I don't even think the call was from his apartment."

"Well," Thorndyke grunted, slipping into bed. "I'll guess I'll just see him tomorrow."

"If you'd like, I'll ask some of the other units in his neighborhood if they've seen him tonight. Perhaps I'll get lucky."

"No, whatever it was, it'll have to keep. Wake me at seven."

"Bath and breakfast, as usual?"

"Yes."

"Very well, sir. Would you like me to order kitchen to serve you a relaxing cup of tea before you retire?"

"No, thank you. It's late, I need to get some sleep."

"Yes, sir. I understand completely. You need to be diligent about your health. Oh, sir, just one more thing."

"What?" Thorndyke replied wearily, lifting his head from the pillow.

"A registry unit from the Roosevelt Quadrant contacted me about an hour ago. It wanted to pass on a message that the file you requested requires a Level Three authorization, and your authority is only Level Two. It will not be possible to—"

"I get the idea," Thorndyke sighed, returning to his pillow. "What does it take for a guy to get a girl's phone number?"

"If you don't mind my continuing," the voice resumed. "The registry also said that an addendum was made to the personal directive sub-matrix governing the file's protocol no more than five minutes after your request was issued and denied."

"Addendum?"

"Yes. It gave a Mr. Paul Thorndyke... that's you, sir... specific access to the information contained within it, should an inquiry be made. I was alerted by one of the asymmetric relay channels connected to the main information network that—"

"Wait—she gave *me* specific access," Thorndyke smiled, propping himself on his elbows.

"Yes indeed, sir. But you'll have to initiate the inquiry again. I'm only a 650 series Interactive Home Security Unit. It won't accept my inquiries unless—"

"Consider yourself authorized."

"Very well, sir. I'll have the information ready for you by morning. Oh, and sir?"

"What now?"

"I don't believe I was supposed to tell you that the protocol had deliberately been adjusted to accept your inquiry. The registry was just being efficient in notifying me that an amendment was made so soon after your initial inquiry was rejected. It's really just shop talk among the IHSU's. I hope I haven't violated any confidences."

"No, it'll be our little secret," Thorndyke smiled, locking his fingers behind his head and gazing out the holographic window. "Close us down 'til wake up."

Lights dimmed to a soft glow. The almost imperceptible static presence of the IHSU ceased, dropping the room into total silence. Thorndyke stared at the ceiling, unable to suppress a smile widening across his face.

"Sharla *Russell*," he whispered to himself.

With a soft chuckle he flipped to his side and went soundly to sleep.

"IF WE CAN'T TRUST OUR OWN EYES"

Every truth has two sides; it is well to look
at both before we commit ourselves to either.

-Aesop

Steam rose from the cup of black coffee sitting on top of Margaret Zhow's desk. Cluttered with old books and scraps of newspaper, personal journals, and other fragments of the past encased in protective sheathing to preserve and protect them, the desktop looked every bit like the organized chaos it was. From these remnants of history, she pieced together the dates and times of historical moments that made her the premiere Jumper of her time. For over ten years the elegant, forty-year old Zhow had dazzled the scientific community with her brilliance and precision. Whether the subject was pre-revolutionary American history, the early days of the industrial revolution, or post-cataclysmic North America, her forays into times past had re-written much of the world's knowledge. Now, having discovered the location of the Shibboleth Project—her most important discovery yet—she was preparing to venture into another time strata and bring back new images of the once-living past.

"Oh, Margaret, sorry. I didn't mean to disturb you," an elderly voice pulled her from her early morning reading. Dropping a folder full of papers onto the corner of her desk, Charles Emory grinned an awkward smile. "I didn't think you'd be in yet. I just wanted to return these."

"Charles, please stay," Zhow called, pulling him back as he started to leave. "We need to talk."

Emory tapped the sensor pad on the edge of the door to seal it shut. "Privacy option engaged," a hollow voice called out over the audible click of the locking mechanism snapping into place. The feeble, white haired man took a seat on the opposite side of her desk, folding his hands delicately across his lap.

"There were two men in your office last night," Zhow said, her voice unusually edgy.

"Yes. They were from the Authorities."

"Authorities! The DPO—what did they want?"

"Investigator Grimes and his partner, a detective Webber, were making some inquiries about James Robenalt."

"What did you tell them?"

"That he was most vociferous in his belief that the time viewing technology should be used as a tool of social reproach."

"And?"

"That I suspected he was making unauthorized jumps."

Zhow stood up. She paused briefly before moving slowly from behind her desk. Emory watched passively while she paced the floor in front of the computer link connecting her office to the database of images stored in the National Records Center.

"Have they seen the jump file yet?"

"I suspect so, but they didn't say officially. From the tenor of their conversation, I believe they were seeking confirmation of things they already knew."

"This whole affair makes me very uncomfortable, Charles."

"I wouldn't worry," Emory said. "The Authorities have their man. Justice will be served, and we can all go back to resuming a normal life."

"Yes, justice," Zhow mimicked.

"The work you did on the Haley jump was outstanding, Margaret," he continued as if the previous conversation hadn't even taken place. "First rate, all the way. Why don't you take a few days off and get some rest. You look fatigued."

"No, I'm all right. I want to stay here, keep on doing... what I'm doing."

"Put this whole, unfortunate affair out of your mind. It will all be over soon, and we can get back to the business of making this world a better place in which to live."

"I'll try to remember that," Zhow's voice trailed as Emory rose and opened the door. "It isn't easy knowing that another life will come to an end."

"It never is, my dear. But what you did was the right thing. Without your jump to procure the necessary evidence, there is no telling where the investigation might have led. Take a few days off from work. I insist on it."

The door closed, leaving Zhow alone in her office. She let her gaze wander to a miniaturized holographic bubble, like an old-fashioned water-filled dome, sitting on a shelf in the corner of the room. Inside was the image of The District circa 2022. The pedestrian walkway in front of the White House was alive with tourists wandering by, posing for pictures and pointing to unseen places beyond the scope of the bubble. It was her favorite toy, one of the earliest images she retrieved from a long ago jump when even this complicated world seemed simpler. Watching the tiny people endlessly repeat their movements, she could only imagine what life was like when the country, strong and united, seemed ready to seize its own destiny. Now, only the hollow shell of a once glorious nation remained, weak, ever divided, a prisoner of fate unwilling to again test its own greatness.

As abhorrent as the thought was of one, two—even a dozen or more deaths—Margaret Zhow tried to take solace in the belief that what she and others were doing was preparing the way for a return to the past, in spirit and practice, and with it, ushering into the world a new age of human development.

08:14 HOURS

Seated at a console, absently scratching his beard while scanning the monitor perched atop his desk, Ed Kolby saw a familiar figure out of the corner of his eye searching through stair-stepped rows of the Microtech Library Archives.

"Can't get enough of this place, Thorndyke?" Kolby called out with a bemused smile, turning Thorndyke's head and leading him toward him. "I thought you B.E.T.A. boys pretty well kept to yourselves."

"You haven't seen Jim Robenalt, have you?" Thorndyke asked.

"No, should I?"

"I just thought he might be here. I called his apartment this morning, but he wasn't there. His IHSU wasn't any help—wouldn't even tell me when he left or where he went."

"Yeah, he's got one of those old 500 models. Those things won't tell you anything unless you're pre-authorized, and even then it's like pulling teeth. They're a real pain to work with."

"I've been looking all over for him, but no one's seen him anywhere."

"Well, it's only a quarter past eight. Hell, most everyone stays late and closes the place down. Me, I like to get up early and have it all to myself. This place'll come alive in another hour or so—but I still don't think you'll find Jim here. Doesn't he have classes to teach on Tuesday?"

"Yeah, maybe that's where he is."

"You haven't forgotten the routine already, have you, Thorndyke?" Kolby chuckled. "It wasn't that long ago you were slogging through the trenches like the rest of us poor slugs, then B.E.T.A. knocks on your door and before anyone knows it, you're heading for higher ground. You know," he continued seriously, "I always thought you'd stay on and get your Ph.D., Paul. Maybe grab a teaching post or a top research slot here at the Institute. Down deep, I never really thought you'd leave."

"Too much competition," Thorndyke winked in his direction.

"Me? Hardly!" Kolby's laugh was loud and embracing. "You ran rings around us, and you knew it. Maybe Quentin was a better mathematician or I had the edge when it came to third-tier isolinear equations, but you put it all together better than anyone. I suppose that's why B.E.T.A. came after you."

"It was a mutual thing, really," Thorndyke struggled to accept the compliment.

"Only Paul Thorndyke could describe five months of the most intense recruiting I've ever seen as 'mutual' interest. Jim sends them your paper on the use of multi-phasic quadratic variables to help isolate random-sequenced Beta Light sub-strata fluctuations, and the next day *Hollock, himself,* is inviting you to his dinner parties."

"Party—I met the man once."

"Yeah, well you must have made a heck of an impression! You remember we shared an office that semester. There wasn't a day go by that someone from B.E.T.A. wasn't calling to take you to lunch, invite you to speak at some conference, or just ask how you were doing."

"Don't exaggerate, Ed," Thorndyke blushed.

"I wish I was! I started answering every call with 'Paul Thorndyke's office,' just to save time. Seriously, Paul, it was an amazing few months. I thought you might actually hold out at one point, but I guess I wasn't really all that surprised when you finally accepted. The truth is, no one was. The golden hand reached down from B.E.T.A. to pluck Paul Thorndyke from obscurity, and damned if you didn't do what *any one of us would have!* You just did it with a lot more finesse than us other poor slugs!"

"Yes, well, anyway, if you see Jim, just tell him I got his message too late to stop by."

"What message?"

"I don't really know," Thorndyke wrinkled his brow. "It was kind of... mysterious. I got a call last night to meet him here, but he didn't say why."

"Finals were last week. Maybe he wanted you to help grade some papers, just like old times," Kolby laughed.

"No. It sounded serious. What's he been doing lately?"

"Oh, the usual. When he's not out trying to save the world from its own stupidity, he's teaching Emory's classes, grading Emory's papers, running Emory's errands—you know, important doctoral candidacy stuff. I'll tell you, the more I find out about all the shit work and nose-wiping I've got to do to please my committee, the smarter you and the others who bailed out of here seem to get."

"Well, I can't complain so far," Thorndyke's face softened, and he broke into a smile. "Particularly, if the next few weeks are anything like the first two."

"Yeah! Quentin told me you got to witness the Haley jump."

"It was incredible! Come on by the pub tonight. I'm meeting up with Quentin and another friend of mine, Brian Russack. I'll tell you all about it."

"Brian Russack? Isn't he that friend of Jim's who helped you get into B.E.T.A.? Maybe he knows where he is."

"That's a thought. I'll ask him when I see him. Anyway, I gotta go Ed. I'll be late for work if I don't get moving."

"I'll see you at the pub."

"Great. And if you see Jim, tell him to stop by too."

10:30 HOURS

"Your ten-thirty is here, Mr. Hollock," Carla's voice cut through the silence in the cavernous office.

"Send her in."

The tired in Scott Hollock's eyes showed as he stood from behind the swept wing desk and made his way across the room, greeting Secretary of State Lillian Dorr when she passed through the entrance way and stepped into his inner sanctum.

"Lillian," Hollock gushed, taking her outstretched hand and squeezing it tenderly. "So good to see you. What's it been—a month?"

"Three, but who's counting?" She allowed herself to be pulled into a gentle kiss before returning to her professional demeanor. "I see you've redecorated some."

"Every week somebody brings me a new artifact or nick-knack from the excavations. The Smithsonian can't handle the overflow so they parcel the second class stuff out to me, Sherwood, and Held. If I'm not careful, pretty soon this place will look like a museum, too."

"Not bad for 'second-class,'" Dorr smiled, fingering the lattice work on a gold-plated funeral mask retrieved from a Mayan expedition.

"Even though it's worthless stuff now, gold's still pretty impressive, I'll admit. They found this mask after we cross-located the site of a burial mound in ancient Peru. Held sent a jumper to capture the burial images, then the museum folks authorized a surface dig to retrieve the artifacts once we discovered the mound wasn't looted."

"It's getting harder and harder to work on the surface," Dorr sighed. "Europe, North America, and all of Asia are pretty well buried in ash, but the southern regions still have some relatively pristine areas. You can't breathe the air there, but it doesn't take as much protective gear to walk around above ground. At the rate things are going though, they'll be covered in ash within the next decade or two. Then we'll just have to content ourselves with cataloguing the things we already have."

"So, why the visit?" Hollock smiled. "I was pleasantly surprised to see you on the calender this morning. I hope things haven't slipped enough between us that we have to resort to this kind of thing to see each other."

"Official business, I'm afraid," she chuckled, a slight edge to her words. "Not that I haven't thought about pinning you down this way. Really Scott, three months and not even a call."

"I know, I know, I'm a shit. It seems like I live here at times."

"Well, you're my date to the Resurfacing Ceremony this Sunday. Atlanta and Phoenix are announcing it officially today. Robert's already locked me into your calendar."

"That's great. It's hard to believe the day's finally come when we'll be able to go outside again. Maybe I'll even open this window," he said, nodding toward the triple pane glass overlooking the Washington Mall, "—if I can get someone to break the hermetic seal."

"After the ceremony, you and I are going to sneak off and have a scandalous reunion in the Willard Hotel. I've seen the restoration and it looks just like it did in the 1880s. Imagine, sitting in bed in a surface building, looking out onto grass and trees in the Mall."

"Sitting?"

"After three months, you'd better think about doing some talking, too."

"Lillian," Hollock grinned, taking her in his arms and kissing her passionately. "You never fail to surprise me. Now to what do I owe this 'official' visit?"

"President Echeverria of the U.S. West will be traveling to The District from Phoenix. President Drees will be coming up from Atlanta to represent the U.S. East. It's the first time the two leaders have been to The District since the New Federation Agreement was signed in 2065 splitting the country into two parts. All of their cabinets and other dignitaries will be in attendance as well."

"What does this have to do with me? I mean, you said the visit was official. Want me to give a speech?"

"Hardly. You're brilliant at what you do, but I'd leave the public speaking to someone else on your staff."

"Okay," he grinned, enjoying the interplay. "You don't want my mind... and you already have my body present and accounted for. So what's left?"

"Is this room secure?" she asked quietly, her expression suddenly serious.

Hollock lifted his eyes to a slender, blinking probe protruding from the ceiling. "Room, inaugurate a Level 5 privacy clearance. Hollock, Authorization 2462-5."

"The room is now secure," a monotone voice returned. "All electronic and visual surveillance apparatus are neutralized. No one will be permitted to enter or leave without the approval of Betalight Electromagnetic Technology Applications Director Scott Hollock."

"Okay, we're secure. Now tell me what's going on."

12:22 HOURS

The noonday crowd drifted through the rounded tunnels, their colorful clothing seemingly illuminated by its pristine whiteness. As separate corridors converged into wide junctures of activity, sterile walls blossomed into dozens of restaurants and shops carved out of the surrounding bedrock. It was here most of the community's social interaction occurred. People ate, shopped, or enjoyed the Theaters that were created specifically to showcase the Beta Light images retrieved from the past. In a world where few animals survived and little plant life flourished, a person could enter worlds brimming with life—or at least the remnants of what life once existed. An old growth forest, a Midwestern prairie, the slopes of an Appalachian foothill, the images were vibrant and real. Only the absence of smell or the out-of-sync movement of leaves on a tree from an unfelt wind gave lie to the beauty which surrounded them.

Everything in the underground city was connected through a subsurface network of corridors and passageways. They were so much a fixture of everyday life, like roads once were on the surface world, that few gave them any real thought. Like capillaries branching off veins they reached into every part of The District. Hundreds of feet wide at their broadest point, their temperature and environmental conditions were regulated by millions of tiny vents embedded in their ceilings and walls that re-circulated air or added coolness or warmth. Every twenty feet or so, a square-shaped tile popped out from an overhead perch to bathe the corridor in soft, yellow warmth. The artificial lighting system was at least a hundred years old, more in some of the older sections of tunnel, yet it never seemed to require maintenance of any kind. There were no bulbs to replace, no working parts to fail, just an endless series of electro-chemical reactions that gave light—and life—to the people who traveled beneath them. Few even bothered to think any more about the rows of eternally glowing squares. They were simply there, serving as testaments to the ingenuity of man as he was forced to adapt to life below the surface, creating a world that mimicked the essentials of the one he left, but was as sterile and empty of purpose as this underground existence had become for many of them.

"You want to get a food bar, or you in the mood for something more exotic?" Brian Russack asked, a short, somewhat stocky man with a receding hairline.

He stood at the juncture of two connecting tunnels surveying the choices he and Thorndyke had. A senior member of the Targeting Support department, he had helped bring the new man to B.E.T.A. and was fast becoming his constant companion. After only three days on the job, Thorndyke had solved a targeting coordination problem that had stumped Russack and others for years. The simple intuitive judgments and almost uncanny gift for piecing information together that made Thorndyke famous at the Time Research Institute served him equally well in his new position. Many saw him as a rising star at B.E.T.A., even before Hollock tapped him to witness the Haley jump.

"Something simple," Thorndyke replied absently, his attention directed elsewhere.

Russack spied a nearby foodshop and grabbed Thorndyke's arm. He was surprised when the gentle tug met with resistance, pulling him back instead of easing Thorndyke forward.

"You hungry or not? The line's short over there."

"You go ahead."

"Well, okay. But we've only got a half an hour left, then we need to get back to work. Ballard wants those Miller's Crossing coordinates by the end of the day. I still need to cross-reference a few index files and tap into the central data base to refine my calculations. You know, there must be twenty others working on the project, not counting you and me."

"You go ahead, Brian. I see someone over there, by the fountain."

"Jim?"

"No, someone else. I'll catch up with you later."

"Want me to bring you a sandwich?" Russack called out with no

53

reply as Thorndyke headed off in the opposite direction, weaving his way through the crush of surrounding people until he had vanished from sight.

There were only a few empty seats near the fountain promenade, a popular site to eat and talk as the inhabitants of the underground world took time out from the bustle of their busy schedules. It was somewhat ironic that a society whose technology produced a seemingly never-ending stream of labor saving devices would be populated with individuals who scurried from one task to the other, always consumed by the need to push themselves harder, never allowing themselves a moment's rest. Even leisure time was carefully planned to maximize every second and seize hold of every opportunity. It was as if the entire society was afraid to stop—even for a moment—to reflect on who they were and what they had become. The busier they kept themselves, individually and collectively, the less time there was to contemplate the truly desperate situation mankind had driven itself to.

"Hello, again," Thorndyke announced, trying to mask the nervousness in his voice as he stood next to the round glass table where Sharla Russell and two of her friends were seated. A fourth chair remained empty and he pulled it out as if inviting himself to sit. "Mind if I join you?"

Claudia and another young woman from their department exchanged quick, furtive glances and stood almost in unison. They grinned at Sharla while their eyes danced between her and Thorndyke.

"We were just leaving," Claudia giggled. "See you back at the office, Sharla."

"You don't have to go," Sharla said. "Mr. Thorndyke probably just lost his way again."

"No. I know *exactly* where I am."

"You're very forward, Mr. Thorndyke," Sharla hid her smile. "Is everyone at B.E.T.A. as self-assured as you?"

"Only when we know what we want."

"Don't mind us," Claudia chuckled. "You have your hands full with this one, Mr. Thorndyke. Be careful, she's broken many hearts."

"Paul," he grinned, taking the seat as Sharla shot a darting stare at her now-laughing friends who were walking away. "And I like a good challenge."

54

"Oh, so you think I'm a 'challenge?'"

"As a matter of fact, I do. But you're also the most beautiful and interesting woman I've ever met. I'd like to get to know you better, if you'll let me."

"How did you know I'd be here?" Sharla found her mouth suddenly dry. Thorndyke leaned back casually, catching her eye and grinning contentedly while she blushed and looked away.

"I talked to one of your friends."

"Claudia? Yes, now I understand why we had to... forgive me, Mr. Thorndyke, but I don't want you to think—"

"Call me Paul. And don't be angry with your friend. I'm glad you're here. I wanted to talk with you, get to know you better. Let you get to know me."

"And why do you think I'd be interested in doing that?"

"Are you always this difficult?" Thorndyke sighed.

"Yes."

"Maybe this was a bad idea," he said, sliding the chair back and starting to stand. Before he could leave she spoke softly.

"I didn't say I wasn't interested."

The growing smile on her face was matched by his as he settled, once again, into the contours of his chair.

"Why don't we start this over again? I'm Paul Thorndyke. Call me Paul."

"Pleased to meet you, Mr. Thorndyke. Paul."

"Would you like to have dinner with me?"

"Yes. I would."

"Tomorrow night, around six? We'll go to the Time Pavilion."

"The Pavilion! I thought only Time Jumpers went there. Are you a jumper too?"

"Hardly," Thorndyke laughed easily. "But working for B.E.T.A. has its rewards."

Her smile faded to a puzzled frown when she noticed his attention drifting toward a table on the other side of the fountain. After a long moment's silence she exhaled loudly, bringing his focus back to her.

"Not even our first date and already you're ignoring me."

"No, I'm sorry. I was looking for somebody, a friend. I thought I saw him, but it was someone else."

"Was he supposed to meet you here, *too*?" Sharla smiled emphasizing the last word, but the teasing jibe was completely lost on the somber-faced man sitting across from her.

"No. I missed him yesterday and couldn't find him this morning. I thought, maybe, he'd show up here. I guess it was just wishful thinking."

"You look worried. Is your friend in trouble?"

"I don't know," Thorndyke said after a long pause.

"Well, I'm sure you'll find a way to connect. You seem to be a very resourceful fellow."

Thorndyke caught the smile on Sharla's face and returned it with a broad grin. The nervousness he'd felt earlier at being in the presence of such a startling beauty had long since disappeared. Instead, he felt more relaxed around her—and sure of himself—than he had with any woman he'd ever known. The chemistry between them was immediate and physical, but it was also more than that. He could feel in his heart that she was the perfect soul mate, a woman who could share his life as a partner and equal in every way. He'd always thought that finding a mate would be a long, scary, analytical process, full of confused and conflicting emotions, but what he was experiencing at the moment was so right and so natural that he immediately recognized it for what it must be. He wondered whether Sharla felt even the slightest way about him as he did about her.

"Dinner at six then," she said, their eyes engaging one another as if they were the only ones there. "I'll meet you at the Pavilion."

15:05 HOURS

"Secretary of State Dorr on the Vid-Link," the President's assistant announced.

"Scramble the signal and patch it into the small conference room," Jonathon Drees replied in a friendly voice. Turning to the others seated around the table, the white-haired, distinguished-looking man stood and nodded graciously, excusing himself. "This won't take more than a few minutes. Please continue and I'll rejoin you momentarily."

Several of the young staff members nodded in return. They had followed the charismatic leader through his rise up the political ladder, joining him in Atlanta after his commanding election the previous year.

Only two other presidents in the three hundred and fifty-year history of the U.S. East had surpassed his electoral total. Popular with the press as well as the people, he was widely perceived as one of the most dynamic political figures of the present time in either of the two countries.

"Lillian, how are you," Drees chimed, settling into his chair while the Vid-Link picture sparkled to life. "How's old Washington?"

"Magnificent, sir. I've toured the dome area and everything looks ready for the ceremony Sunday. Even the damaged buildings look remarkably well preserved. There's been a very aggressive restoration program in place for the last five years. I think you'll be very pleased."

"It's amazing when you think about it," Drees sighed dreamily. "Returning to the surface."

"Yes, sir. There's grass and trees on the Mall and plans to install a solar imitator next year to mimic the sun. The dome covering even has a bluish tint to it. It looks like the old sky in the holograms we've seen. Well close enough to it, anyway."

"So, I take it you're satisfied with conditions for the Resurfacing Ceremony to take place as scheduled?"

"From a logistics standpoint, everything seems in order. The District government has been most cooperative in accommodating our needs. And of course, President Echeverria's advance team has been over the same ground. I met with my counterpart last night, and he's completely satisfied."

"But?"

"Sir?"

"I can hear it in your voice, Lillian. What's troubling you?"

"I—it's nothing I can put my finger on sir, yet."

"So, give me your best guess. I trust your instincts, Lillian. What do we have, political problems? Echeverria's still insisting on more access to The Machine? Is he going to use the ceremony to embarrass me somehow?"

"No, sir. This is something more... sinister."

"Now there's a word I hadn't expected," Drees said in a concerned voice.

"There was a murder in the National Records Center, an Archivist. It happened three days ago. They've arrested the young man

57

responsible for it."

"A murder! How horrific!"

"He'll be brought to trial tomorrow and sentenced. The issue will be behind us by the time you arrive in The District Saturday night."

"But you're not convinced it's settled?"

"No, sir. Some of the pieces just don't fit. I met with an old friend earlier today. Took him into my confidence. We shared facts, but some things still just don't add up."

"This 'friend,' he's trustworthy? There's still a good deal of tension between our two countries, unfortunately, particularly where The Machine is involved. Sometimes, I almost wish the technology had never been discovered. I wouldn't want to see things stirred up between Echeverria's people and ours unnecessarily."

"He's very trustworthy, sir."

"So, then," Drees drummed his fingers. "What do you recommend?"

"I think we should increase your security detail sir, until we know for sure what happened."

"You think this incident is somehow tied to my appearance in The District?"

"I don't know. But there hasn't been a murder here in fifty years. The Ceremony is rekindling a lot of emotions about reuniting the country. It could be an isolated incident, or it could be something deeper."

"But you don't know for sure, and I don't want to risk a further incident over speculation. There will always be factions that want to force a recombining of the U.S. East and West. The simple fact is we have been a divided country longer than we were a single nation. The people of both countries are satisfied with this new arrangement. No, I won't let the hollow threats of a few extremists mar this ceremony. We share a common heritage with the West, centered around The District. It's the first spot of land to be reclaimed from that disease-plagued ash. I will go to old Washington and attend the Resurfacing Ceremony with my good friend Jorge Echeverria. There will be no increased security, not until you bring me something more specific. But I do appreciate your continued vigilance in this matter. If any solid evidence to the contrary arises, contact me again immediately. Otherwise, Mary and I will see you in The District Saturday morning."

"Very well, sir."

"Oh, and Lillian?" Drees grinned as the Vid-Link was about to be terminated. "Say hello to Mr. Hollock for me the next time you see him. I do enjoy the semi-annual briefings he and the other Directors of T.I.M.E. and P.A.S.T. give to Echeverria and myself on the management of the time viewing process."

"I will, sir," Dorr blushed, tapping a sensor and ending the transmission.

16:25 HOURS

There was very little to distinguish the living quarters from the work areas in Henry Sherwood's apartment. A large, cavernous structure carved out of bedrock ten levels below the surface, it was a mini-complex of different-sized rooms linked together through a network of private corridors and hidden access ways. At one time most of the innovative work performed by Sherwood and his staff took place within its walls, but as the importance of P.A.S.T. to the time viewing process grew, he was forced to seek other accommodations to support the growing size of his labor force. Now, as part of the large BETA TIME PAST complex, his company was a fully integrated unit of the giant megalith—and no longer subject to his absolute control. By retaining a small private staff and working out of the old assembly shop in his residence, he was still able to tinker with new ideas in relative privacy, exercising a measure of control over his own destiny that the advancing years had otherwise denied him.

"Henry, this place is wonderful," Scott Hollock admired as he walked around the central assembly room. Off in the distance, he could hear the machine tools of a small number of workers laboring in their private areas. Except for him and Sherwood, the big room was deserted, looking more like a museum picture from fifty years earlier than the still-active manufacturing plant it was.

"Don't like to spend much time at the main shop," Sherwood grunted. "I just show up enough every now and then to let 'em know who's in charge. Some of my best work is still done right here, inside these walls."

"Are you sure it's safe to talk here?"

"Don't mind them," Sherwood motioned with his head. "Not a one of 'em I wouldn't trust with my life."

"You may well have to."

The older man looked at Hollock, drinking in the unspoken words that completed the thought. "Come on," Sherwood's jaw tightened. "We can talk in my private quarters."

Hollock was led to a small room, one level up. Cluttered with mechanical schematics and half-completed models of strange looking equipment—the purpose of which couldn't easily be fathomed—he watched Sherwood scrape the debris off a careworn chair and offer it to him. Hollock took the seat as the old man settled into a second chair, its contents unceremoniously deposited on the floor.

"I think I'm right, Henry" Hollock began. "God only knows how, but I think I'm right."

"Well, this is serious, then."

"I think we should bring Knoble and Escobar into the discussion."

"Them!" Sherwood laughed. "Those two dandies haven't done a lick of work since they hired you to run their business. There are applications to their work they haven't even dreamed of. You'd never convince 'em anything like that was possible."

"But, they're—"

"They're worthless," he spat. "You're talking about a technology that doesn't even exist, least not anything I've heard of. You'd need a computer the size of the Transmission Center just to keep the image stable. Nothing like that's been thought of, least invented. I'd know it if it was. Hell, you might as well try and convince 'em that that fool *interactive breach* theory works too, and you can enter the past and change it up."

"I know it sounds fantastic."

"Maybe there isn't anything more to it. Maybe things really happened the way they seem."

"The Secretary of State for the U.S. East came to my office this morning. Her people have picked up rumors too. She can't tie it together yet any better than I can, but she feels it in her gut too, like me."

"Secretary of State? That the woman you courted before she took off to Atlanta to run that fellow's campaign?"

"You mean the President?" Hollock hid a smile. "Yes, that's her."

"Well, if she were here I'd tell her the same thing I'm telling you. There's no computer big enough to do the things you'd need it to do to change around a Beta Light image. Every molecule in that strata is bound to the others. Change one, and you'd have to change 'em all. The result would be such an obvious forgery it wouldn't hold water with a ten-year-old child."

"Unless someone figured out a way to do it differently."

"How, differently?"

"We've made some significant breakthroughs the last few months in translinear equations. We're able to pinpoint the strata in a Beta Light swirl with greater precision in half the time. I think it's possible to apply some of the same techniques to a retrieved image and alter it in small, but significant ways."

"Holo-blend the damn thing? Are you serious? You'd need a whole new system of mathematics to account for the shift-phase fluctuations that are bound to occur. Tweaking what we already know won't solve even half the problems. No, you're talking about a breakthrough almost as significant as discovering Beta Light itself. You can't keep something like that under wraps."

"Maybe not," Hollock sighed dejectedly.

"That boy Robenalt, what did that young fellow who works for you say he did?"

"He was a mathematician and computer programmer. A brilliant one, by Mr. Thorndyke's assessment."

"Hmmm, well, have you talked to him about this theory of yours? What does he think?"

"The authorities won't let anyone near him. He's going to be arraigned tomorrow and tried."

"If you're right about your suspicions—and Lord knows I don't know how you can be—there's a world of trouble ahead. If we can't trust our own eyes to see the past, what use is the technology? Might as well shut down every scientific inquiry and turn it into one big fun house."

"You always had a way of making your point, Henry," Hollock laughed.

"Now you better get on back to that office of yours before people start asking where you've been. Damn knows Held is paranoid enough as it is about any of us meeting outside the management team structure. He heard I went to see you yesterday and raised holy hell about protocol and procedures."

"I'll get going, Henry. Keep a sharp ear out and call me if you hear anything new."

"That I will, Mr. Hollock. But don't hold your breath waiting for fairies to appear."

19:22 HOURS

Sweet sounds of Herbie Chaffin's sax floated through the air, pulling at the senses like an exotic fragrance.

On stage the tall, distinguished-looking man closed his eyes and played a tune from the big band revival of the early twenty-first century. The mellow sounds of strings and woodwinds were somewhere in the background accompanying him, their images hidden by the dark shadows of the *Deep Ellum* nightclub where he and his band played their music in 2022. Retrieving music, culture, and other ordinary events was becoming an increasingly popular use of the time viewing technology, which competed with the demands of scholars for more investigation into the mysteries of the past. The full sized holographic images were projected onto a stage or an open area and like the perfect recordings they were, played back sights and sounds in vivid detail. Except for the slightly transparent quality of some of the earliest retrievals, the holograms looked and sounded as real and solid as the individuals whose images they captured. The past was alive, in all its depth and color, even if the future seemed to offer an increasingly limited and dismal path for humanity to follow.

"So let me get this straight," Quentin laughed, taking another swallow of beer while Thorndyke, surrounded by two other friends, who were grinning with anticipation, smiled benignly. "You're standing there in Henry Sherwood's presence... *the* Henry Sherwood, and you mumble 'glad to meet ya'—and leave!"

"It was more like, 'pleased to meet ya,'" Thorndyke chuckled. "And it wasn't a mumble. It was a clear, unmitigated choke."

"So what did he look like?" Ed Kolby asked sincerely, once the howls of laughter finally died down. "I heard he's a frail old guy. Did he walk in on his own power or does he have to use a hover-cart to get around?"

"I hope to look that good when I'm his age," Thorndyke said with admiration.

"Yeah, you can't believe all that stuff," Quentin grunted. "Sherwood's a tough old coot. He'll be around for a long time, you'll see."

"Well, I hope so," Russack said. "He's the only thing keeping T.I.M.E. from swallowing us all up. I don't want to take orders from Held or anyone else who isn't part of B.E.T.A."

"That's not necessarily a bad thing, if the right person's in charge," Kolby thought aloud. "We can't go on like this, doubling the number of Beta Light jumps every year unless we work some economies of scale into the calculation. Combining redundant operations and consolidating resources is just good planning and makes a lot of sense. Otherwise the whole thing will collapse of its own weight and then where will we be? The day will come when one man runs the whole show. Whether it's Held or someone else, who knows? But sure as we're sitting here, that day is coming. Of course," he shrugged with self-mocking humility. "I'm just a lowly grad student without a job. What do I know?"

"What do you think, Paul?" Quentin asked. "If Ed's right, Held's probably going to end up on top, one way or another. Sherwood's strong, but he can't run T.I.M.E. forever, and Knoble and Escobar only show up at B.E.T.A. for the Christmas party. Who else would it be?"

"I don't know, and try not to think about that stuff," Thorndyke replied dryly.

"Yes, that's Paul Thorndyke! The most apolitical man I know."

"And I intend to keep it that way. I do my job and leave the rest of the world's problems to be solved by greater minds than mine."

"Don't let this guy kid you," Quentin said. "I've known him since Kinderblock. Whether Held takes over or not, one day we'll all be working for him. Paul Thorndyke, Managing Director of B.E.T.A.–T.I.M.E.–P.A.S.T. Has a nice ring to it, don't you think?"

"Quentin, you're drunk."

"Not entirely! But drunk or not, I've seen you charm the frown off a DPO's face. Why won't you just admit it? Everyone knows you're a born leader."

"And you, Quentin Cottle, never could tell a lie with a straight face."

"No, Paul, I really mean it. And it's not just the beer talking. You've got a rare gift. People like you, listen to what you say. Hell—who else but Paul Thorndyke could get plucked from anonymity two weeks onto the job to represent Scott Hollock at the most important jump in the last twenty years!"

"Cassidy should have been the one to go, but he was sick. I just happened to be in the right place at—"

"And did I mention modest? Let me tell you about this man, the things he's done. Did you know he climbed out on a juncture point rafter in one of the tunnels when he was only nine to save a stupid kid... a year *older* than him... who was about to fall and break his neck?"

"You *are* drunk, Quentin."

"Maybe so. But I'm here today to tell about it because of you."

"No kidding, Paul," Kolby reacted. "You saved Quentin's life?"

"Anyone would have done the same thing."

"But *anyone* didn't. *You* did. Like it or not, Thorndyke, you're a man of destiny. You may try and hide behind that 'let the others do it' malarkey, but you're always the first in line to tilt at the windmills. Remember that time in the Institute when—"

"Enough, Quentin—please," Thorndyke pleaded.

Straightening in his seat, Quentin Cottle smiled and lifted a silent toast to his friend who touched glasses and drank along with him.

A small servo waiter placed some food on their table. Noticing one empty seat, it began gathering up the eating utensils to give them all more room.

"Hey wait," Thorndyke called. "Leave those."

"Expecting someone else, Paul?" Quentin asked.

"Yeah, Jim Robenalt. I left word on his Vid-phone that we'd be here tonight. I'm hoping he'll stop by."

"*That's* not likely," Kolby snorted, taking a bite of the tasteless food and washing it down with a sip of beer.

"What does that mean?" Thorndyke asked.

"You haven't heard?"

"Heard what?"

"It's all over The District—Jim's been arrested."

64

"Arrested! For what?"

"Murder."

Thorndyke was on his feet, almost knocking over a pitcher of beer on the edge of the table.

"Yeah, Paul," Quentin said quietly. "He's the one who killed that Archivist they found last week. It's been the only thing on the news since two o'clock today when the DPO announced it. I thought you knew, but just didn't want to talk about it."

"I haven't heard anything! I was down in Targeting Support all afternoon."

"The news said the DPO authorized a jump to the crime scene," Russack said. "They came back with the full holographic evidence."

"I know this man! He's not capable of anything like that!"

"I've known Jim for ten years," Russack continued. "I couldn't believe it either, at first. But Beta Light doesn't lie. There's no doubt about it. He did it."

"Who did the jump?"

"Margaret Zhow. She's one of the best."

It was as if the wind had been knocked from Thorndyke's lungs. He sat back in his chair, the shock and disbelief openly registered on his face.

"Jim Robenalt... is not capable... of hurting anyone. He's not a murderer."

"I'm sorry, Paul," Quentin put his arm around Thorndyke's shoulder. "I know Jim was your mentor. He was a good friend of mine, too."

"They're arraigning him in The District court tomorrow," Kolby said quietly.

"I have to leave," Thorndyke mumbled, again rising to his feet. Russack started to stand, intent on joining him, but Quentin tugged gently on his arm.

"He needs to be alone, think this through by himself," Quentin said as Thorndyke headed for the door.

"You know him best," Russack conceded, returning to his seat.

"JOURNEY TO NOWHERE"
Wednesday, September 25, 2416 AD
09:52 HOURS

He who, from zone to zone,
Guides through the boundless sky thy certain flight,
In the long way that I must tread alone,
Will lead my steps aright.
                                    -William Cullen Bryant

His wrists and ankles bound by electronic restraints, Jim Robenalt was hurried into the crowded courtroom. A dozen District Police Officers formed a human barrier to hold back the crush of frenzied reporters calling out to the thirty-year-old man, who struggled to maintain his dignity while he was placed in a clear glass booth facing the judge and prosecutor.

Throughout The District, video screens broadcast the proceedings to a spellbound population watching in shock and disbelief. There was so little crime in the twenty-fifth century that even mundane disturbances—public drunkenness, petty vandalism, the rare domestic dispute—were newsworthy events in their own right. No one could remember the last time a charge of assault, let alone *murder*, had been brought against anyone.

"Is the prosecution prepared to present evidence in this matter?" the judge spoke over a restless din which hung over the courtroom, bringing immediate quiet to the media and spectators alike.

"Yes, your honor, we are. If the Court please, the defendant is accused of the intentional murder of Benjamin Warren Mitchell, Senior Archivist in the National Records Center, on the night of September 21, 2416."

"How does the defendant respond to this charge?"

"I didn't kill anyone," Robenalt protested defeatedly.

"The evidence, your honor, is incontrovertible," the prosecutor continued. "A special jump was authorized to 22:14 hours on the date at issue. Beta Light recordings were retrieved and will be presented to the Court as proof of the defendant's guilt."

It was almost impossible to find an opening into the crowded courtroom, but Paul Thorndyke pushed his way past the logjam of people blocking the door and forced his way inside. He could see the anguish in Jim Robenalt's eyes as the even-toned prosecutor paced the area in front of the judge's bench. No counsel for the defense was present, not because of any inherent injustice in the court's proceedings, but due to basic reforms introduced into the criminal justice system many decades ago. It was no longer the job of a prosecutor to seek convictions of those charged with a crime. Instead, they "prosecuted" the facts of a case—allowing video, audio, DNA, and forensic evidence to establish an individual's guilt or innocence to society's satisfaction. Thus the innocent were cleared of false charges, and the guilty proven so beyond a reasonable doubt, without the capriciousness of human emotion tainting the verdict. A defendant appeared in court not to weigh the evidence of his crimes, for that had already been established, but after a public viewing of the evidence to allow for mitigating factors to be introduced that might influence the particulars of his sentence.

"If the Court please," the prosecutor began, "I would like to play a holo-record of the events in question. It will clearly establish the defendant's criminal culpability so that we may proceed to the sentencing phase of the trial. I must warn the Court that the images are particularly brutal and caution those watching it to exercise their judgment in viewing the evidence as it is presented."

All eyes focused on a twenty-by-thirty foot space at the center of the room. The lights in the empty space grew dim and the image of Benjamin Mitchell shimmered into view. Hunched over a table top viewer in the catalogue room he studied the miniature replay from a Beta Light file flickering out of view.

"This is the murdered Archivist, Benjamin Warren Mitchell," the prosecutor's voice sounded in the background, "three minutes before his death at the hands of James Robenalt."

"What is that file he is viewing?" the judge asked.

"Nothing of consequence, your honor. Archivist Mitchell was very conscientious about maintaining his records. On the night in question, he was reviewing a recent batch of Beta Light recordings to prepare their further cataloguing and cross-indexing with the master files."

Dark-haired, slightly built with a pleasant, easy going personality, Mitchell leaned back in his chair and rubbed his eyes. Reacting to the sound of footsteps he turned to face someone who had walked into the room. Hidden by deep shadows in the dimly-lit room, the person's identity, even sex, could not immediately be discerned.

"Oh, hi," Mitchell grinned awkwardly. "Didn't hear you come in."

"You're here late," Robenalt's voice could be clearly heard.

"Yeah, just finishing up." He took the disk out of the machine and slipped it into one of the storage units next to his console as the shadowy figure, dressed in black, moved toward his desk. From Mitchell's body language, it was evident that he was uncomfortable being in the other man's presence. "Like I said, I was just getting ready to go."

Still hidden by the shadows, the visitor passed his hand over a sensor point and dimmed the lights further. He moved steadily forward, approaching the now-standing Mitchell—his face lit by the table top viewer—who reacted in obvious fear.

"You... know why I'm here."

"Yes," Mitchell's voice quivered. "I know about the unauthorized jumps. I stumbled across a discarded file in the Central Archives two weeks ago, something you meant to delete, but overlooked because it was so small—just a fragment of a larger file. If I were looking for it, I'd never have known it was there. It wasn't encrypted like the others I found when I knew what to look for."

"A mistake."

"Yes, but it told me enough. I know what you're doing, and you have to be stopped."

"You're going to... report me."

"I should have gone to the authorities before. I just couldn't believe it was possible."

"Can't let you do that."

Mitchell started to push past him, but the still-shadowy figure grabbed him by the arm and swung him around roughly.

"It's over!" Mitchell shouted, yanking his arm free. *"I* know about it! It's only a matter of time before *others* find out too! It's—" The image flickered, then reset, like a video recording playing through a damaged section of tape.

"The Beta Light recording became degraded at this point, your honor," the prosecutor explained. "The last five seconds of Archivist Mitchell's statement were not retrieved, but all subsequent action was fully captured. Efforts are presently underway to compensate for and remove the interference. The final court transcript will reflect the full seven minute recording."

"Very well, proceed."

The two figures began to struggle, crashing into equipment as Mitchell flailed about helplessly, trying to defend himself against Robenalt's sudden attack. It was difficult to see in the darkened room, but the guttural, gasping sounds that came from Ben Mitchell were sickeningly real. Staggering into a swath of light from one of the small overhead guide lamps that lit the exitway, the magnitude of his injuries were clear to see. His throat spilled blood from a deep, spurting gash along the side of his neck. Amid audible gasps from reporters and spectators alike, Mitchell collapsed against a wall support and then fell to the floor with a heavy thud.

Into the light stepped the shadowy figure, blood dripping from a knife he held in his hand. Jim Robenalt's face was strangely serene while he stood surveying the gasping figure writhing on the floor. The holographic image wavered, then dissolved in finality, returning the courtroom to its normal state.

"The people have presented their evidence, your honor," the prosecutor spoke solemnly. "The Beta Light recordings are incontrovertible. We ask the state to impose the maximum penalty allowed by law."

There was no sound in the courtroom, not even the whisper of muffled speech. All eyes focused on the clear glass booth as Robenalt turned toward the crowd, his face blank and expressionless. His eyes met Thorndyke's and he shook his head as if to deny what all had seen. Thorndyke let his gaze drift downward, unable to look his friend in the face. Before him and all other citizens of The District, the proof of his guilt was beyond question.

"Mr. Robenalt," the judge said quietly. "Before I impose sentence, you have the right to make a statement."

Slowly, as if weighed down by a great chain, Robenalt faced the judge and prosecutor, his mouth struggling to form words, but saying nothing. When he did speak it was in a soft, almost passive voice. He knew there was little, if anything, he could say or do to alter the course of fate that was about to befall him.

"I did not kill Ben Mitchell. He was my friend."

"The Beta Light images prove you are his murderer," the judge stated flatly. "You have an opportunity, under law, to give the Court some reason to explain your actions. I will listen to whatever mitigating circumstances you may offer, but I will not retry the basic facts of this case. What have you to say to give account for your actions?"

"I didn't kill Ben. It wasn't me."

"James Robenalt," the judge said, bringing the proceedings to a close. "You have been found guilty of the heinous crime of murder against a fellow human being. For this you will pay the ultimate price under the law. Do you have a choice for the execution of your sentence?"

"Today. An hour ago. I want to stay in this time strata, here, in The District."

A hush fell over the courtroom while the prosecutor and judge quietly conferred.

"The court will grant your request. You are to be taken immediately to the Transmission Center where your body will be demolecularized and inserted into a Beta Light strata one hour prior to that time. You will remain in this transitional state until reconstitution to flesh and blood is no longer possible. You will live out the remainder of your conscious existence in stasis, neither dead nor alive, existing as thought without substance, until God, having mercy on your immortal soul, calls you to your final judgment. Before I conclude these proceedings, is there anyone with whom you wish to spend your remaining few moments—a loved one, family member, friend? The Court will grant you thirty minutes to conclude your affairs."

"Yes, your honor. I do want to see someone."

"If you will give their name to— "

"He's already here. Paul Thorndyke."

The words were like fists slammed into his chest, taking away his breath. Everyone's eyes were riveted on him as Thorndyke, still in shock, pressed his way to the front of the courtroom. The judge motioned him toward the bench.

"Very well. The proceedings are adjourned. Mr. Thorndyke, if you'll please accompany these gentlemen into the other room."

A phalanx of District Police Officers ushered Robenalt out of his booth, sweeping Thorndyke into the rushing stream of arms and legs that pushed back into the secured area of the courtroom. The judge's gavel sounded sharply, almost drowned out by the clamor of overlapping voices as once again the crowded room was returned to bedlam.

11:02 HOURS

"Thirty minutes," the guard announced brusquely. "Finish your business, and be quick. If it was up to me, I'd have sent you back to the beginning of time and let you rot there the second they found you guilty."

Robenalt barely showed any reaction while the guard deactivated his bonds, leaving him alone with Thorndyke in the windowless room. As the solid white door closed with an echoing thud, they could hear the slight, humming buzz of the security field generator activated on the other side, sealing them inside.

For a long time neither man spoke. Thorndyke watched with puzzled concern as Robenalt stared into the distance, his eyes fixed on nothing, his body seemingly frozen where he stood. Condemned to an existence without meaning—a living hologram unable to interact with his surroundings—the fate he faced was, in many ways, more terrible than death. No one knew how long the human mind would survive once the body that encased it could no longer be retrieved. Days, months, years—an eternity? Robenalt would be able to see and hear everything around him, be a part of the life he once knew, but he would be robbed of any ability to interact with the people he observed. Were he faced with a similar choice, Thorndyke didn't know if he could have chosen a time period so close to his own. Would it be a comfort to watch the people he once knew grow old as they lived their lives, or a torment to see them, knowing he could never again be a part of their world—any world?

"I didn't kill Ben," Robenalt began slowly, still facing away from Thorndyke. "I know what the Beta Light showed, but I was never there. I was alone, at home, in my apartment." His upper body rigid and unmoving, he turned his head like an automated doll, seeking Thorndyke's eyes and locking onto them. "Do you believe me?"

"Yes," Thorndyke replied in a barely audible voice. A thin smile pierced Robenalt's lips.

"No. You always were a bad liar. But I am telling you the truth. I'm not a murderer."

"Jim, help me," Thorndyke exhaled mournfully. "Tell me something, give me something I can use to get you out of this. I don't understand any of this either. I know you couldn't do that, but I saw... we all saw—"

"The images were changed, somehow. I don't know how."

"Changed? That's not possible!"

"I don't have all the pieces yet, but they're there in my mind. I need your help, Paul."

"I'll do anything I can, but you've got to help me too! What does Ben have to do with this? Why would somebody want to kill him? And why frame you for the murder? You guys were friends."

"The people who did this to me, they'll come after you, too," Robenalt said softly. "It's dangerous. Maybe deadly."

"I'm not afraid."

"You *should* be." The words were cold and sent a chill through Thorndyke, who kept his eyes locked on Robenalt's piercing gaze.

"If what you say is true, I'll find a way to get the truth out."

His face transforming with emotion, Robenalt choked back tears as he and Thorndyke grasped hands, then pulled each other into a crushing hug. They both knew that even if he was successful, there was probably nothing anyone could do to rescue him from the twilight world he had been condemned to. Thorndyke would be putting himself at risk to clear his name and right a grave injustice, but Robenalt's fate would be sealed forever.

"I found something strange a few weeks ago," Robenalt said quietly. "I tried to make sense of it myself, but I couldn't put it together. After Ben's death, I started to think about it differently and some pieces began to fall in place—but I still couldn't see the whole picture. I'm still not sure what it is, but I know it's connected to this somehow."

"What is it? Where is it?"

"I downloaded it into a hidden file in the Central Archives. No one can access it but me, unless they have the code. I can't give it to you; there is not enough time. You'll have to decrypt it. Once you do, you'll see everything I know. It's part of the puzzle. Piece it together, find out who did this to me—who really killed Ben."

"This file, where—"

"You'll find it. Think back to the work that you did for me last summer. You'll know where to look."

"Time's up," a guard announced unceremoniously, entering the room with a contingent of somber-faced support techs, who had come to prepare the prisoner for his jump.

Robenalt was handed a bright red suit without a jump pack, which he put on with as much dignity as he could muster. Drinking in his last breath of fresh air, he stood passively while a clear bubble-like helmet was fitted over his head and sealed into place. As the support techs working on him made the final adjustments to his suit, he looked at Thorndyke and mouthed a silent goodbye.

"Are you ready, Mr. Robenalt?" the judge intoned, standing in the outer corridor.

Robenalt nodded weakly. Thorndyke's eyes were so clouded by tears that he could barely see his friend being led in chains through the open door. A barrage of flashing lights and overlapping shouts met his appearance as a second guard, himself deeply affected by the unfolding drama, placed his hand on Thorndyke's shoulder.

"Are you going to witness the—"

"Execution?" Thorndyke replied automatically.

"I know he was your friend," the man said.

"I'm sorry," Thorndyke mumbled. "Yes, I want to be there, need... to be there."

Silently, the guard led him to the observation booth overlooking the main launch area. A sober delegation of elected officials and judicial representatives had already taken their place, each pair of eyes riveted on the red-suited figure now standing at the center of the ball-shaped room. Energy from the unfolding spiral had already charged the air,

73

causing most to back away uncomfortably from the clear glass barrier separating them from the room below. Only Thorndyke, oblivious to the painful prickles attacking his flesh, stood passively next to the glass.

"We're one minute from launch," the voice of Abraham Held broke through the static-charged air. "Begin final countdown on my mark."

To the left of the observation booth was a communications monitor broadcasting the unfolding scene throughout The District. Off camera a barely audible announcer described the final seconds of Jim Robenalt's life.

"Once inserted into the spiral, convicted murderer James Robenalt will be transported one hour into the past. After a final systems check to insure that he is properly stabilized in the correct time strata, jump officials will close the vortex without retrieving him from the Beta Light sedimentary layer. Any link to the present will be severed, condemning James Robenalt to serve out his sentence in a world of images without substance, emotions without feeling, life without meaning. Such is the fate of a condemned murderer, who would take the life of another with no remorse or acknowledgment of his actions."

A whine built as the core to the great Machine approached critical mass.

"Pulse generator on-line," Held announced.

With a barely perceptible nod, the presiding judge signaled Held to throw the switch. A blinding flash lit up the room and a huge, spiral warp sprang up from the core of the Transmission Center, swallowing the red-suited figure and sucking him into a void from which, for him, there was no return.

12:39 HOURS

The call to Emory's office came in on a little used line, bypassing the central registry and proceeding directly to a secure phone in his office. He tapped the touch pad at the base of the viewer and waited for the image of a man in his thirties to fill the screen.

"The sentence was just carried out," Harmon Bright said in a matter-of-fact voice, drawing a muted reaction from Emory, who stared back blankly at the screen.

"Yes, a most unfortunate, but necessary—"

"What about this person from B.E.T.A.... Thorndyke?"

"No one of any concern. He and Robenalt were friends when Thorndyke was a student at the Institute. Thorndyke knows nothing."

"But he works for Hollock."

"He's been on the job for less than three weeks. He hardly knows where the restrooms are, let alone understand—"

"Hollock sent him to witness the Haley jump Monday. Pretty strong stuff for someone with his head up his ass, don't you think?"

"It's not like you to panic, Mr. Bright," Emory replied coolly.

Bright's jaw tightened, and he spat his remarks back with a threatening wave of his hand. "Don't patronize me, Emory. Without my brains, and GUTS, you'd be nowhere, just a sad little man sitting in his room plotting greatness—and dying in obscurity."

"I apologize if my remarks offended you," Emory immediately retreated. It was difficult to tell from the tone of his voice whether his sentiments were genuine or nothing more than a palliative to Bright's ego. Bright smiled smugly, enjoying the seeming respect the elder man displayed while they eyed each other across their view screens.

"Robenalt was close to stumbling on to us, too. Mitchell didn't understand what he had. Robenalt found the same files, but didn't have time to analyze them. That's the only thing that saved us. But Robenalt isn't a fool. He knew the files meant something. We don't know what he told that friend of his when they were alone together."

"There's nothing to worry about," Emory soothed. "Even if he suspects something, too, Thorndyke can't do anyone any harm. Not now—not before Sunday. After that, it doesn't matter what he learns."

"That's what you said about Mitchell. If I hadn't found out what he was doing, he'd have gone to the authorities."

"Mitchell was a mistake, I admit it. I underestimated his resolve to push forward with his investigation. That's why I arranged to get you a job on his staff, to keep an eye on him. Not kill him."

"There wasn't any time to 'consult'," Bright stated flatly. "He'd found out I was altering Beta Light records and was going to expose us. I had to act then, and I did."

"Well," Emory sighed. "What's past is past. Our work remains on schedule. Nothing can stop us now."

"Our work?" Bright laughed. "Don't you mean *my* work? That's the problem with you people. You sit there in your ivory tower thinking the world comes to you, and some guy who isn't even good enough to sit in your classes creates a whole new mathematical process that allows holo-images to be blended together without anyone detecting the change. Without me you'd be nothing, and your little scheme would be so much hot air."

"There is no question about your contribution to science."

"Just remember, I'm the one who got you where you are—all of you," Bright puffed, encouraged by Emory's deferential manner. "When Sunday comes, you'll have all the evidence you need to support your claims. Drees and Echeverria will be 'exposed,' and you and your friends can put the rest of your little Tea Party into action. *The Second American Revolution.* I've got to admit it has a nice, patriotic ring. Should go a long way in quelling any public outcry when the new government takes over. I almost wish I could be there when you play the recording of them plotting to end constitutional government and set up a joint dictatorship of both countries. You know what they say," he laughed. "Absolute power corrupts absolutely."

"What we do, we do for the future of our people. Once again the country will be united under a single flag, a single leader—"

"Save the speech, Doc. I could care less about your politics. One country, two—a hundred. I'm sure you'll be holding new elections right away." The silence from Emory was deafening as Bright, enjoying himself, laughed out loud. "Don't worry, I don't care what you do, as long as you guys keep up your end of the bargain. Unlimited funds to continue my research, and the public recognition I deserve for showing all of you who the better man is."

"At the proper time, Mr. Bright."

"Sure Doc, just remember, I'm not stupid. Never work a dangerous job without an insurance policy."

"Is that a threat?" Emory responded passively.

"I just don't want any *misunderstanding* after Sunday. Are we clear?"

"You have my word. Everything you've been promised will be delivered."

"Good. I still think you ought to do something about Thorndyke. That Robenalt tape was a hurried job. I even had to cut a few seconds out of it that I couldn't 'fix.' Zhow made dozens of jumps to get the right images for Sunday, and it took me months to blend them all together seamlessly. As good as my new system is, I still need actual Beta Light images from other time strata to insert into the new recording. There's only so much I can do to compensate for the rough parts."

"The Robenalt tape was good enough. As long as the Sunday tape is flawless, that's all that matters."

"Even Drees' own mother would disown him after what I put together," Bright chuckled. "And Echeverria, I made it look like he's going to double cross Drees—take over the whole country himself. What's this world coming to when there's no honor among thieves?"

"We'll meet Saturday, as scheduled, to review final details of the plan. Have everything ready by then."

"I'm ready now. Just make sure you're there."

The Vid-phone snapped off with sudden finality. Emory sat in his chair for a moment, staring at the blank screen, when the link suddenly re-engaged. The face of Abraham Held came into view, sequestered in his office as he poured over a data chart printout from the Robenalt jump.

"Emory," Held grimaced. "There's been a complication."

"What kind of complication?"

"That old fool Sherwood has been meeting with Hollock, twice in two days. I don't know why. We may need to find out."

"It's too soon for another jump," Emory said. "Everyone will be on alert, particularly after the Robenalt incident and so close to the Resurfacing Ceremony."

"I control the jump schedule. I can hide anything I want. The authorities have already been over to talk to me. They only found what I wanted them to see, evidence of Robenalt's jumps which we 'discovered' together. I used four of your person's jumps to create a phony document trail for Robenalt. The others she made are still hidden, and nobody's going to find them unless I want them to. We have to know what Hollock and Sherwood suspect. If they're getting close, we need to shut them down."

"I'll talk to Margaret. I don't know what she'll say. The Mitchell murder and Robenalt sentence has her pretty shaken up."

"I thought you said she was reliable?"

"She is. But she didn't bargain for this, neither of us did. It was supposed to be a bloodless coup. No one was going to get hurt."

"We're making a revolution, Charles," Held's voice was cold and analytical. "Robenalt was the perfect patsy. He knew Mitchell professionally, had access to his work station and his personal beliefs, which he announced repeatedly and publicly, gave him a credible motive to commit a crime. Every war has its casualties. This one is no different."

"When do you need her there?"

"Tonight, at ten. I'll bury any trace of it in the last jump of the day."

"We'll be ready by ten o'clock."

"Good. Until then."

"Until then," Emory echoed, tapping off the viewer.

18:05 HOURS

"I've never seen anything so beautiful," Sharla gushed, taking in the massive, high-ceilinged room as she and Thorndyke stood outside the main entranceway to the newly constructed Time Pavilion.

The interior of the building was clearly visible from the enclosed glass annex, where they and dozens of other couples waited for a table to clear. The walls were made of carved, ornate wood hundreds of years old, salvaged from buildings destroyed in the nuclear conflagration during the mid-twenty first century. A high dome looked out onto a holographic projection of stars bathing the room in their gentle glow. Music captured from Beta Light performances from years gone by wafted through the air, pulling the waiting crowd toward the single set of doors restricting entrance to the main area.

"Gee, I'm, um, sorry about this," Thorndyke mumbled, peering over the heads of the people in front of him in line. "I didn't know you needed a reservation."

"You don't go here much?" she teased, the joke going completely past him.

"No, I heard it's a wonderful place, but, er, I guess the jumpers get first priority."

A servo-host trolled by, offering drinks to those waiting in line. When it approached their position in line, Thorndyke bent forward slightly and mumbled a question.

"Excuse me, but how long do you think we'll have to wait."

The little machine twirled around as if sizing up the crowd, then spun its upper torso back to face Thorndyke. A small speech port on its oval-shaped head snapped open.

"Two hours, twenty seven minutes."

"Two hours!" Thorndyke shouted to the amusement of the couple ahead of them.

"—and twenty seven minutes. Would you like a drink?"

"I'm sorry," he stammered, turning to Sharla, who despite the confusion seemed to be enjoying herself.

"Why don't we just go someplace else," she offered, touching his arm.

"I really hate to make you miss something like this."

"I'm sure there'll be other times."

"Why Miss Russell," Thorndyke beamed. "You're being rather forward."

"Perhaps," Sharla grinned mischievously, gently leading him by the arm toward the exit.

Stepping out into the brightly lit tunnel, Thorndyke put his arm around her waist and folded her into the arc of his body. She felt so natural walking along his side that it almost scared him. His throat tightened and mouth went dry while he fought to maintain at least a small measure of calm, and not betray the blissful nervousness that still crept over him whenever he looked at her. It was only when he detected the slight tremble of her own body as she glanced up into his eyes that he allowed himself to relax, content to let the natural course of events guide their future together.

"I'll be glad when they open up the dome," Thorndyke said, hailing an electric cab that slowed to a stop at the motion of his hand. "I never knew how claustrophobic these tunnels were until I spent some time on the surface."

"You've been outside?"

"Inside the dome."

"I've never been up there."

"It's perfectly safe. Has been for some time now," he smiled as the side door opened, and he helped her get inside. "I think it was ready

79

for habitation a year ago, but the government wants to be perfectly sure. Anyway, all the cautions will be removed on Sunday, and you can see for yourself."

"Where to, please?" the mechanical voice of the driverless cab asked.

"Good question," Thorndyke grinned. "You have any place special you'd like to go?"

"Take us to the Theater, please."

"Great idea! What do you like? Pirates, gangsters, maybe the Crusades?"

"You forget, Mr. Thorndyke," she replied playfully. "It's my job to catalogue most of the new Beta Light images. I see them first in the raw form before they're edited."

"Edited? Thorndyke's attention peaked. "You can do that? Change them around?"

"No, not like altering the contents. Just culling the best images, cutting and recombining them and cleaning them up. Some of the early recordings have a fair bit of static. Even the newer ones still have a lot of noise. We put them through a processor and tighten them up, boost the color clarity and image parameters. I never really see the final results unless I go back to the archives and retrieve a disk for playback."

"Who does all this processing?"

"Department of Entertainment. They work closely with some of the corporate interests that market to the public. The companies that buy the images and repackage them for sale do final editing, but DOE usually works hand-in-hand with them even during the post-production process to insure quality control. "

"What about non-entertainment?"

"Well, that would be Archival Studies. But there isn't much editing there. The High Types like to keep the data raw, just as it is, to get a clearer, more accurate picture."

"Do you think someone could manipulate the images," Thorndyke thought aloud. "Insert something—or someone—into a Beta Light image who wasn't really there?"

"Not likely," Sharla shrugged after pausing for a moment to consider the question. "I remember seeing pictures in old books around the time photography was invented. Some of them had obvious holes where images were cut out or things inserted into them. It looked pretty laughable, and I guess it fooled a lot of the people at first, but it didn't take too long for everyone to see how fake they were. Remember those pictures of the man who killed one of the old U.S. Presidents—Oswald Harvey or something—where they cut his head off at the chin and put it on another man's body. It fooled more people until digital technology came along and exposed it all. The fakes were easier with still photos, harder with film and tape technology, and really tough to detect with lasercut images. But all those were two-dimensional, even the moving pictures. Beta Light is 3-D with stereophonic sound. I can't imagine a process that would produce even a reasonable fake."

The cab rolled to a gentle stop in front of the Theater. Thorndyke and Sharla stepped out and headed into the building where an attractive young woman seated at a wrap-around desk met them.

"Welcome," she smiled brightly. "Have you been here before."

"Yes," Thorndyke replied.

"Good. Then you know how things work. Please don't walk around once you've been seated. The size of the room will not change, but depending upon which Beta Light image you select, it may appear to take on greater proportions. Will you be seeking entertainment, wholesome images, voyeuristic pleasures, or dining?"

"Dining."

"Excellent. Any particular time period?"

"Is King Henry the Eighth accepting guests this evening?" Thorndyke smiled.

"Just a moment and I'll see," the woman said as she consulted a small monitor recessed in her table. "Yes, you're in luck. Booth 9."

A young man dressed in waiter's garb led them to a row of rooms, each nine- by-twelve feet, lined with metal cloth that glittered in a soft, seamless sheen. They entered the featureless area and sat at a non-descript table slightly to the left of the door.

"Tonight you'll be feasting on representations of boar, goat, pheasant, and lamb, with select seasonal vegetables indigenous to sixteenth century England. And of course, fresh brewed ale and mulberry wine. The food will emerge from within the table as soon as the hologram begins. If you have need of any other services, please throw a resin-polymer rib bone at the candelabrum in front of the King. You'll strike a sensor pad behind that spot that will signal someone from customer services. Enjoy."

The man left, sealing the door shut. A soft whine built into a higher pitch, soon disappearing into the clamor of voices, song, and ambient clutter as the dining room of an old English castle encompassed them. Their table became an extension of the King's table, Henry the Eighth appearing to wink and nod their way as he welcomed the assembled guests to his feast. Emerging before them were plates of food fashioned to resemble the meats, fruits, and vegetables of the time. Biting into a rack of lamb, Thorndyke looked at Sharla and chuckled, his comments almost lost amid the noisy revelry around them.

"I'll bet this stuff really had some taste. Can you image the sensations in this room? Smells, tastes, the stifling air, the grimy dirt on some of those plates."

"Please," Sharla grimaced theatrically. "Ours may not have much flavor, but I doubt if we'll risk getting any of the diseases they got from their food. I can't imagine really living in a time like that, but it's fun to pretend."

Soon the banquet was in full force with minstrels playing and jugglers entertaining the crowd. King Henry and one of his wives were enjoying the diversion, filling their cups with wine and ale while they accepted an endless stream of toasts, each one more saccharine and fawning than the one before it. Sharla raised her glass in mock approval, clearly enjoying the festive occasion, when she noticed that Thorndyke had suddenly become very pensive. She stopped and set the cup of wine back down on her table, speaking to him softly.

"Elizabethan England not your favorite time strata?"

"No, I'm sorry," Thorndyke replied sheepishly. "This is really wonderful. I guess I'm still pretty shook up about what happened earlier today."

"We didn't have to do this tonight, Paul," she threaded her arm in his. "I would have understood if you needed some time to yourself."

"No, I didn't want to be alone. I'm really glad you came with me, Sharla. I just can't help wondering what it's like right now for Jim. An hour from now he'll be able to see and hear all of this. I wonder, will any of it bring him comfort?"

"It's still hard to believe what he did."

"I can't believe he'd actually kill somebody," Thorndyke said. "A lot of this still doesn't make sense."

"I doubt it ever will. How do you ever reconcile something like that, deliberately taking another life?"

"No, you don't understand, Sharla. I know this man. He's no more capable of murdering someone than, well, I am."

"People act in extreme ways when they're under pressure," Sharla said compassionately. "I've seen a lot in the Beta Light recordings they bring back. Mild, meek people turn violent, others succumb to the heat of passion and do things that are totally out of character. It doesn't matter what time strata it comes from. Stone age, Renaissance, Industrial Revolution, Age of Information—it doesn't matter. Even a highly civilized society isn't immune to acts of barbarism, collectively or individually."

"Not Jim Robenalt."

The rough and tumble of a drunken brawl breaking out on the other side of the room momentarily distracted them. King Henry looked on with amusement while two of his guests hurled oaths at one another. The guests then pushed back from the table, stood and crossed swords only to stagger and fall—one backward onto the earthen floor, the other face forward into his food—too drunk to support their own weight let alone carry through with the attack.

"There's something Jim said to me, just before they took him away," Thorndyke said softly as the room returned to relative quiet. "I've been thinking a lot about it. I want to follow up on it, but I need to get into the Central Archives."

"Why don't you just do this from B.E.T.A.? You've got full access to every holo-record ever collected."

"If there is something more to this, then whoever is behind it will be watching anything done at B.E.T.A. Especially by me."

"This friend of yours, Jim Robenalt. You really knew him well?"

"I'd have trusted him with my own life."

Picking up a synthetic rib bone, Sharla tossed the heavy object toward the crest of melting candles resting in front of the king. Almost immediately the image snapped off, returning the room to its normal state. She stood and wiped her hands on a shard of cloth resting on top of the table.

"I didn't mean to spoil your evening," Thorndyke said contritely.

"You haven't. I had enough to eat. Besides, we've only got a few hours to access the Central Files from my workstation before they power down Archival Records for the night."

"You're going to help me? It might be dangerous."

"You're risking your life to help someone you love, aren't you?"

The gentle touch of his hand against her cheek was all the reassurance Sharla needed to know that her decision was the right one. She cupped her hand to his and allowed herself to be pulled into a deep, soulful kiss. The tenderness of their brief union spoke more to both of them than any words either could possibly utter.

"We'd better be going," she whispered as the door to the Theater opened, and a bright young hostess awaited their request.

"All right. But first we need to call one other person."

"AN EYE ON THE PRIZE"
Thursday, September 26, 2416 AD
06:10 HOURS

*All is riddle, and the key to a riddle
is another riddle.*

-Emerson

The gentle chime pulled Thorndyke out of a deep, satisfying sleep. Nestled in his arm, Sharla barely stirred, drawing her hand across his chest and tightening her hold on him. He listened to the rise and fall of her breath as she molded her body into his, feeling more content than he had ever been at any moment in his life.

"The time is now six hours, ten minutes," a soothing voice accompanied another chime, this one more persistent than the last.

"Give us another ten minutes," Thorndyke said to the alarm, pulling Sharla even closer against his body.

"Very well. Ten minutes of additional rest time has been programmed."

The room fell back into quiet. Thorndyke let his eyes play over Sharla's face, content to watch her sleep while she lay in his arms. Even though they'd only known each other for a few days it was difficult to imagine what life would be like without her. He remembered smiling when Quentin Cottle described the first time he saw Ruth, and how he knew he was going to marry her. *No one can be so sure that quickly,* he laughed. Quentin never replied, just smiled enigmatically in a way Thorndyke didn't understand, until Sharla came into his life. Now he understood, and as he watched her slowly begin to awake, he knew as certainly as Quentin had known about Ruth that he and Sharla would be together, forever.

"Mmmm, good morning," she smiled, opening her eyes. "What time is it?"

"A little after six."

"We should get up," she sighed, beginning to move.

"No, lay with me a little longer."

He brushed the hair from her face with a soft, gentle sweep of his hand, not wanting the moment to end. With a deep, satisfying smile, Sharla let her head sink back into his chest. They lay together in silence, the touch of their skin against each other's body the only communication they needed, until the call of a woman's voice from the other room drew them out of their private world.

"Hey, wake up sleepy-head. You're going to be late for—"

Cut off mid-word, Claudia stopped dead in her tracks as she burst into her roommate's quarters. A sheepish Paul Thorndyke smiled awkwardly while the bemused young woman let her eyes flit between him and Sharla. "I didn't know you had... company," she grinned. "I didn't hear you come in last night."

"It was late," Sharla mumbled, smiling at Thorndyke.

"Just how much sleep did you two get?" Claudia replied mischievously.

"It's not really what you think, Claudia," Sharla stretched. "We were working until two."

"Working? I thought you went on a date?"

"We did."

"You have an interesting way of showing a girl a good time, Mr. Thorndyke," Claudia's grin widened.

"I, er, need to get out of bed," Thorndyke mumbled. Motioning with his head, he drew Claudia's attention to a pile of clothing on a chair across the room.

"Well, I have to finish getting ready," she backed away, enjoying the situation. "Shall I tell them you'll be a little late this morning, Sharla? I don't think Mr. Connoly will mind. Seems like you put in some long hours yesterday."

"You *are* a wicked person," Sharla chuckled.

"Important announcement," the room interrupted. "A news bulletin has just been released by The District Information Services. Would you like me to access the public information and entertainment viewing network or record the broadcast for future playback."

"Show us now," Sharla said. A flat viewing screen descended from the ceiling, displaying the face of a middle-aged broadcaster.

"Repeating our story, the nation mourns the loss of one of the truly great men of our time. Henry Sherwood, Nobel Prize Laureate and founder of P.A.S.T., died in his sleep at 4:30 am this morning. His body was discovered a short while ago and taken to The District hospital where doctors pronounced him dead. Sherwood designed the device that projects a human being into Beta Light layers, and with Constantine Knoble and Michael Escobar, created the time viewing process we know today. The eccentric Sherwood had just completed work on a new system to block the dangerous electromagnetic pulses that accompany the insertion process. He was to have been on hand this afternoon to personally witness the first use of his new invention, which was installed at the Transmission Center only yesterday. Secretary of State Lillian Dorr, visiting The District on official business, issued a statement on behalf of President Drees calling Henry Sherwood a 'brilliant innovator, good friend, and national hero whose passing will leave a great void in our hearts and spirit.' A spokesman for President Echeverria lamented the loss of the 'great man's mind, who had so much more to contribute to the advancement of our society.' A state funeral for Sherwood will be held Sunday in which the leaders of both the U.S. East and West are expected to attend.

"In accompanying news, sources officially confirmed today what everyone in The District has known by rumor for some time now. The surface beneath the great dome will soon be opened to public use. A Resurfacing Ceremony had already been scheduled for Sunday afternoon, during which both Presidents of the United States and other national and international dignitaries will be present. The occasion will mark the first time a surface section of land has been reclaimed from the ash. Atlanta, Phoenix, London, and Madrid have encased individual buildings against the ash, but these structures are used primarily as laboratories to further study the outside environment. Santiago Chile, and Melbourne Australia remain the only world cities to have constructed surface domes prior to significant ash contamination, but these extend over relatively small areas. The great dome of The District is the largest self-contained structure in the world, and dwarfs any other dome currently in existence. If The District experiment is successful, it will serve as the prototype of a vast new network of domes gradually enabling mankind's return to the surface."

"Video screen off," Sharla said when the broadcast began to transition to another subject.

"I can't believe Henry Sherwood's dead," Thorndyke shook his head. "A heart attack. He looked so vigorous when I saw him."

"You met Henry Sherwood?" Claudia's mouth dropped.

"Just the other day."

"Well, I'm impressed. Sharla, he's a keeper," Claudia grinned, turning to leave.

"Don't mention to anyone I was there late last night," Sharla called as Claudia was about to exit the room. Her friend turned and looked at her, a thin smile crossing her lips.

"You weren't doing anything naughty on my desk, were you?"

"Claudia!"

"You are full of surprises, Sharla Russell," she giggled while her hand reached for a sensor pad, sealing the door shut.

Thorndyke gave Sharla a quizzical look, who lifted her eyes toward the ceiling. He swept back the covers and stepped from the bed, then crossed the room. She took in his thin, but finely-toned body, watching admiringly as he pulled on his trousers and reached for his shirt. Finished dressing, he faced her again. She let the bed sheets fall away and stood, nude, her legs apart and arms folded teasingly across her chest.

"Leaving so soon?"

"Not that I wouldn't like to stay," he sighed, his gaze never leaving her. "But I've got to get back to my apartment and shower and dress for work."

"We have running water here, too."

He crossed back to where she was standing. Running his hand along her smooth, soft skin, he pulled her into a tight embrace.

"Better get dressed, too, or you'll be late."

The kiss was as long and passionate as the ones they shared the night before, and it left both of them dizzy with anticipation. Sharla blushed while she gently slipped from his grasp and wrapped herself in a robe, certain he could read her innermost thoughts. Thorndyke reluctantly started for the door, but the sound of a computerized voice pulled him back.

"Incoming Vid-phone message for Paul Thorndyke."

"Yes, I'll take it."

"A call for you, here?" Sharla said.

A flat, egg-shaped monitor rose from a slit in the room's furniture and blossomed into the three-foot wide screen. Ruth Parker blinked back surprise when she focused on Thorndyke and the evidently curious woman standing in the background.

"Paul, I'm sorry. Am I disturbing you?"

"No, Ruth. What is it?"

"I, er, Quentin asked me to get in touch with you. I thought I was calling your apartment."

"My phone's on skip."

"Oh, I see. Well, he said to meet him at his office as soon as you can. Something about what he found last night. He said you'd understand."

"Thank you, Ruth."

"A friend?" Ruth smiled, moving her head slightly to see around him.

"I'm Sharla."

"Ruth Parker. Nice to meet you, Sharla. I'll see you later, Paul." The image shut off and the viewer began to recede into the table.

Sharla tightened the cinch on her robe and smiled at Thorndyke. "She seems nice," she said. From the look on her face he couldn't tell if the comment was genuine, or if she was probing for his reaction.

"Ruth's a great girl. She and Quentin have been seeing each other for years. It's one of those 'love at first sight' relationships."

"How romantic," Sharla smiled. "Just how did she know where to find you?"

"Like I said, I put my number on automatic transfer. My apartment re-routed the call here."

"How could it do that? I didn't change my registry protocol."

"You didn't?"

"No."

"But it was changed a couple of days ago."

"Registry," Sharla spoke to the room. "Has the privacy protocol for this residence been altered?"

"The protocol was amended on September 23rd at 21:03 hours to permit incoming calls from Paul Thorndyke. Transfer privileges are an automatic byproduct of any such modification to the personal directive sub-matrix."

"Who authorized this change?"

"Claudia Morales."

"It wasn't you?" Thorndyke puzzled.

"It appears there's been some serious matchmaking going on here, Mr. Thorndyke."

"So it seems. You upset about it?"

"No," she tried to hide her smile.

"Well then, I'll see you again tonight."

"Tonight."

The outer door opened and Thorndyke stepped into the building corridor, winking back in her direction before moving out of sight. The door re-sealed with a snap. Sharla stood silently in the center of the room, her eyes alive with thought as she turned slowly to the door leading into the adjoining bedroom.

"Claudia, darling. We have to talk."

08:15 HOURS

The laboratory was located three hundred yards beneath the surface, carved out of solid bedrock and reinforced with enough steel and concrete to survive a direct hit by a twenty megaton thermonuclear explosion.

Seventy people lived within its cramped confines, foregoing contact for months at a time with anyone but the other scientists, technicians, and security personnel guarding the complex. Every so often a new team would arrive to replace select individuals, giving them a spate of well-earned rest before returning to their grueling lifestyle again. It wasn't so much that the work was tiring. For most of the scientists and technicians, the intense intellectual exchange was a reward in itself. It was the seclusion, cut off from the rest of the world—even from news of mundane current events—that made life difficult. But such extreme measures were necessary to guard against accidents in a high security biogenetic facility. And, to protect its secrets.

"This is truly amazing," Janet Kimball blinked, looking up from the eyepiece to an electron imaging scanner and staring at her colleagues huddled in a semi-circle behind her. "It's gone. All of it."

90

"You mean to tell me, there isn't even a trace of toxin?" Dr. Hubert, a portly man in horn-rimmed glasses scoffed. "Take the imaging field down another ten angstrom units."

"It's as tight as it can get," Kimball replied. "There's nothing there. Nothing."

Hubert bent over the microscope, searching with his own eyes. "By God," he whispered, righting himself slowly and turning to face the anxious stares of six other men and women crowded together in the sterile, equipment-filled room. Harry Gardner, a white-haired, respected member of the group, stepped from the side of the laboratory table and clasped his hands together. Unable to suppress a broad smile, he spoke eagerly to his fellow scientists.

"Three weeks ago, using a process perfected by Dr. Somerall and myself, we introduced a highly toxic residue into a closed ecosystem. The control culture was quickly overrun by the virulence and all organic life destroyed. But here, in the experimental culture, not only has life survived, all traces of the poison have been eliminated. We cannot find it in any cell of any organism, in any spectrographic reading of any element, or in any measurable quantity in any site within the experiment's physical confines."

"What accounts for these results?" a man in his thirties asked.

"GS-2035/BCLF—the Gardner-Somerall bio-chemical life form. A genetically engineered virus-sized organism that can be introduced into the stem cells of plants to migrate to their leaves, then bind with the plant's own genetic material to fundamentally alter its indigenous respiratory process. Instead of simply scrubbing carbon dioxide from the air, the altered plants will take in even the most virulent form of airborne pollution, break it down chemically into harmless components, and then excrete it into the soil where it will remain a harmless constituent of the earth."

"You said a 'bio-chemical life form?'"

"Yes, using nuclear acceleration technology we genetically-altered a virus, stripping all but several hundred thousand haploid sets from its original DNA. Then we injected its modified chromosome sac with a chemically-enhanced solution of DNA extracted from the chloroplastic cells of a typical long stemmed plant. Within fifteen hours, the new virus had replicated itself with the exact genetic makeup of the original hybrid. It functions on both an organic and chemical basis—drawing life from photosynthesis as well as from purely chemical processes. What we have here, ladies and gentlemen, is a new life form capable of survival by itself or in a symbiotic relationship with a host plant. When injected into a higher level organism, the plant's original metabolic and respiratory functions remain unaffected. Carbon dioxide is converted to oxygen in the same proportions and concentrations as before. But in addition to that, the plant's respiratory process now also cleanses the air of all toxins, whether man-made or natural. And, there are no discernible side effects."

"Incredible! A water hyacinth of the air."

"Congratulations, doctor!" Hubert could barely suppress his glee. "You and Somerall will win the Nobel Prize for Science hands down! When do you begin field testing?"

"Soon. We want to run a few more controlled experiments through the middle of April to verify our results. Then, starting in June, we can begin the first open-air trials. With any luck we should be finished with all our research by the end of the year and go to full scale production in early 2036."

"Can you show us the process you used to create the hybrid virus?"

"Certainly, Doctor," Gardner beamed. "It's relatively simple, given the complexity of the concept. Somerall and I worked from notes we discovered in the Fermilab in Chicago three summers ago. The research by a Dr. York was brilliant in its insight— she was on the verge of discovering the essence of the bio-chemical transfer process when her work was abandoned. Had she persevered, no doubt she would have achieved the success we've demonstrated here today in another year, at most."

"The ironies of fate," Hubert shook his head. "She probably ran out of funding or, more likely, changed the focus of her work to pursue some other more relevant project. I can't say I blame her. The environment was hardly in the state back then that it's come to today."

"Yes. It's a pity that the country stopped funding basic ecological research shortly after the turn of the century; but, after so many exaggerated claims about global warming, a new ice age, the depletion of the ozone layer—even the effect of the trade winds on long term weather patterns—there was bound to be a backlash. What was it they called it? Political correctness? Can you *imagine* actually working under conditions where basic research was so heavily influenced by the personal prejudices of petty politicians who were bound and determined to make science conform to their own preconceived notions? The ozone layer wasn't affected by sunspots and other natural climatic processes... just aerosol spray cans and old air cooling technology. Well, we stopped the spray cans and changed cooling systems, but the ozone layer kept getting thinner. So we curtailed fossil fuel emissions and other byproducts of technological advancement, but still the problem worsened. It was only when the solutions became more and more perverse, and their anticipated beneficial effects farther and farther away, that the public finally began to see the pronouncements for what they were—tools to advance a private, social agenda."

"It's amazing how blind we can be when we stop believing in logic and substitute preconceived philosophy for the scientific method," Hubert agreed.

"Yes, but the true pity is that before we could get to where scientific pursuit was truly unfettered by political dogma, we had to suffer through years of backlash against the old ways. Once the people saw through these lies and distortions they abandoned respect for scientific evaluations of any kind. Reasonableness was cast to the wind—there were no controls, no restraints on activities that might adversely affect the environment. Poisons were literally pumped into the air without further thought until today the air is difficult to breathe in many of our cities, large *and* small."

"Which makes this discovery all the more significant," Hubert slapped Gardner's back. "If we can convince the government to spend enough money to fully back your wonderful discovery, we can wipe out every trace of pollution nation-wide in twenty years, and world-wide in another fifty."

"I just wish things were a bit more stable politically, Dr. Hubert," Gardner sighed. "I don't know much about what's happening topside these days, but what I hear troubles me. I think we're in store for some difficult times ahead. I just hope Witherspoone's up to the challenge."

"Witherspoone's no Haley, not with that stunt he pulled last November! Launching a surgical nuclear strike—what does he think the old Soviet's are going to do, just sit there and take it? I agree, there's trouble ahead, but no sense worrying about things we can't control. Think positive! Now, let's see this new process of yours."

"Certainly. Ladies and gentlemen, if you'll follow me into the acceleration lab where Dr. Somerall is waiting, we'll show you everything you need to know."

The image on the center screen monitor began to distort as the small group headed through an open door into the adjoining room.

"What's that noise on the viewer?" Greene was on his feet. Like the others monitoring Zhow's jump to the Miller's Crossing research facility, he watched the unfolding drama with a dry mouth and pounding heart. In the next room was the secret to creating a technology that could remove the poisonous ash from the surface of the world. Only seconds separated them from this knowledge, but the image on the monitor was beginning to seriously degrade.

"It's the nuclear accelerator," someone shouted. "It's blanking out the Beta Light images."

"No!" Greene screamed as the picture rolled and degraded, the sound winking out completely. "Send a signal to Zhow on her pulse generator. Tell her to back off. Don't let an energy cone develop. It will cut us off completely and we'll never get another chance to return to that time strata."

"Radiation doesn't cause an energy cone to develop," a technician said. "Beta Light blackouts are caused by second-level vibrations that—"

"We don't know what causes the damn thing to do it, but I'm not going to take any chances! Get her to back off, now!"

"It doesn't matter," the technician replied in a soft, almost unemotional voice. "Energy cone or no, the group went into the accelerator room. Whenever there's radiation present, the Beta Light images never record in the first place. There'll be no pictures or sound from there. We can only hope they'll move their files to a shielded area before they shut down in the next few weeks."

"Don't hold your breath," Greene slumped back in his seat. "This was our best hope. It'll take a miracle for someone to come out of that room with the information we need to see. This is just great—my first shot at the helm, and it's a total fuck up. Where's Held anyway?"

"He still hasn't checked in, sir."

"Zhow's waiting for further instructions, Mr. Greene," a voice called over the open link.

"Might I suggest, sir," the first technician responded, "that we consider a complete round-the clock surveillance of all activity outside the accelerator room? We might be able to pick up enough ambient conversation to piece together some important information."

"It's worth a try," Greene agreed half-heartedly. "But we need to rethink and prepare for our next series of moves. There's a lot of ground to be covered, most of it probably wasted. Signal Zhow, bring her home. This jump's over."

Rising slowly, Jerry Greene walked over to the observation window at the Launch Director's station, looking down at the floor below. It was almost eerie to see ground support technicians sitting at their stations without their protective gear. Henry Sherwood's energy baffles were working perfectly.

"This is really great," Greene muttered under his breath while he watched the crew prepare for Zhow's re-emergence from the Beta Light swirl. "York's research in the twentieth century was incomplete, and even that eludes us. Now three and a half decades into the future we find the site where they successfully brought her work to completion, but we can't see how they *actually did it!* "

With a furious wail the energy spiral reappeared, reforming Zhow, who stepped out of the vortex and stalked down the ramp. Two technicians rushed to help her, but she pushed them aside, almost ripping her helmet from the neck brace and tossing it onto the floor.

"Why was I brought back? The mission wasn't complete!"

"Dr. Zhow," Greene soothed over the intercom. "We'll complete your debrief in the red room."

"Damnit, Greene!" Zhow exploded. "Send me back, NOW!"

"The mission has terminated," Greene's voice was controlled, but insistent. "Report to the debriefing room."

Technicians stared at the woman, her tired eyes staring back, watching the confrontation with apprehension and confusion. Tensions often ran high on a complicated jump, especially one as important as this, but never before had Zhow seemed so completely out-of-control. She let her eyes focus on the lone figure standing in the Launch

Director's booth overhead, then turned abruptly and stormed out of the Transmission Center.

"Want me to go after her?" a nervous voice called over his communication link.

"No," Greene said. "Shut it down, ladies and gentlemen. There'll be no further jumps today."

As the enormous machine was powered down Greene looked out over the small army of technical staff scurrying about their stations below, and let out a long, heavy sigh. "This is just not my day."

09:29 HOURS

"The Director's been looking for you, Paul," a pleasant looking woman said to Thorndyke who was hurrying through the inter-office corridor on his way to Quentin's cubicle, stopping him in mid-stride.

"Director? Hollock?"

"Know anyone else who's the top guy at B.E.T.A.?" Brian Russack called as he was passing by, drawing laughs from the surrounding cubicles whose occupants were eavesdropping on the conversation.

"What does he want?" Thorndyke replied earnestly.

"I don't know," the young woman said. "He didn't tell me. All I know is he's looking for you."

"Everyone's been trying to find you," Russack continued. "I even called you at home, but you'd already left for work. You're apartment said you didn't leave until 8:45. What happened, you oversleep?"

"Something like that."

"Well, whatever Hollock wants, it sounds important. Seems like you and him are becoming good buddies. He asking your advice on how to run the department? Or maybe how to keep Abraham Held out of our business!" Russack laughed, enjoying his own joke.

"I gotta go," Thorndyke said, heading down the hallway.

"Don't forget your friends when you're running the show," Russack shouted, drawing more laughter as Thorndyke raced out of view.

* * *

It was the second time in four days that Paul Thorndyke found himself entering through the massive polished brass doors to Hollock's office. If anything, the nervous pit in his stomach had grown larger, not smaller, in the intervening period as he approached the great eagle-shaped desk with Scott Hollock behind it.

"Paul, isn't it?" Hollock motioned to a pair of chairs near the center of the room. "Have a seat, I'll be right with you. Room security, activate privacy option, Level Twelve. Hollock Authorization 2462-5."

"Level Twelve, sir?" Thorndyke repeated.

"Complete and total—it even throws a Beta Light shield around the room. We use low-level radioactive pellets embedded in the office superstructure. The lead shielding is pulled back temporarily to blank out any sounds and images that could be recovered at a later time. There's not much more exposure than a good dose of clinical X-rays, so not to worry."

"I'm not worried, sir."

"Well, Mr. Thorndyke," Hollock became deadly serious as the room activated the security measures. "You should be."

"Have I done anything wrong, sir?"

"No, Paul." Hollock came out from behind his desk to join him. "I suspect you already know you're in some danger. I'm sorry to put you in even greater peril, but I don't have any other choice."

"I'm not completely following this, sir."

"Jim Robenalt was your friend. You spent his last moments together. You've been to see me with Henry Sherwood in my office. And now Henry's dead."

"Yes," Thorndyke replied sadly. "I saw the news this morning. Heart attack."

"Henry Sherwood didn't die of a heart attack. He was murdered."

"Murdered! How—"

"I can't prove any of what I'm about to tell you, but every intuition I have tells me that death wasn't natural. I've requested that The District authorities conduct a full autopsy instead of allowing the preliminary findings to stand before the body is cremated. There are lethal drugs that can only be detected by a more thorough analysis than the one the medical examiner would initially perform."

"Lethal drugs! What's happening here, sir? First Ben Mitchell is murdered, now you say Henry Sherwood was killed. What madman is doing this?"

"That's what I want you to find out, Paul. You don't believe James Robenalt is guilty of the Mitchell crime, do you?"

"No, sir, I do not. I know what the Beta Light images showed, but they're wrong! Jim isn't capable of doing anything like that."

"You know this because he's your friend?"

"I know this because it isn't possible for him to take another life—not that way, not that brutally. Not any way. It's my intuition, too, sir."

"I trust your instincts, Paul. I don't know how, but someone's found a way to alter Beta Light images. You know what that means? In the wrong hands, it could re-write history, bring down governments with manufactured evidence—"

"—even convict innocent people of another man's crime."

Hollock leaned forward, putting his hand on Thorndyke's shoulder, and staring him in the eyes.

"Even if my request is approved to autopsy Henry's body, we won't know the results for another day or two. Maybe not until next week. I need answers now, Paul. That's where you come in."

"What can I do?"

"This is my personal access code," he said, handing him a small circular disk. "It doesn't require a voice check or retina scan. The disk, plus what I'm about to tell you to activate it, will give you access to any computer file, any data bank in B.E.T.A., or any Level 10 security file anywhere in The District. Be careful what you do with it."

"I will."

"Use it to find out what's going on, who's behind all of this. I can't make inquiries; I'm too visible. But you can. Are you up to the task, Paul, because I have to know? There's no shame if you're not."

"My only regret, Mr. Hollock, is that whatever I do is probably too late to help Jim Robenalt."

"You're a good man, Paul, with decent instincts. I only hope Jim Robenalt is watching all this somehow. Maybe it will give him some sense of comfort."

"I hope so, too, Mr. Hollock."

"Call me Scott. Now let me tell you what else you need to know."

10:18 HOURS

It looked as if Quentin Cottle hadn't slept in the last twenty-four hours. Sitting in his cubicle, he rubbed the tired from his eyes, opening them again to see a somber-looking Paul Thorndyke step inside and close the door.

"Where've you been?" Quentin frowned. "I've been looking for you for the last two hours. Didn't Ruth get a hold of you?"

"Come on, Quentin. Let's go for a walk."

"Walk! You drag me out of bed, get me involved in some ball-busting search of the Central Archives for a hidden file, which, by the way, I find just as they're about to shut off power for the night. So I download the data into a portable unit and head for home where I spend the whole night decrypting the file so you can read it... and you want to take a walk?"

"Now, Quentin."

"The man wants to take a walk," he mumbled, gathering up a portable reader and following Thorndyke out the door.

*　*　*

"Entering surface area," a mechanical voice intoned as the small, square-shape lift came to a stop at the top of the turbo shaft. "Please put on enviromasks and take all other necessary precautions to guard against ash contamination."

"Where are our masks?" Quentin looked around nervously, seeing Thorndyke's hand about to tap the sensor pad to open the exterior door.

"We don't need any. The air's clean enough to breath now. They're opening the dome up to unrestricted use in three days."

"Yeah, but... that's Sunday."

"Quentin, if it's clean enough for Sunday, it's clean enough for now."

"Well, I guess," he muttered, looking as if he wanted to hold his breath while Thorndyke broke the airtight seal. There was a slight pop as the dome air rushed inside.

"You smell that, Quentin?" Thorndyke paused before stepping outside.

"Oh God! I knew it was a mistake—"

99

"No, breathe deeply. That fresh, wonderful smell."

Wincing, Quentin allowed the sweet smell of grass and trees to filter through his nose. He looked in wonder at Thorndyke, who stared back equally in awe.

"What *is* that? I've never smelled anything like that before."

"Whatever it is, it's wonderful. I'm going to be spending a lot of time up here."

Along asphalt-surfaced roadways connecting the deserted buildings of the strange surface world, Thorndyke and Cottle strolled through the old city of Washington, D.C. Most of its buildings had been damaged during the Big War, but the city—no longer the capital of a united nation—was spared the full brunt of attack. Atlanta, the new capital of the U.S. East, was almost completely destroyed, as were strategic industrial and transportation centers throughout both countries. Washington, which had been transformed into a cultural and historical center, suffered less destruction than it might otherwise have. Many of its damaged buildings were meticulously restored while the two nations struggled through the Great Recovery, the period of rebirth and re-development following the war. But any further work was abandoned early in the twenty second century when the ash became more virulent and more pervasive, eventually forcing the population underground. Only in the last ten years, since the great dome was completed and the decontamination process begun, had any further work been done to restore the damage that remained to the city. Washington—now *The District*—would never again be the city it once was, but in a world increasingly devoted to images of the past, a relic, even one as damaged as this, was still regarded as a national treasure.

"I think that's the White House," Quentin pointed to a boxy white building surrounded by an iron fence.

"Yeah. Come on. Let's go have a look."

"You know, Paul," Quentin said as they pushed their way through a creaking gate and headed across the circular driveway leading to its entrance. "As cool as this is, I still need to talk to you about what I found."

"I want to hear it, Quentin. But we couldn't talk below. They'll never think of searching this strata to find us, if they're looking."

"If who's looking?"

"The ones who killed Mitchell. It wasn't Robenalt, he was set up."

"I know," Quentin said. "And I think I know how."

"You cracked the code?"

"Well, I found the hidden file—and some of it was encrypted like you thought," Quentin recounted blandly while they moved through the building's vacant interior, occasionally letting their eyes drift to some unique feature or important historical room. "My guess is Robenalt stumbled onto something while he was fooling around with another problem, and downloaded part of it into his personal data files until a security program kicked in and shut the dataflow down. He didn't fully understand what he had, but knew it was something big."

"How big?"

"Jim's a fine mathematician... was a fine mathematician," Quentin's voice trailed. "But this is something that's beyond even me. Best I can figure, it's an active logic system—new, completely revolutionary, really high concept stuff. It's like making the jump from an abacus to a mainframe supercomputer in one single step. And here's the best part. It's internal symmetry is so simple, so clear when you first understand it, that it's really revolutionary only in the way it takes already existing theorems and stands them on their heads to get an entirely new logic system. I'm still not convinced it really works, but if it holds up, you can find algorithmic shortcuts to do things with it you'd never even *dream* of before!"

"Like playing with Beta Light images to put a new face on someone else's body?"

"Yes, that would be possible. A system like this could handle the multi-quadrillions of variables a second necessary to insert a 3-D image into a holographic scene."

"And invent something that didn't happen."

"Sure. It's just a matter of cutting and pasting snippets of images from different events into the target image. The more you have to work with, the more convincing the blend. With enough data, it could appear seamless. Of course, the real trick will be to computer generate an entirely fictitious event, you know, create some kind of interactive hologram by taking the essence and personality of some real figure from the past, then combine it with a formula that interpolates the missing action. That's probably not going to happen until the *next* new revolutionary system comes along, but for the time being, yeah. If it really works, you could pass off a pretty good fake, as long as you had the data."

"And if there aren't enough images to recombine?"

"It'd look pretty fake, if you knew what to look for. That's the key. I imagine the first time it's done no one would really suspect unless the flaw was so obvious it looked suspicious. But something that's less than perfect, yeah, you could still get away with it until everyone caught on that there *was* a new logic system and knew what to look for."

"Where did this new theory come from? Whose work is this?"

"I don't know. I don't know anyone at the Institute—faculty or staff—who's capable of something like this. It's beyond even Ed Kolby, and that's saying something. He's the best mathematician I know. Whoever thought this up was a real genus."

"Well then, if not someone at the Institute, who could it be?"

"Don't be an elitist, Paul." Quentin chided playfully. "Remember, Einstein was a patent clerk."

"I want you to go back to the archives, Quentin, dig deeper. There's got to be a trail buried in there somewhere."

"*Lo siento, amigo.* No can do. I've maxed out everything I've had access to."

"Try this," Thorndyke said, handing him a small disk.

"What's this?"

"It'll take you any place you want."

"Just how does a GS3, two weeks on the job, come into possession of a magic key?" Quentin pondered, turning the dime-sized disk between his thumb and fingers. "I've been at B.E.T.A. over a year and my security level's a 5. This thing had to come from someone at Hollock's level."

"Not 'someone.'"

"*Hollock* gave you this? Just handed it over, like that?"

"I've left a partial code-strand with Ruth, the missing piece to the key. You'll need that to activate it. She doesn't know what it is— no need to tell her. She thinks it's an access marker for a file I control that you want to skim through for your work. I left a voice-call with her apartment so she'll get it when she comes back tonight, or you can call the apartment and retrieve it yourself. I'm sure you share protocols."

"You left the code on a home security unit information channel?"

"Sometimes it's best to hide things in plain sight. It's the last place anyone looks."

"You are just a bundle of surprises today, my friend," Quentin chuckled, glancing around. "Say, know where we are?"

"Judging by the shape of the room, the Oval Office. Imagine what it must have looked like back then."

The room, like most surface building interiors, was a hollow shell stripped of its furnishings. In many buildings, all that remained were bare walls—usually with large gaping holes, stripped-down floors, and crumbling ceilings. Piles of debris were often scattered about with twisted shards of glass or metal poking through the dilapidated walls to tear at flesh and clothing. The White House had been restored better than most, but it was still little more than an empty caricature of its glory days. All that was missing were the light fixtures, carpets, wall hangings, and furniture destroyed in the war or looted in the chaos that followed—and the people who inhabited it. The ghosts of every president of the old United States from John Adams, its first occupant, to Gregory Dauchot, its last, still walked the halls, brought out from time-to-time and put on display by the Beta Light images that recorded their every movements. But like everything else in the restored city, they were not real, only shadows of the past.

Wordlessly, the two intruders took one long, last look around the room, and left the shadows to themselves.

11:59 HOURS

"Will you just settle down, Abraham," Emory tried to calm the furious man.

"Who authorized that little shit to kill Henry Sherwood!"

"We agreed we wanted him out of the way," Harmon Bright replied calmly. "You gave the order—"

"—to *silence* him!" It looked as if Held was about to physically strike the smarmy young man standing directly in front of him. "You were to inject him with a drug and put him in a coma, enough to keep him unconscious until after the Resurfacing Ceremony on Sunday. No one said anything about putting him into cardiac arrest!"

"The old coot was stronger than I thought. I gave him the injection, and he fought it. I used more, and, well, I'm as sorry about this as you are."

"Spare me the maudlin self-pity," Held spat in disgust. "You enjoy killing, Bright. You liked what you did to that Archivist. It gave you a rush like the sick psychopath you are. I bought the excuse for what you did to Mitchell, but I'm not going to condone this! Henry Sherwood was an old man, who—"

"—hated your guts, just like you hated his. Don't pretend you're sorry he's dead."

"I will not be party to any action that shows such a blatant disregard for human life!"

"You're not speaking for history, are you Held?" Bright smirked. "Just in case anyone jumps to this time strata and recovers these images to use at your trial?"

It was all Held could do to control himself as he locked eyes with Bright, still taunting him with his smile. Emory stepped in to defuse the situation, speaking in a soft, soothing voice.

"Gentlemen, please. I know tensions are running high. Whether we approve of Mr. Bright's actions before hand or in retrospect, we all knew the dangers manifested in our decision to embark on this course of action. It will serve no purpose to second-guess last night's unfortunate event."

"I missed my jump this morning, waiting for him to show up here," Held complained like a little boy, gesturing toward Bright. "I've never missed a jump before. This whole situation is getting out of control. The authorities aren't stupid. They'll autopsy Sherwood and come looking—for what or who, it doesn't matter. They'll shut everything down and tighten security Sunday, maybe call off the whole event. And then where will we be?"

"There won't be any autopsy," Bright stated blandly. "Who do you think is going to authorize cutting up the body of a man like Henry Sherwood, taking out his organs, weighing them, dissecting them? It's not going to happen."

"Hollock's already asked the government to do it."

"He can ask anyone he wants, but there isn't a chance in hell they'll agree before Sunday. After that, what does it matter?"

"I have to agree, Abraham," Emory said. "There was no sign of struggle, no bruising on the corpse, no puncture wounds, just a clean dermal contact. Henry Sherwood was an old man. He died peacefully in his sleep."

"But now we've got another problem—Hollock," Bright snorted.

"Looking for another person to kill?" Held snapped.

"If I have to."

"Hollock isn't our immediate problem," Emory tried to change the subject. "Margaret's on the edge. I don't know how much more of this she can take."

"She knew the consequences of her actions when she joined us," Held replied unsympathetically.

"Margaret isn't like us. Her motives are not entirely political. She's been my colleague for twenty years. She admires and respects my work. She joined us because I asked her, not because she believes in her heart it's the right thing to do."

"We need one more jump from her, Charles," Held said firmly. "We need to know what Hollock knows, what he suspects."

"And who he's been talking to," Bright added.

"Then she can get out if she wants," Held continued. "We're making a revolution, building a new country. A united country. If that principle isn't worth fighting, or dying for, what is?"

"You know, Held," Bright laughed. "You crack me up. You almost sound like you believe that stuff."

"I will not stand here and be insulted by some idiot savant!" Held fought to control his temper.

"Well, without this 'idiot savant,' you and Chuck would be meeting every Tuesday night in a conspiracy of two, instead of about to pull a coup of not just one, but *two* governments!"

"Coup is such an ugly word," Emory sighed.

"Call it what you want, but by Sunday afternoon Drees and that old hack from Phoenix will be cooling their heels in The District jail, thanks to my Beta Light re-write of history. And who, of course, will ride in on his white horse—or at least a damn fine holographic representation of one—and save both countries from civil chaos? Abraham Held! You should thank me, Held. Without Sherwood, it'll make it easy for you to take over T.I.M.E. and B.E.T.A. That is what

105

you want, isn't it? That's what this is really all about. Total power." Bright began to circle Held as he spoke, enjoying watching the older man twitch while he continued his pronouncements. "I'm sure you'll decline the call to step in and assume the formal trappings of power. I mean, why take the pay cut just for the title? No, the way I see it, you'll let someone else be the front guy. Maybe old Doc Emory here, as long as you hold the real power—the Time Machine."

Held's nostrils flared as Bright continued to speak, staring daggers into him while he leaned against the wall and crossed his arms in front of his chest.

"Kind of makes you salivate just thinking about it, doesn't it, Held? Absolute, total control. You'd never be allowed that kind of authority as long as the country is fragmented. If the West didn't veto it, the East would. But a single country, hey that's a whole new ball game! I'm guessing you think the country will be too busy putting itself back together to notice what's happening with The Machine. By the time everyone figures out what's been created, it'll be too late to pull back. Not a bad little analysis for a guy without a lot of formal education. But then, you don't need a Ph.D. to understand people like us, do you Held?"

"Aren't you afraid something might happen to *you* once this so-called power play works itself out?" Held spoke contemptuously.

"You know, it's amazing how great minds think alike. Chuck and I were talking about the same thing not too long ago. No, I don't worry about things like that. I know whoever takes over won't forget his friends, whether they're out in front or behind the scene pulling the strings. I'm no threat to anyone, Held," Bright laughed. "Pain in the ass maybe, but what's life without a little pain? Makes you appreciate the good times even more. Besides, anyone clever enough to invent a way to rearrange holographic images should also be smart enough to save some of the cuttings from the edit room floor... just in case he needed them for future reference, don't you think?"

"Nothing's going to happen to you, Bright," Held said, trying to keep his voice even. "You're too important to us. We all know that."

"Let Emory make the speeches," Bright dismissed the patronizing remark. "He's better at it. Now, what are we going to do about Hollock?"

"Please. We can't afford another killing," Held pleaded.

"I'll ask Margaret to make one more jump," Emory said. "Then we can decide the appropriate course of action to take. Abraham, how soon can we have access to your facilities?"

"I'll talk to our man at B.E.T.A. He's been keeping an eye on things for us over there. He can supply us with the jump coordinates before the day is out. We can do it at midnight, like before, when they shunt the main power grid over to maintenance. That will hide the power surge. I'll hide the jump time itself by folding it into the Miller's Crossing matrix. As long as we keep it under ten minutes at a time, no one will find out. They'll chalk any anomaly up to normal system variance."

"See if you can catch Hollock talking with that friend of Robenalt's," Bright said. "I don't trust that guy."

"Yes, I agree," Emory said. "With all that's happened, I think Mr. Thorndyke now bears some watching."

"We don't have anything to worry about from some kid who's still wet behind the ears," Held dismissed their concern.

"Maybe so," Bright mused. "But humor me—if you don't mind, that is."

"Okay," Held sighed resignedly, avoiding looking at the silly grin on Bright's face. "I'll see what we can find out on the kid, too. But only if we have enough time."

15:15 HOURS

"How long have they been in there?" Carla smiled, glancing at the sealed double doors leading into Hollock's office.

"At least an hour," Robert sniffed.

"With a *full* privacy blackout this time. I understand they're old friends. Very good friends."

"What the Director does with his personal life is his own business."

"You made reservations for him at the Willard Hotel this Sunday—at her request?"

"Been snooping through the restricted files again, Carla?" Robert cast a sideway glance.

"I just think it's so romantic. And scandalous! The Secretary of State of the United States East and Director Hollock alone in his office,

107

on full privacy status, doing who knows what? He's even blocked out all Beta Light recordings." Leaning against the top of her desk she stared dreamily toward the door. "I wish George had a romantic streak. All he ever wanted to do was—"

"I don't really think I need to hear this," Robert blushed. "Besides, this isn't the only time today he's called for a Level Twelve authorization."

"Oh, right," Carla seemed disappointed.

"I think it all has to do with the Resurfacing Ceremony this Sunday. The President is going to attend. They're probably discussing security arrangements for him and the other officials."

"Well, I still think it's romantic anyway."

"What?"

"The two of them in there. She likes him, I can tell it."

"Go back to work, Carla," Robert sighed, returning to his monitor as another routine request for a few moments of Hollock's time scrolled across his screen.

* * *

"I've pulled in every chit I have, but I can't expedite your request, Scott," Lillian Dorr said while Scott Hollock looked back at her with a disappointed frown. "The Central Council said they'd take it under advisement, which means the funeral will go ahead as planned. But at least Sherwood won't be cremated as soon as it's over. It's the best I can do. They plan an open casket and don't want to do anything to disfigure the body while it's on public display. After that, well, I think you have some negotiating room."

"After that, it won't make any difference."

"I need evidence, Scott. Give me something to show the President, then I can get him involved. He won't intervene in a District matter unless he has something solid to go on. There are too many ramifications down the road. We're heading into a difficult legislative session next year. He wants to save his favors for that."

"Politics. God, how I hate that crap."

"Don't go moral on me, Mr. Hollock," Dorr chuckled teasingly. "There's no one better at the game than you. I've seen you shmooze the bureaucrats and politicians in Atlanta *and* Phoenix to keep your funding intact—and Held's hand off your controls. Why is it any different when the subject is hydroponics policy or social services?"

"I know something bad is going to happen," Hollock remained serious. "I can feel it in my gut. Things just aren't adding up."

"Are you telling me that the President's life is in danger?"

"I'm telling you that the President needs to be careful," he struggled for the words.

"Well, that certainly clears it up."

"Look Lillian, you know as well as I do District Intelligence has been picking up rumors of a plot to overthrow the government for months now. Your own security service has heard the same things. You told me that."

"We get rumors like this all the time," Dorr said without emotion. "Somebody doesn't like our trade agreement with the West, or the ContenentalTrans isn't running on time, or they think their taxes are too high—or going to the wrong programs. Or maybe they just don't like the way Drees combs his hair, or the way his teeth show when he smiles. So they make a threat against the government. We send somebody to talk to them, calm them down, and let them off with a warning and thirty hours of civics retraining. If they do it repeatedly, we take stronger measures. But we don't mobilize the security forces every time some crazy makes a complaint."

"These aren't 'complaints,' Lillian. They're serious threats."

"This is a democracy, Scott. People complain. Sometimes irrationally, sometimes in private, sometimes in very public places. But we don't take action against a citizen unless there's a real threat, and words by themselves aren't threats. Even if a thousand people—ten thousand—banded together to overthrow every single elected official, the country wouldn't tolerate it. There hasn't been a serious coup attempt since Peter Haley was killed almost four hundred years ago, and that was when we were one combined country. Since the New Federation Agreement was signed, dividing us into two nations, the population of each country has been more homogenous, and these tensions simply haven't percolated to a threatening level."

"So you don't see any problem?" Hollock said with thinly disguised irritation.

"Yes, I do as a matter of fact. But not enough to warrant extreme measures. I came to you the other day and shared my concerns. You gave me your take, and I took everything back to my people. There still wasn't enough to pin anything down. My hands are tied. This is too important for the President of the U.S. East not to be there, especially with Echeverria attending. I'm sure there'll be protesters, but the DPO and our people can handle them."

"Protesters! Is that all this has been about for you? Protecting Drees from protesters!"

"Don't patronize me, Scott," Dorr's temper flashed. "I believe there's a more serious threat. I believed that before I came to see you Tuesday, and I believe it even more strongly now. But what I believe is irrelevant until I have some proof. So now we're back to where we started. The President of the United States East will not alter his schedule—or permit greater security—unless there's a good deal more to this than an Archivist's murder, questions about Henry Sherwood's heart attack, and the rumblings of a few deluded citizens who want to see someone else running the country. Unfortunately, as popular as Jonathan Drees has been, twenty-three percent of the electorate don't share that feeling. We can't lock everyone up, and we sure as hell can't keep Drees under lock and key in Atlanta because a bunch of people don't like him or his policies."

"I'm very disappointed, Lillian."

"Don't be. I'm doing my job."

"Maybe so," Hollock let out a slow, steady breath. "But at least promise me you will act if I come up with something."

"I'll shut the ceremony down in the middle of Drees' address if there's a reason to. You know that."

"Yeah. Let's just hope it never gets that far."

15:39 HOURS

The door to her apartment unit was locked. Margaret Zhow sat alone inside a room that looked like a miniature Theater, gazing out onto a holographic garden.

She had the most extensive private collection of Beta Light images of anyone in The District, and had built the room several years earlier to showcase them. Some were elaborate constructions of important historical events, others sweeping, majestic landscapes from prehistoric times to the years before the Big War drove everyone from the surface. But the image she enjoyed most was her garden. Simple, colorful, it made her seem as if she was sitting on the back porch of some Antebellum manor with not a care in the world, watching bees buzz about, insects crawl, and birds occasionally land to pick at the seeds or drink the nectar of the vegetation surrounding her.

"Visitor at the main entrance," the room announced, drawing her out of her deep-seated thoughts.

"I said I didn't want to be disturbed. What's wrong with you? Are you malfunctioning?"

"Dr. Emory has overridden the privacy code. He has access to this apartment through an amendment to your personal security protocol from August 7, 23—."

"Enough!" Zhow interrupted, standing. "Close down Beta Light file 1602."

The image blurred slightly, then vanished, leaving only an empty white room in its place. Zhow left and closed the door, entering the main living area where Emory, resting his frail, weary body, was already waiting.

"I always admired your taste in artifacts, Margaret," he said, looking at the works of art and ornamental vases scattered around the room. "I do wish I'd come here more often."

"You've come enough, Charles," she said unemotionally.

"You were my best student, the finest mind I ever taught. And there have been many good minds over the years."

"Those compliments got you into bed with a twenty-year-old girl. They no longer work as well on a forty-year-old woman."

"I know this whole affair has you upset, Margaret," Emory spoke calmly. "I wish I never had to ask you to become involved. But I did."

"Yes. We can't change the past."

"We need another jump. A last one."

"Henry Sherwood was supposed to be the last."

"Yes, poor Henry. His passing is a great loss for all of us."

"Bright killed him, didn't he?" Zhow stated flatly. "Why? You heard what Sherwood said on the jump file I brought back. He didn't believe Beta Light images could be altered. He wasn't a threat to you."

"Henry had a weak heart. His death was a natural one, a tragic coincidence. You have my word on it. No one in our circle did him any harm," Emery lied.

It was so quiet he could almost hear Zhow breathe while he waited, stone-faced, for her to respond. Slowly, as if trying to sort everything out in her mind, she turned her back on Emory and stared off into the distance.

"Who is it now?"

"Scott Hollock. We suspect he knows more than he should. We have to know what he's told that Dorr woman."

"No more after this, Charles. I'm finished. I want out."

"I won't ask you again."

"I don't want to see you again after this," Zhow continued, still not facing him.

"I understand," Emory replied softly, looking even more frail than he had when he first entered. He rose from his seat and headed toward the door, pausing before he instructed it to open. "You know I don't have much longer to live. I won't see the culmination of this great work, only it's beginning. I believe in what we're doing. I wouldn't have asked you to become involved if it was only for my personal gain. This country's greatness can only be restored by reuniting with the West. All our troubles, all our ills can be traced to that cursed day when petty minds surrendered to expediency and ripped apart a great heritage. Was Lincoln wrong to fight to preserve the union at any cost? You were there, you saw him anguish over sending those young men into battle. But he did what had to be done, and history recognizes him as a great leader."

"Lincoln commanded an army," Zhow faced Emory again and spoke evenly. "The men who fought and died, on both sides, did so to preserve a truth they believed in. Tell me, Charles, what army did Jim Robenalt fight for? What crime did he commit for which he deserved to die?"

"I'm not here to argue, Margaret. Held needs you there at midnight."

"I'll be there for you, Charles," she whispered under her breath as he stepped into the hallway and left her apartment. "I always am."

20:41 HOURS

"So, how long have you known Paul?" Ruth Parker asked, drawing a curious smile from Sharla who glanced at him and Quentin huddled together at the opposite end of the room.

"Just a few days."

"But long enough to know you love him."

"That obvious?" she chuckled with faux resignation.

"It is to me."

"I am in love with him, Ruth," Sharla sighed. "Madly. He's the most interesting, most amazing man I've ever met. Brilliant, compassionate, kind, perceptive, self-sacrificing—and you know what makes him even more extraordinary? He really has no idea how truly exceptional he is."

The two women glanced at Thorndyke and Quentin bent over a stack of Beta Light files downloaded from the Central Archives. Both were locked in deep conversation while they fine-tuned a program that Quentin had been working on for most of the evening.

"It doesn't take more than a moment if you know it's right," Sharla continued dreamily. "I knew we'd be together forever the first time I saw him. I feel so complete when he's around. You don't think it's crazy, do you, to feel this way so strongly, so soon?"

"It was the same way with Quentin," Ruth said. "I'm a strong believer in destiny. If something's meant to be, there isn't anyone, or anything, that can stop it. Or even slow it down."

"I only hope he feels about me, the same way I do about him."

"Oh, I think he does," Ruth giggled with a nod and a wink.

"I like you, Ruth," Sharla whispered, ending the conversation when Quentin and Paul brought an armful of data disks and a portable viewer over to the coffee table and laid them down in a pile.

"You won't believe what Quentin's come up with," Thorndyke shook his head in admiration.

"I'll go fix us something to eat," Ruth smiled, rising from the sofa. "I think we could use a little snack before you two take us through your night's work."

"Oh, no," Thorndyke sighed. "Look at the time. I'm sorry, Sharla, I didn't—"

"Ruth and I had a great time getting to know each other. Don't

113

worry about dinner, we can go out another time. Show me what you found."

"You may want to see this too, Ruth," Quentin called, pulling her back into the room.

Ruth took her seat next to Sharla while Thorndyke slipped the first disk into the viewer. Immediately a full-sized holographic image of Benjamin Mitchell, minutes before his death, flickered into view. Quickly, Quentin tapped a sensor pad on the viewer, muting the sound. Only the image remained, playing back the Beta Light recording as it had appeared at Robenalt's trial.

"Where did you get that?" Sharla stared at the image, her mouth agape. "That's a judicial file. No one has clearance to get into that."

"You'd be amazed what Paul's got in that bag of tricks of his," Quentin grinned.

"Look at this disk," Thorndyke said grim-faced. "At first the evidence is damning. But on closer examination, it doesn't hold up. The image flickers and resets at one point... there. Quentin, freeze the image and back it up to that point. There, see?"

"It's just noise," Sharla said quietly. "We see it all the time. The first images are rough and sometimes distorted. We run them through a re-processor to clean them up and get a stable picture. The full image is always there, just not tracking right with the viewer. Sometimes it takes a couple of passes to get rid of all the clutter, unless, of course, it's not a calibration problem and the jump pack itself is out of phase with the Beta Light strata. I've seen one or two files where the noise from that was so bad they had to do the jump over."

"But every file gets cleaned."

"Sure, those we save, always. Especially a judicial file. You know, Paul," Sharla paused to reflect. "It has been a couple of days. They should have processed all the noise out by now to get a completed file."

"The missing image didn't seem to materially affect the facts of the case," Ruth offered. "I guess there's just no hurry."

"What if it isn't 'noise?'" Thorndyke asked.

"Not noise?" Sharla replied quizzically. "I don't think there's an image in a hundred that comes through without some clean-up needed. What else could it be?"

"The image was cut, here," Quentin said, slowly advancing the recording. "A small splice was made, maybe a second or two, enough to cut out the last couple of words. Look at the shadow on the table made by the other person. It's here, then here, just like that, jumping a foot or so instantaneously."

"That's not distortion," Sharla could barely speak the words.

"Watch it again with the sound."

In the center of the room, the Beta Light image of Jim Robenalt grabbed Mitchell by the arm and swung him around roughly.

"It's over!" Mitchell shouted. "I know about it! It's only a matter of time before others find out, too! It's—"

The image flickered, then reset. Quentin stopped the playback.

"The rest of what Mitchell says is wiped out, only the action continues. Then it picks up again as they struggle. I think someone stopped the recording at that point and deliberately erased the sound. But it was a rushed job. They didn't get all the words out, so they had to go back and do it again. This time they didn't just remove the sound overlay, they took out some of the image pixels too, probably by accident. They phonied up the whole thing by making it seem like the image got noisy at that point. But a noisy image doesn't jump time. It isn't like removing frames from an old style photolight projection, it just blanks out a few seconds of sound or image then resumes at that later point. That's where they made their first mistake."

"No one noticed because everything was happening so quickly at that point," Thorndyke continued. "And, no one was looking for any tampering. I'm not surprised no one picked up on it. Quentin didn't even see it the first time he looked at it."

"You said 'first mistake?'" Ruth spoke in a hush.

"Watch here, just before all this took place."

The playback was rewound to the point where Robenalt, his face hidden by the shadows, passed his hand over a sensor point and dimmed the lights further. He approached the now-standing Mitchell, who reacted in obvious fear.

"I know about the unauthorized jumps," Mitchell said. "I stumbled across a discarded file in the Central Archives two weeks ago, something you meant to delete but overlooked because it was so small—just a fragment of a larger file. If I was looking for it, I'd never have known it was there."

"Here," Thorndyke interrupted, advancing the file. "Listen to Robenalt's voice."

"You're going to... report me."

"I should have gone to the authorities before," Mitchell said. "I just couldn't believe it was possible."

"Can't let you do that."

"There," Quentin said, stopping the playback again. "Watch the image when I slow it down and replay those parts. You can't see Jim's face clearly, but listen to the voice—especially where he seems to pause. At first you think it's just stress, but every pause has a small amount of almost imperceptible noise... like this."

The image froze and a thin band of distortion cut across the view. Quentin walked toward the holographic image, moving into its field, and let his finger trace along the jagged edge radiating out in all directions from Robenalt's head.

"Sound is captured in a Beta Light recording much the same way images are. Each subatomic component of the Beta Light recording is woven into a highly integrated and interrelated tapestry of particles that together make up the sights and sounds of the images. Alter even one sub-unit, and you leave a noticeable hole at that point. This is because instead of dealing with a two-dimensional surface, Beta Light recordings exists in three dimensions—four when you count the passage of time. Theoretically, you might be able to insert or subtract an image if it was small enough and self-contained enough, and if you were willing to spend a month or two editing the image so it would show up convincingly. But remember, you're dealing with trillions of data points per three-dimensional centimeter that have to be manipulated *every second* to get a convincing image. And it gets even harder if you're trying to insert an image over occupied space instead of, say, letting it float in thin air. Even then you still have to contend with background bleed-through from all images up, down, and sideways. Frankly, I don't think it's ever been tried, even with the best computers. It's just too difficult to do.

"Now, it gets even more complicated when you deal with sound. You can't just add to or subtract from a recording like you would with an image. Sound is everywhere! You have to replace *every single audio data point* for that specific sound without affecting the other

116

ambient noises. With the technology we have today that simply isn't possible. You might get away with it the first time you play it, but as soon as someone really listened they'd hear the bleed-through of the original sound. It's only marginally better if you're just adding net-new sound without trying to erase an existing sound. There would still be enough overlap with existing noise when you try to fit a different pitch of the same sound for every conceivable point in the image that it wouldn't sound natural.

"But there," Quentin pointed. "Look at this distortion band. It only appears for a fraction of a second and then it's gone. It is amazing, really! Almost too much to believe! What you're looking at is the only visible evidence of a new sound element being inserted over an existing track in the original recording. Whoever did this probably only left the trail because they were rushed. It's less than a millionth of a percent of the total volume of the image. Do you understand what I'm saying? Somebody took an image that was, at best, a day or two old, and altered it in a way that wouldn't be possible if every computer in The District worked on it for a month! And they did it near-flawlessly! But wait, there's more! Each one of these distortion points is a mathematical cincture—a patch-point literally sewn into the subatomic structure of the image by an algorithmic formula so advanced it doesn't... exist. But it does, and I'm here looking at it! The new words are literally stitched into the old image, atom-by-atom, point-by-point, where the old words once existed. The mathematics to do this is so sophisticated it transforms itself from an abstract representation to something that actually has substance."

"You can't be serious, Quentin," Sharla gasped.

"Don't ask me how, but I can see it. It's a quantum leap in mathematics that literally revolutionizes the way computers can be used to broadcast images, like when light was first used to carry sound instead of wires or air waves. There's no needle, no grooves, no magnetic fields, just an emanating source and a target matrix. The computer becomes an active tool in translating the properties of each component into sight and sound. Instead of simply enhancing the quality of a recording, in this case, it becomes a functional part of the recording itself."

"I don't understand any of this," Sharla grunted.

"Look, here, back the image up to when Robenalt first speaks. You see it again, only this time the pixels are in a different location... there, and there."

"What does it mean?" Ruth asked apprehensively.

"It means," Quentin took a heavy breath, "that someone lifted a few words Jim Robenalt said on one occasion, then combined them at a second point with words from a different sentence and patched them both together to make something new. Then the whole thing was overlaid over the original speech, which was mathematically removed. You don't notice it as much when he first starts to speak because there's no break. It's the start, but there is a slightly noticeable pause when the words are recombined. My guess is the whole thing is processed even further to refine out the differences in the two different strands of speech. Even though it's the same person, their voice will be slightly higher or lower if they're fatigued, a little stressed, or it's early in the day instead of later. That leveling helps explain why Jim's voice seems somewhat subdued."

"And since there's no visible face in most of the Beta Light recording," Thorndyke said, "there's no problem with matching lip movements to words. Look at him carefully the one time you get a clear view of his face. Maybe it's my imagination, but the expression doesn't match the heavy breathing of the body. The guy just finished a fight to the death and he looks like he's watching a Vid-show. His skin isn't even flushed."

"Like to know what I found when I looked at the face?" Quentin smiled.

"I'll bet more pixels," Sharla guessed aloud.

"Thousands of them. Small, tightly compact to reduce the noise. It must have taken hours to process. In fact, I'll bet that's why the other stuff was kind of rushed. The face was the key—"

"—to forging Jim's identity," Thorndyke concluded triumphantly. "With this new process, you could coordinate face and mouth movements, if you had enough images to work with, and enough time to run the numbers."

"If you two are right, Paul," Sharla said carefully, "and I'm beginning to think there's something to this, think of what it would take to pull something like this off. It isn't just this new mathematical system Quentin talks about. Somebody would have to make Beta Light jumps into the recent past to bring back Robenalt's image. Only the government can do that."

"Or some people in very powerful positions."

"Who?"

"I don't know," Thorndyke confessed.

"And why Robenalt?" Ruth added. "Why frame him? What did he do to deserve that?"

"All they needed to make this image work was Jim's face," Thorndyke replied. "And a body about the same size and shape of his to put it on. I'll bet you Jim was picked because he's similar physically to the real killer, and he's someone Mitchell knew. Maybe there was something else to it, too, but that was the main reason."

"I'm more interested in why Mitchell was killed," Quentin interjected. "Maybe it had something to do with what he was looking at. It's too convenient that the Beta Light recording stopped short of including his view monitor while it was on. A jumper would almost have to contort themselves to make sure that part of the strata remained outside their image capture range."

"None of this adds up," Ruth said. "Except to spell trouble. You have no idea what you two are getting into."

"Jim was my friend. Somebody did this to him. I want to know who."

For a long moment the four thought in silence, each mulling over the options— and dangers—of becoming even more involved. Finally, Sharla turned to Thorndyke and spoke.

"Maybe we're going about this the wrong way. Mitchell was killed because of something he knew, or did. Or was going to do. Find out what was going on, and we'll have a pretty good idea of who's behind all this."

"Great. And just how do you propose to do that?"

"Ruth, can you access Central Files from your viewer?"

"Yes."

"Call up Archival Research Index Records. Whatever Mitchell was viewing at the time he was killed will be recorded in the index, not to mention every other Beta Light file he's accessed in the last twelve months. I'll bet you whatever is in that index will lead us in the right

119

direction."

"You know," Thorndyke smiled broadly. "You're not only beautiful, but very clever too."

"You should expect no less, Mr. Thorndyke," Sharla replied coquettishly. "I certainly don't."

"Sharla," Ruth called from the view screen across the room. "I'm getting something strange, here. It says I'm locked out. Something about authorization needed for a 'File 24.'"

"That's a judicial file. They must have sealed everything for the investigation."

"Well, it was a good idea anyway," Ruth sighed.

"Your magic bag, can it break a Level 8 data access restriction?" Sharla asked Thorndyke.

"Yes."

"I've already tried it," Quentin said, standing over Ruth and punching in the appropriate authorization code. "Still nothing."

"Now that's really odd. I've never seen a judicial file higher than Level 7. Level 8 should be more than enough."

"I can get us into a Level 10 security file," Thorndyke said.

"Level 10! Something is definitely wrong here."

"Well, whatever it is, there's nothing more we can do tonight. It's getting late. Maybe we should call it a night. Quentin, why don't you stay with Ruth tonight, here, you know, just in case."

"You think something might happen?" Quentin's jaw tightened.

"I don't know what to think. I'm going to go see Hollock in the morning, tell him what we've found. Maybe he'll have a better feel for what's going on and make some sense of it."

"Stay, Quentin," Ruth softly urged.

"Sharla, it might make sense for you to stay here, too. You know, safety in numbers."

"What about you?"

"I'll go back to my place. If they're looking for anyone, it's going to be me. No sense getting you all involved."

"But we are involved," she replied in an irritated voice.

"Yeah, I guess," Thorndyke agreed.

"So it doesn't make a lot of sense for you to wander off by yourself and leave us alone, does it?"

"Well, no, I guess not," Thorndyke said.

"Safety in numbers? That's what you said. Right?"

"Yes, well—"

"So maybe you should stay here with me, *too?*"

"Well, yes, I guess you're right," he relented.

"I'm glad we could finally persuade you," Sharla said coolly

"She's a real toot," Quentin laughed, watching Thorndyke shift uncomfortably. "See you guys in the morning."

Ruth hid a smile as she and Quentin drifted off to the other room, sealing the door behind them.

"You know," Thorndyke said, grinning impishly. "Maybe this wasn't such a bad idea."

He put his arms around Sharla's waist, expecting her to fold herself into his embrace. Instead she moved away and opened a closet door, taking out a blanket and pillow and tossing it to him.

"You can sleep over there, on the floor. I'll take the couch," she said in a matter-of-fact voice. "Unless you'd rather have the couch instead?"

"No, er, the floor's fine," Thorndyke replied, thoroughly confused.

As Sharla made her impromptu bed, Thorndyke walked over to his spot and began to slip off his shirt. Glancing furtively in her direction he watched her undress and slip under her covers, then order the lights to dim.

"Good night, Paul," she cooed, her voice light and sweet.

"Night," Thorndyke mumbled, building himself a pallet.

He listened to her breathing become steady and slow as she fell off to sleep. Boosting himself slightly on his elbows, he stared at her through the dim, ambient light of the apartment's electrical devices, all whirling and clicking in a soothing sympathy while they went about their various duties. Chuckling appreciatively, he shook his head and lay back against his pillow, looking in her direction one last time.

"High maintenance—but definitely worth it."

"RENDEZVOUS WITH A DEAD MAN"
Friday, September 27, 2416 AD
09:05 HOURS

That is at the bottom the only courage
demanded of us; to have courage
for the most strange... and most
inexplicable that we may encounter.
                    -Rainer Maria Rilke

Many aspects of life had changed dramatically since the dawn of the Industrial Revolution when people began to congregate in factories or office complexes to go about the task of earning a living. The type of work they did, how it was performed, the nature of the products or services they created—all these were transformed with each new social or technological innovation.

But throughout it all, one component of this process remained unshakably consistent. Monday, the traditional starting point of the new work week, was always accompanied by a certain amount of dread as the blissful relaxation—or frantic quest for amusement—of the weekend came to an end. By Wednesday, though, even those who disliked their jobs had settled into a routine, working efficiently and productively. But as soon as Friday morning came, thoughts of a two, sometimes three day respite from work began crowding everyone's mind. Just as it was in the nineteenth century, so it still was half a millennium later. Fridays were a much anticipated, much welcome marker for the men and women who now, more than ever, looked to the present for some meaning to their lives, since the future of all mankind was growing more and more uncertain with each passing day.

"Hi, Carla," Thorndyke said, eying the young woman sitting at Robert's desk. It was his third visit to Hollock's office in the last five days. Despite his relatively new status at B.E.T.A., he was fast becoming a familiar figure among the staff who jealously guarded the entryway to the Director's office. "Where's, er—"

"Robert? Off. In fact, you won't find many people here today at all."

"Really? Did I miss the memo?"

"Memo? I don't think there was any—"

"No, I don't mean a real memo," Thorndyke chuckled. "I mean, what's going on?"

"Oh, yes... I get it. That's funny! No, most people took a personal day to get ready for the festivities this weekend. They've announced all sorts of parties and gatherings before for the Resurfacing Ceremony Sunday. Haven't you been watching the news?"

"No. I've been kind of busy."

"They've even shut down a lot of work at T.I.M.E. and P.A.S.T. The Historical Records team downstairs is still refining the jump coordinates for another try at Miller's Crossing today, but the rest of B.E.T.A. is a skeleton crew. I'm leaving at two, myself."

"Carla, you are a wealth of information."

"Thank you! Are you here to see Mr. Hollock?"

"Yes. Is he free?"

"He's not in yet," she suppressed a grin.

"Oh. When's he expected?"

"He was supposed to be here at seven. That's his normal time. But he didn't show up and he hasn't called."

"I see. You wouldn't have any idea—"

"Know what I think?" she leaned forward conspiratorially.

"What?"

"I think he's off some place with the Secretary of State, Lillian Dorr. They're... old friends, I understand."

"So, you think he's—"

"Yes! Isn't it so romantic? He never does anything spontaneous like this. It just shows you how a good woman can change a man's life. You can wait here, with me, if you'd like. I'm sure he'll be by soon. He has a ten o'clock with his department heads, their regular Friday morning meeting."

"I can't stay," Thorndyke seemed distracted. "Can you tell him I was here when he comes in?"   •

"Certainly," Carla said. He turned to leave but she called to him as he was about to exit the room, drawing him back momentarily.

"Mr. Thorndyke, Paul. May I call you Paul?"

"Sure. Paul's fine."

"Paul, I live in the Constitution Quadrant, Level 27, on Madison."

"Yes," he replied, puzzled.

"I'm going to adjust my security protocol when I get home, you know... to allow new friends to call... if they want to."

"I, er, I'm seeing someone, actually," Thorndyke stammered, finally realizing what the young woman was saying.

"Oh," she replied sadly, then brightened theatrically. "Well, I'm sure I'll be seeing more of you here, anyway. Until next time, Paul. Goodbye."

Carla couldn't quite understand the awkward, barely intelligible mumble that passed from Thorndyke's lips, but there was no mistaking the crimson red blush that all but consumed his handsome face. She watched him turn and leave with a delightful smile, dreaming of the next time the serious young man would return to the office.

* * *

The hallways were all but deserted as Thorndyke made his way through the sprawling underground complex to level G where his office was located. Except for the occasional cubicle with a solitary figure laboring to meet a project deadline, there was no one around. Half way down one of the brightly lit corridors, he pulled up short at the sound of a familiar voice calling from behind.

"Are we the only two human beings stupid enough to come to work today?" Brian Russack boomed, his voice carrying down the empty hallway.

"Hey, Brian," Thorndyke smiled.

"I've been looking for you, Paul. Where you been?"

"Oh, you know," Thorndyke looked around, not answering the question. "Boy is this place deserted."

"They suspended all jumps while everyone looks at the new Miller's Crossing data. There's nothing to do, unless you're in Historical Research. Once HR figures out the exact time sequences they want to access, we'll need to refine the coordinates. But until then, it's just hurry up and wait. Say, what do you say we go grab us some downtime at the Theater? There won't be anything definitive for us today, and even if there is, the whole city's shutting down for the big ceremony this weekend. There's a new Beta scan on the Roman chariot races D'Angelo brought back. I hear it's unbelievable! They configure the Theater like you're actually in the Coliseum stands. If you want, you can even sit down by the track itself and watch them go by. They added fans for special effects, you know, like the breeze of the animals as they race by. And here's the kicker. They've created an ester that's supposed to smell just like horse dung. You know, to add realism!"

"I think I'll pass," Thorndyke said. "I still have a few things I need to do."

"Boy," Russack kidded. "You are bucking for Hollock's job!"

"You haven't seen him today, have you?"

"Me and Scott, we hang together off-hours. Here, it's strictly work."

"Okay, okay," Thorndyke smirked. "Stupid question."

"But I will tell 'em you're looking for 'em if he drops by my cube for a chat," Russack laughed as Thorndyke waved and began walking away.

Russack watched the tall, gangly looking man continue down the hallway, his eyes never leaving the disappearing figure until Thorndyke was completely out of sight. Then, stepping into a nearby empty cubicle he sat behind the desk and tapped on a motion-sensitive switch to bring a Vid-link monitor to life.

"This is Russack," he spoke quietly to the screen, waiting for the rainbow of colors to congeal into a face on the other end. "He's here, looking for Hollock."

"Yes," Emory sighed. "I'm not surprised."

"What should I do?"

"Keep tabs on him, like we discussed yesterday. But discretely."

"I will. But Paul's very bright. He suspects something. If he's starting to piece things together, he can be trouble."

"Caution is advised, Mr. Russack," Emory agreed. "But there's no need to worry excessively about a junior level analyst at B.E.T.A. Even if he starts asking the right questions, it's too late to do any good."

125

"But if he—"

"There's nothing he can do, even if he stumbles across the truth. Mr. Hollock won't be coming in today."

"I understand," Russack replied grim-faced.

"Still, I think it's best that you come to the shelter once your work is finished at B.E.T.A. We're certain to need your help there, once things begin to heat up."

"I'll be there as soon as I can," Russack nodded, tapping the switch and shutting off the signal.

09:27 HOURS

"Well, what did he say?" Quentin whispered, poking his head inside Thorndyke's office. Thorndyke pushed the pile of datasheets and readouts cluttering his work station off to one side and folded his hands across the edge of his desk.

"He wasn't there."

"Not there? Where was he?"

"Carla thinks he's... she doesn't know."

"I don't have a good feeling about this," Quentin took a seat across from him, his eyes furtively searching the door for anyone passing by.

"Neither do I. I just accessed news and information. Hollock's not dead. At least they're not reporting it."

"Paul, do you know how crazy this whole conversation sounds?"

"I know."

"I am convinced we're on to something," Quentin said. "I don't know what it is, but I can tell you one thing. It's dangerous, and whatever it is, it's completely out of our league."

"I'll understand if you need to back off, Quentin," Thorndyke said, his chest rising and falling with a heavy sigh.

"Did I say anything about bugging out? That is right, bugging out? Or is it buggering?"

"No, I think you got it right," Thorndyke couldn't help but smile. "Buggering is a *nineteenth*—and it doesn't really mean the same thing."

"Well, pre-industrial native civilizations of South America are my field of study anyway. So, what do we do?"

"The key is Mitchell's murder. It ties everything together, somehow. Robenalt, the doctored images, I'll bet even Henry

Sherwood 'heart attack' and Hollock's disappearance are connected to it as well. It's all there. I just can't put the pieces together yet."

"Maybe we should take our findings to the District Police? Let them sort it out."

"No. Nothing's clear enough yet to get the authorities involved."

"So what do you propose, Paul?"

"I think we ought to have another look at Mitchell's death. This time without the manipulations."

"What! How?"

"The Transmission Center is shut down while HR works out a new jump scenario for Miller's Crossing."

"You can't be serious!" Quentin's mouth dropped. "Make an unauthorized jump?"

"We can get into the Transmission Center using Hollock's access code."

"Getting in isn't the problem! Who are you going to get to make the jump?"

"I will."

"You! What training do you have?"

"What training do I need? You know as well as I do they don't really need jumpers to bring back Beta Light images. Everything could be done with a remote controlled probe, probably with greater efficiency. The jump suit and jump pack have everything you need to recover images. The jumper's just along for the ride. We didn't have to put people into the equation. We *wanted to!"*

"Yeah, sure, all that's well and good. But where are you going to get forty other people to go along with this little idea of yours?"

"I don't need forty, Quentin. I only need one. This is a simple jump into the near past. There's no complicated targeting, no need for redundant ground support. We're not doing a complete strata survey, so there's no image banks to monitor, no extended uplink to maintain. Most of what needs to be done can be handled by the computers. All it takes is a jumper and someone to ride herd over the process on the other side to make sure I get back."

"The place is still guarded, Paul. We'll never make it past the front door."

"I know another way in. Meet me at Archival Records in one hour."

127

"I hope you know what you're doing," Quentin said while he watched Thorndyke rise and head out into the corridor, leaving him alone in the empty cubicle.

10:41 HOURS

The corridors of Archival Records, one of the myriad of quasi-independent agencies created to support the vast time viewing complex, were as empty as any of the offices in B.E.T.A., T.I.M.E., or P.A.S.T.

Only Sharla and two other archivists remained at their work stations. The rest of the department had joined the thousands of others who took the day off to prepare for the upcoming celebration. An eerie, almost haunting silence hung over the powered down equipment and vacant cubicles dotting the underground complex. Except for the occasional click or buzz from some still-active piece of machinery, the only noise heard was the faint sound of human conversation coming from a far off corner of the room where Sharla, Thorndyke, and Quentin stood quietly conversing.

"I called again, like you asked," Sharla said. "He still hasn't come in."

"I'm more convinced than ever that something's terribly wrong," Thorndyke lowered his voice, looking around conspiratorially. He spotted a lone woman walking down a far corridor and watched until she disappeared, unnoticing, into another section. "Sharla, it's not safe for you to stay around any longer. We can use Hollock's code to get access to the Transmission Center through your area. I just need you to make sure no one sees us go in, and lock up after we enter. Then get out of here. Take the day off like everyone else. I'll meet you back at your apartment as soon as we're finished."

"I'm going with you."

"No," Thorndyke's voice hardened.

"I'm in this as much as—"

"Will you just listen to me for once?" he snapped in frustration. "You are the most *exasperating woman!* This is something Quentin and I can do alone. It's dangerous enough without dragging you into it, too! You've already helped me more than I had any right to ask. Now let me do what I need to do for my friend. I don't want you to get

128

hurt."

For a long moment Sharla's eyes fixed on his. Quentin couldn't tell if the look she was giving Thorndyke was one of anger or love, but there was no denying the intensity of the emotion. Towering over her, Thorndyke held her gaze with equal passion, his jaw fixed tightly, lips stretched and thin, as if every muscle in his body was being called upon to bolster his resolve. Finally, after what seemed like minutes, Sharla let a thin smile creep across her face and folded her arms delicately across her chest.

"You'd better come back to me safe and sound, Paul Thorndyke. I've already made up my mind about you, and I have no intention of letting you get away."

"That's one thing you'll never have to worry about," Thorndyke took her gently in his arms.

"I hate to break in on this tender moment," Quentin said seriously. "But if we don't get going soon, we're not going to have enough time to program the Machine and get in a jump before the guards do a walk through of the Transmission Center. I used Hollock's code to run a check on the security schedule and we've got about 45 minutes to get in and out. And that includes programming the right coordinates into the command logic center while you're suiting up and I'm getting the energy spiral up to full force."

"Be careful," Sharla whispered, her voice breaking as she kissed Thorndyke forcefully, then slipped from his grasp.

"I'm coming back," he said, forcing a smile.

"You better. Because if you don't, I'm coming after you."

12:17 HOURS

"Are we almost ready?" Thorndyke shouted over the growing din.

The bluish-grey crackle of an energy spiral continued to build off the end of the ramp, drowning out every other sound in the Transmission Center.

"I've still got a few more systems to bring up," Quentin yelled, scurrying between a half-dozen banks of equipment scattered throughout the control room. "I fed the jump coordinates from the justice file disk into the main computer, but I still have to calibrate the warp strength to match the resonance of the Beta Light strata we're aiming for. Damn, these baffles still need some fine tuning! My skin's crawling."

"You can grab a ground suit from the back," Thorndyke shouted while he fitted the clear glass helmet of his jump suit onto his collar and locked it in place.

"No time! We've already got a sub-vortex. Thirty seconds to launch. You ready?"

"Ready!"

Thorndyke turned and faced the crackling tornado of raw, swirling energy less than twenty feet away. Growing in size, changing in colors, it was at once both terrifying and compelling, a doorway to the images of another time beckoning him to enter. He took a slow, halting step forward, feeling the energy pull at his body, its tendrils wrapping around his torso and legs like some living, breathing animal.

"We're going critical," Quentin yelled into his throat mike. "God, I hope I did this right."

. Now standing at the center of the platform, the red suited figure began to glow with sparkling light. Thorndyke caught his breath as he felt the fibers of his very being begin to slip apart and dissolve into a disconnected mass of electrically-charged particles. Where his body intertwined with the now bluish-white swirl of energy he felt neither heat nor cold, pleasure nor pain, nor sensation of any kind. It was as if every nerve in his body was becoming desensitized to its surroundings, and the only thing left was the empty shell of his corporal form encasing his still-active, conscious mind.

"Now!" Quentin screamed, throwing the switch to fire the pulse generator and send Thorndyke's demolecularized body, now completely engulfed in a huge, spiral warp, into the core of the Transmission Center.

Immediately, the room returned to silence. The sound was so deafeningly quiet that Quentin could actually hear the thump of his own heartbeat as he fought to control his breathing.

A bank of monitors tracked Thorndyke's movements. Quentin looked up to see the red suited figure hanging against a backdrop of totally black void like a 21st century astronaut walking in space. "This isn't right," he said nervously to himself. "The coordinates are right, but there's some kind of interference blocking out the Beta Light images."

"It's an energy cone," Brian Russack said blandly, his voice coming from behind. Spinning, Quentin turned to face the steely-eyed man, who was holding a weapon pointed at his chest. "If you overpower a jump you black out sections of the Beta Light strata, like cutting frames from an old-style film. Once it's gone, it's gone. You can never get it back. We wiped it out just after Zhow made her jump to get the original images."

"Margaret Zhow!"

"And others. Lots of us, really. You really shouldn't have interfered, Quentin. You and Paul are in way over your heads."

"I've got to bring him back," Quentin reached for a sensor on the control panel, only to find another hand slam down hard against his. He looked up into the smirking grin of a large, heavily muscled man who was pinning his hand to the console. Behind him another two figures emerged from the shadows, surrounding him on all sides.

With quiet efficiency, one of the men entered a new set of coordinates into the control panel. Quentin was pulled back and forced to stand a short distance away, watching with concern while his friend, disoriented and confused, drifted helplessly on the screen.

"What are you going to do? You can't just leave him there."

"It's not my decision," Russack said, his face grim.

"You can't just leave him there—in nothing!"

"I've already given the order. He'll be moved to another time strata. But he won't be coming back."

"Brian, please—"

"Just consider yourself lucky that I don't put you in there with him!" Russack exploded. "It'll all be over in forty-eight hours, and then it won't matter. We can bring him back then. In the meantime it's going to be enough trouble to deal with you."

"Forty-eight hours! You don't know if he'll even be alive! Nobody's ever been in stasis for more than a day. You're sentencing him to death!"

"Nobody asked you to interfere! Nobody asked you to stick your nose into something you don't understand! I'm giving him a chance to survive, which is more than they'd give you if they thought you really knew anything." Motioning toward the door with the barrel of his gun, he shouted to the big man. "Shank, get him out of here. Take him to the Subterranean."

Tossing Shank the weapon, Russack turned his back while the heavily muscled man ushered Quentin from the room. Still drifting and turning aimlessly on the screen, Thorndyke was in a total state of confusion. Unable to communicate with the control room, all he knew was that something terrible had gone wrong and precious minutes had slipped by without the problem being corrected.

"Look at this guy's vitals," one of the two remaining men laughed, noticing Thorndyke's accelerated heartbeat and frantic breathing on the jump screen indicator.

"Move him to the new coordinates," Russack ordered. He grew impatient as the laughing man continued to watch the monitor.

"I'll bet he's scared shitless. Look at those numbers!"

"That man has more guts than you'll ever have, you witless moron," Russack slammed his hand on the console. Reaching over, he initiated the command himself.

The man eased back, thoroughly chastised, and watched in silence while the image on the screen faded and Thorndyke was transferred to a different time strata.

13:32 HOURS

The Transmission Center was eerily quiet. Except for a dull humm from the master control panel, every other piece of equipment was powered down between jumps.

Only a few seconds earlier, Thorndyke was floating though a pitch black void when he suddenly found himself pulled back from his jump. Now, standing on the edge of the ramp he peered down into the cold dark core of the enormous Time Machine, then let his eyes take in the silent, empty room.

"Quentin, what happened?"

Thorndyke waited at the edge of the precipice, unsure whether to brace himself for another bone-shaking energy spiral to sweep up and engulf him, or move off the long narrow platform. Expecting Quentin to step out from behind a console and give him direction he strained his eyes to see, but couldn't detect any motion in the dimly lit room.

"Something went wrong with that last jump, Quentin. You sure you got the coordinates right? Quentin?"

Again only silence returned. As he moved down the ramp and stepped onto the polished smooth floor, Thorndyke felt a strange sensation in his arms and legs. It was as if, somehow, they weren't connected to his body. He brushed the sleeve of his suit, expecting to see a flurry of carbon flakes litter the floor, but the material was as clean and free of distress as it had been when he first put it on.

"Paul," Quentin's voice broke the silence. Thorndyke faced the direction of the sound.

"Quentin, where are you?"

"Paul, over here. I found it."

"Found what?"

The lights in the room suddenly brightened and a smiling Quentin Cottle emerged from behind a large panel, making his way to the master control console. Thorndyke was about to call out when the sight of a second figure carrying a bright red jump suit took away his breath. Heading toward him, fumbling with the latches that opened and sealed the suit, was *his own image* just as it had been one hour earlier when he and Quentin used Hollock's code to bypass security and enter the Transmission Center.

Too stunned to react, Thorndyke watched the tall, gangly man walk to the edge of the platform and begin slipping on the suit. It was only when he stepped back and his arm and hand brushed against the edge of an equipment bay, passing easily through it, that the full realization of where he was, and what had happened to him, finally sank in.

"I'm here, in the Transmission Center, where we started," he muttered. "But why? What happened to the jump?"

"I'm sorry I got you into this, Paul," said another familiar voice.

Thorndyke spun around to see Jim Robenalt, his face visible through his jump suit helmet, walk through the Transmission Center wall and make his way toward him.

"Jim! My God!" Thorndyke rushed to meet his friend. He grabbed him forcefully by the arms and pulled him into a crushing embrace. To his great surprise, Robenalt was as real and solid as his own flesh. "You got out! How? But you couldn't. We're still... in a jump."

"You've been sent back to my time, Paul. We're the only things real here. Everything else is an illusion."

"I don't understand. Why did Quentin send me here? I was supposed to go back to Mitchell's murder, get the real images to prove you didn't do it. We found—"

"I know. I've been watching you, watching everything. I saw what Quentin found. But none of that will do anyone any good."

"But we can prove you're innocent!"

"Look, up there," Robenalt motioned, drawing his eyes to the observation booth still hidden in deep shadows.

Thorndyke strained to make out the faces of the four men looking down from their observation post watching him and Quentin scurry around the ground level readying the Center for the jump.

"That's Brian Russack. What's he doing here? I don't recognize the others."

"They work for Emory and Held."

"Held! I knew it had to be someone like him! But Professor Emory? What's he got to do with all this? And what are Brian and those others going to do?"

"I suspect we'll find out shortly," Robenalt said.

"Jim, we're in deep trouble, aren't we?"

"Held and Emory are orchestrating a coup to bring down both governments Sunday, at the Resurfacing Ceremony," Robenalt explained. "Held's behind it, Emory's a pawn but doesn't know it. He thinks Held wants to reunite the country, which he does—but under his control."

"Overthrow the governments! How? Oh, my God, they're going to manipulate Beta Light images, just like they did with you. Make it look like Drees and Echeverria are doing something treasonous. Jim, we've got to stop this!"

The howl of the energy spiral building to critical mass drew both men's attention to Thorndyke's image at the end of the long ramp. Thorndyke felt his throat tighten and nervously clutched his stomach, tensing his muscles in sympathy with the figure who appeared to do the same. A brilliant flash of light swept up from the bowels of the great Time Machine, surrounding and encompassing the motionless figure, who immediately disintegrated into a billion sparkling points. Almost as quickly as it began, it was over, and the room returned to purring quiet. The image of a red-suited jumper floating helplessly in a pitch-black void now appeared on a monitor.

"You know," Thorndyke grunted, half-smiling in spite of the seriousness of their situation. "I still don't see why any sane person would want to go through this if they had a choice."

"I think we know what happened to you," Robenalt nodded, casting a glance toward Russack who was now aiming a weapon at Quentin. "I'm sorry, Paul. Truly, I am."

His hand pressed to his side, Robenalt tried to cover a patch in his suit that appeared to phase out momentarily, then return to normal. Slowly, he turned to face Thorndyke, who could barely suppress his shock and fear.

"I think the electromagnetic bonds are beginning to deteriorate at the sub-atomic level," Robenalt's voice was calm and unemotional. "The human body wasn't meant to be placed in stasis for more than a few hours, maybe a day or two at the most. I can feel the basic structure of my muscles and bones beginning to come apart."

"My God, Jim."

"There isn't any pain, at least not yet. As you can probably tell by now, there isn't much feeling here anyway, except for what's in your mind. I'm just becoming more and more like the images around us, empty, hollow—shadows of the real world. My guess is that by this time tomorrow, the process will be irreversible. The electromagnetic bonds will split and not be able to reconstitute themselves. Then I'll just dissolve away."

"Jim, I—" Thorndyke choked.

"I don't dread what's happening; I welcome it. You will, too, when the time comes."

"We're getting out of here," Thorndyke said with resolve.

Robenalt smiled benignly, clasping his friend on the shoulder. They both watched Quentin being escorted from the room and the final settings made to move Thorndyke to Robenalt's time strata.

"They're taking him below to the deepest depths of The District—the Subterranean."

"Subterranean? That's where the first survivors of the ash went underground while they were building the near-subsurface tunnels. It's been abandoned for centuries. How did they get there?"

"There's a channel to the Subterranean right here in the

135

Transmission Center, next to Held's office. I saw them use it the other day. It's a long walk down, but it takes them right into the heart of an old military communications complex. That's where they're holding Scott Hollock."

"Hollock's alive!"

"He put up a real struggle. He's injured badly, but they couldn't afford another death. Not so soon after killing Henry Sherwood."

"This whole thing is so unbelievable." Thorndyke shook his head. "Like some nightmare out of the 21st century."

"Come on, Paul," Robenalt took his friend by the arm, leading him toward the wall. "We may be an hour behind, but we get to see *everything!* I think it's time you and I took a little trip below."

* * *

Standing at the control console, Brian Russack hesitated momentarily before tapping a sensor to close the open link to Thorndyke's jump. Instantly the vortex collapsed and returned the room to deathly quiet.

"So, where'd you send 'em?" the man beside him asked almost absently.

"An hour back."

"An hour? Why that?"

"Held's waiting for us," Russack replied coolly. "Power down the rest of this equipment and we'll meet at D Section."

"Sure. Held ought to be pleased. There's no one left to give us any trouble."

"Yeah. Everyone's out of the way."

The man shut off sensors and dialed back the monitoring gauges to their maintenance levels while Russack walked to the edge of the Transmission core and peered out at the enormous machine. He'd been a member of the team that recruited Thorndyke to B.E.T.A., and after he accepted the offer was pleased to find that Thorndyke had been assigned to his area. He was even friends with Jim Robenalt from their days together at the Time Research Institute. In fact, it was Robenalt who first brought Thorndyke's considerable talents to Russack's attention, which he passed along to upper management at B.E.T.A.

Russack felt no malice toward either man. What happened to Robenalt was an unfortunate necessity. Both he and Mitchell had stumbled across Harmon Bright's secret, though neither fully understood the significance of what they had found. Robenalt had pieced together the fundamentals of Bright's new mathematical system, but didn't fully grasp its implications. Ben Mitchell, a thorough, meticulous archivist, had come upon an altered Beta Light file and was just beginning to make sense of his discovery, when Bright confronted him and took his life. Robenalt was a convenient scapegoat, solving two problems at once. Russack wasn't a part of either decision, just a foot soldier in what he and his fellow conspirators—who numbered less than thirty—had come to think of as the Second American Revolution. He believed in the greater purpose of their actions, and that allowed him to accept the decisions without question.

But even though he truly believed that what he was doing was right, it still troubled him deeply. There were casualties in any war, and this one was no different. Here, though, the enemies were his neighbors, friends, perhaps even family. By sending Thorndyke back to Robenalt's time strata, at least he wouldn't be alone for eternity. And, there was always the hope that once life in the country returned to normal, both he and Robenalt could be retrieved from their Beta Light exile and allowed to resume their life in the present world.

Russack turned slowly and headed toward the exit to the now darkened room, secure in the belief that once the two nations were reunited the people would accept the wisdom of their actions, even if they might still question their methods.

19:55 HOURS

"So, where's this new guy of yours?" Claudia smiled, slipping off her shoes while she settled into the overstuffed sofa and began rubbing her feet. "Don't tell me the romance has cooled after only three days! One night he sleeps over, the next night you don't come home. Now the third night you're pacing the room alone. Do we have trouble in paradise, or have you just worn the poor dear out?"

"This isn't funny, Claudia," Sharla scolded more harshly than she intended.

Claudia immediately rose to her feet, a look of concern evident on her face. The good natured banter between the two roommates was a normal part of their lives, even extending into the workplace. From everything she'd seen, Paul Thorndyke's affection for Sharla was as genuine as Sharla's was for him. She knew she'd touched a raw nerve inadvertently and wanted to make amends.

"I'm sorry, honey. I didn't mean—I was just joking. I thought you two were... is everything okay? That guy didn't turn out to be some kind of creep, did he?"

"No, Claudia, I'm sorry," Sharla whispered. "We were suppose to meet here tonight, and he's just late."

"Maybe he got caught up in some assignment. Everything got really crazy with the short shift today. I'll bet they pulled him on to that special jump they're doing tomorrow."

"Yeah, maybe."

"No, really, Sharla. I got caught down in Archival Records, myself. I thought I'd slip away like everyone else, but I had to clean up another mess. You know, I'm constantly re-filing disks that have been misplaced. People are getting sloppier and sloppier as we bring in more Beta Light files. Can you imagine the grief we'd get if we lost a master file before Entertainment and Science had time to reproduce it? They'd have to do a whole new jump! I tell you, honey, it's only a matter of time before they put servo-units in our department and automate the whole thing. Then can you imagine the no-mind work we'd be left to do? It's hard enough to keep things interesting with machines doing all the detail work."

"I've got to go, Claudia," Sharla said, fitting her waist pouch around her middle and buckling it into place. "If Paul comes by, tell him I went to over to Ruth's apartment."

"You really like him, don't you?"

"Yes, I do."

"Then don't let him stand you up again, Sharla Russell," Claudia giggled as her girlfriend headed through the door.

20:15 HOURS

D Section was a labyrinth of equipment bays and storage compartments located in a deserted Defense Communications Shelter almost three quarters of a mile beneath the city of old Washington D.C.

138

Part of an ancient command and control center that was built to protect the President and other key government officials during a nuclear attack, it was abandoned toward the end of the twenty-first century. Remaining sealed up and unused for over 350 years, it was the perfect hiding place and sanctuary for a group of conspirators determined to once again change the course of human history.

The old communication complex—and the hundreds of other underground facilities linked together by a primitive network of tunnels and causeways—made up what had come to be known as "the Subterranean." It was a little explored area with hundreds of winding, twisting passageways following the natural cracks and fissures in the rock, augmented by a system of man-made tunnels with storage and living areas connected to them. Built over a seventy-year period and kept secret from the press and public, the *Subterranean Integrated Command Complex* was a virtual city beneath a city.

Creation of the first underground bunker began in the 1950's with the construction of a large ball-shaped room three hundred meters beneath the surface. For many years this heavily reinforced structure was the country's primary strategic command and control center in the event of nuclear war, only to be replaced in the early 1990s when a natural cavern was discovered almost a half-mile below it. For the next thirty years, a virtually impregnable fortress of offices, storage facilities, military barracks, and communications infrastructure was built into the natural contour of the rock. But with the signing of a world-wide armistice in 2066 repudiating the use of nuclear weapons, the deep underground complex was no longer needed. Too expensive to maintain and too troublesome to dismantle, it was sealed off and left to history with only the original structure remaining in use as a fortified shelter for select government officials in the event of an unforeseen national emergency. The same construction that shielded the room from nuclear attack would one day, centuries later, serve as the perfect place to house the core of the great Time Machine.

As for the remainder of the complex, officially the Subterranean didn't exist, but everyone in The District knew it was there. Strange stories circulated about bands of genetically mutated humans who lived in these hellish depths, cut off from the rest of humanity, and evolving into a race of their own. They were the stories told by older boys and girls to frighten younger children—made all the more believable because they were based in fact. The first settlers, driven underground in the twenty-second century when the surface ash in North America climbed to deadly levels, reopened the complex and built a life for themselves and their families in these abandoned shelters. Years passed while the near-subsurface tunnels were constructed to allow mankind the opportunity to live a more tolerable existence in these wide, planned-out spaces. But as with every wave of human migration, whether forced or voluntary, when the time came for all to move on, some chose to stay behind and remain in the Subterranean.

An effort was made at first to keep in contact with the lower dwellers, as the inhabitants of the Subterranean came to be called. This contact diminished when friends above and below died off, leaving both worlds to grow more and more distant and isolated. Hydraulic lifts that once operated between the Subterranean and the surface ceased to function through disuse and disrepair; and the only way in or out was by one of the many long, winding stairwells that were used as emergency ingress or egress points into and out of the deep underground complex.

Soon, the Subterranean was little more than a distant memory in The District's collective consciousness, a forgotten outpost in the mythic lore of man's battle to survive the ravages of nature gone awry. Alive only in the history books, every once and a while someone would discover one of its sealed-off stairwells and descend for a moment's adventure, bringing back with them apocryphal tales of human voices sounding in the shadows. But the government discouraged such unauthorized forays into the lower depths, fearing for the safety and well being of their citizens who risked injury, even death, should they fall from a stairwell or become lost in its maze-like passageways.

The Subterranean was a place of mystery and isolation. It became the perfect place for someone to hide.

Or to keep something hidden.

* * *

"It's really spooky walking through walls," Thorndyke grimaced, trying to keep pace with Jim Robenalt a few steps ahead of him. "But

140

solid rock... boy that's something really different. It's *totally* black in here."

"We're almost there," Robenalt called, popping through the cold granite barrier into a dimly lit tunnel. "This leads to D Section, ahead."

Like two other-world explorers, Robenalt and Thorndyke walked along the moist, fungus-caked pathway. They could almost smell the rot and mildew from the leaking walls of the dirty, abandoned section of tunnel. Underground aquifers bled tiny rivulets of water through cracks and fissures in the stone, providing just enough nutrients and minerals to sustain what little bit of life was left that far below the surface. In other areas, where the vast hydroponic gardens were once located, water was more plentiful and more complex forms of plant life still grew under artificial light from generators that were hundreds of years old. But those parts remained unexplored, and even Held and Emory, who had been operating out of the underground fortress for over a year, were unaware of their existence.

A massive steel barricade, like the door to an old bank vault, blocked their way to the interior of D Section. Thorndyke paused at first, studying the complicated locking mechanism for some clue to its functioning until he remembered with a grunt that what he was looking at was the image of that area as it had existed one hour earlier.

"I know," he heard Robenalt chuckle. "It's a little disconcerting. Sometimes I forget, too. Just walk right through it."

"I hope it's not too thick," Thorndyke mumbled. "I hate the black. Where there's no light, there's no Beta Light images."

"Yeah. We're lucky these old plasma-conduit lighting systems still function. My guess is they've been shining ever since they built this place. Once you turn them on, the electro-chemical processes inside keep them firing. You can see they've dimmed over the centuries, but they're still good for probably another hundred years."

The humm of an old civil defense generator caught Robenalt's attention as he emerged first through the heavy metal door and stepped into a brightly-lit complex of rooms. Thorndyke popped through a moment later and looked around in wonder. White walls blended into acoustically contoured ceilings. A smattering of old desks and chairs remained, but mostly the room was empty. Perhaps a half dozen men and women scurried about, two of them recognizable from the

Transmission Center, but otherwise the complex seemed deserted.

A soft moan brought the two men to another sealed-off room. There, lying on a cot with his head swaddled in a make-shift bandage was Scott Hollock. Blood stains spoiled his shirt and another bandage covered a jagged, still-bleeding gash on his arm and chest. Quentin knelt at the Director's side, trying to comfort the badly hurt man.

"You've got to hang on, sir," he pleaded, wiping Hollock's head with a damp cloth as if the act itself was an adequate substitute for the medical attention he so desperately needed.

"How... bad?"

"Don't talk. It's going to be all right."

Hollock's eyes closed, and he let his head lull back on the makeshift pillow. The old Civil Defense cot was careworn and frayed at the edges, but still solid enough to support his weight. Quentin found a box of medical supplies anchored to the wall, but none of the medicines it contained were of any value, having long ago corroded or dried into a solid mass. Only some gauze bandages were still in good enough shape to be used, and that supply was quickly depleted as he fought to stem the flow of blood from deep gashes inflicted on the B.E.T.A. Director by his attackers.

"I wish there was something we could do," Thorndyke said, watching helplessly while Quentin continued to whisper words of comfort to Hollock.

"I don't know if he'll make it, Paul. He looks worse than he did last night when they brought him here. I'm glad that Quentin's with him."

Robenalt gasped audibly as another section of his body phased out briefly, then struggled to reform, sending him to his knees. He drew in deep, anguished breaths while Thorndyke rushed over to help him to his feet.

"Damn! Remember what I said about no pain? That was bad."

"We've got to do something to get you out of here!" Thorndyke cried in exasperation.

"There's nothing we can do, but watch and hope. Maybe someone will figure out you're here and get you back before it's too late. In the meantime, you need to see everything, know everything, so you can tell everyone the truth. Hopefully, it will still matter."

"If only there was a way we could communicate with someone

outside," Thorndyke said. Lifting his arm he shook it forlornly. "These pulse wave bands we're wearing only receive signals."

"Jesus Paul, what an idiot I am!"

"What?"

"The pulse bands—we can use them!"

"Jim, are you okay? They only receive data, they don't transmit."

"*One* doesn't transmit. But *two* might if we use some of the circuitry in our helmet communication systems to redirect the signal."

"Are you serious? You can do that?"

"I don't know, but standing around talking about it isn't going to do any good."

Fumbling with the latch to his helmet, Robenalt broke the seal and started to lift it off the restraining collar.

"Jim, wait—you can't do that!"

"I just did."

"No, stop! You're letting your oxygen escape!"

"We don't need oxygen here, Paul. We don't breathe, or eat, or sleep."

"But when they bring you back, they need all the molecules inside your suit to be there or they can't reconstitute you properly! That's why we wear a suit, not just to protect against the heat but to keep everything contained inside a defined perimeter. Even the air we breathed. Otherwise something might get lost or jumbled during the recovery."

"I'm not going back, Paul. Even if there was a way, I wouldn't make it through the recovery process. I'm too far gone. I can feel it. Now pry your wrist band off your arm and give it to me, but be careful not to break the seal to your suit."

As if in a dream, Thorndyke carefully removed the band and watched Robenalt open up the two devices using makeshift tools scavenged from his own suit and helmet. With as much dexterity as he could muster, he began to link them to the components of his throat mike to construct a makeshift transmitter.

"I can already tell this is going to take a lot of time," Robenalt sighed. "I heard there's going to be another jump to Miller's Crossing at 9:30 tomorrow morning. If we're lucky we'll have something by then that might be able to send a signal to someone on the jump team."

"But if they're all working for Held—"

"Held's only brought a few people into this, Russack, Emory, Zhow"

"Margaret Zhow! Oh my God, this is worse than I thought."

"Zhow's got her own reasons from what I've heard, but with the exception of the three guys that ambushed Quentin, there's no one else from Held's inner circle. The rest are people with certain ideological bents that Emory recruited. And then there's Harmon Bright."

"Bright... Bright? Why do I know that name? Wait a minute, isn't he that strange guy Emory took under his wing before I left the Institute? Gave him a job doing research, or something?"

"It's Bright's work that lets them manipulate the Beta Light images."

"Bright?"

"He's a true genius, but an evil man. I still don't understand what he wants out of this. He's the one who killed Mitchell and Henry Sherwood."

"You've got to make that work, Jim," Thorndyke said with urgency. "These people have to be stopped. I don't care how noble their intentions are, they've got no right to do what they're doing."

"If there's any way, I will," Robenalt answered, busying himself with the components while Thorndyke let his eyes drift back to Hollock and Quentin, wishing there was some way he could reach them.

22:02 HOURS

"I'm really worried, Sharla," Ruth fretted, tapping the control panel on her living quarters Vid-link to check for messages. It was the third time in the last fifteen minutes she had searched her office and other remote sites for any word from Quentin. Like every time before, there was nothing to retrieve.

"I know something went wrong with that jump," Sharla said while she paced the floor. "I knew I should have gone with them."

"Then you'd be missing, too. Paul was right, whatever they stumbled upon is terribly dangerous."

"We can't just wait around doing nothing, Ruth. I think we ought to take the data file to The District authorities. Maybe they can make some sense of it, help us find out who has anything to gain by fabricating a judicial file. Find that out, and I guarantee you it'll lead us to Paul and Quentin."

"You have a visitor," the room announced before Ruth could answer. "This individual is not known to my security protocol."

"Visitor?" she looked at Sharla, puzzled. "Are you expecting anyone?"

"No."

"Unit Security, please identify this person before authorizing admittance."

"Secretary of State Lillian Dorr, United States East."

"The Secretary of State! What does she want?"

"She wishes admittance to your living quarters," the computerized voice replied matter-of-factly.

"Of course, yes. Let her in."

Magnetic locks disengaged and the rectangular shaped access way recessed into the wall, allowing Lillian Dorr to enter the apartment. Alone, she looked nervous but composed while she waited for the solid metal door to slide back and seal itself with an audible click.

"Please forgive this intrusion," she smiled reflexively. "Which one of you is Sharla Russell?"

"I am. How did you know—"

"—you were here? I'd like to tell you it was fancy detective work. But actually, I asked your roommate. She seems to be a delightful, but somewhat scattered young woman."

"I think she was probably just nervous," Sharla replied automatically. "But that still doesn't tell me how you know who I am, or why you were looking for me in the first place."

"Yes, of course," Dorr smiled. "May I sit down?"

"Certainly," Ruth offered.

"Good. It's been a long day, hasn't it, for all of us?" Settling into a comfortable chair, Dorr caught her breath while Ruth and Sharla, darting glances at each other, took seats opposite her and waited for her to continue.

"You're Paul Thorndyke's companion, Sharla?"

"We're, er, friends, yes."

"Forgive me. From what I understood, I'd assumed you and he were in a committed relationship. However, he has confided certain matters to you, hasn't he? I'm sorry to be so forward, but I must know that."

"Matters?" Sharla replied hesitantly.

"I understand your skepticism, Ms. Russell. This all seems so mysterious, perhaps necessarily so. Let me come right to the point. Scott Hollock, the Director of B.E.T.A., has made Paul Thorndyke privy to certain information of a high, national security nature. I need to know if that same information has also been conveyed to you. By your presence here, now, I'm going to assume that if it has, Ms. Parker is also aware of many of these same details."

"Yes," Sharla answered. "Paul told me certain things."

"I'm aware of them, too," Ruth added. "Quentin Cottle is a close friend of Paul's. He's my fiancé. He's been working with Paul on... whatever this is."

"They're both missing, Madam Secretary," Sharla said.

"So is the Director of B.E.T.A," Dorr replied in a low voice.

"This is very bad," Sharla rose, tensing her body as she started to pace again.

"Forgive me for asking, Ms. Dorr, er, Madam Secretary—" Ruth ventured cautiously.

"Please, I know this is difficult for both of you. Call me Lillian."

"Lillian," Ruth nodded. "Has this become a Federal matter? Sharla and I were discussing whether to take what we know to The District authorities. Maybe we should take it to the national government instead."

"Before we do anything, I need to know exactly what we are dealing with," Dorr replied. "We all know some of what's going on. Let's put those pieces together and see where it takes us."

"I agree," Sharla said.

"Good. Let me tell you what I know, and we'll go from there. I met with Scott Hollock the other day. He is a personal friend of mine, in addition to being the Director of B.E.T.A. We discussed certain rumors our Federal Intelligence Operatives had picked up related to the Presidents' visits to The District tomorrow and Sunday. Scott was convinced some kind of effort was underway to disrupt the Resurfacing Ceremony, something political aimed at President Drees or President Echeverria—or both. He took your Mr. Thorndyke into his confidence to help him get the evidence I needed to raise this to a higher level of security. I've been attempting to locate Mr. Thorndyke all afternoon, but to no avail. That's why I've sought you out, Sharla."

"There's something going on all right," Sharla said flatly. "We think it's tied to a manipulation of a Beta Light file Quentin uncovered."

"Manipulation?"

"A judicial file was tampered with. A murderer's identity was changed and an innocent man was convicted of the crime."

"You have evidence of this?"

"We have the file."

"If what you're telling me is true," Dorr's face transformed, "then a lot of things that didn't add up before are beginning to make sense. Where is this file?"

"Here," Ruth went to a drawer and retrieved the disk.

Handing it to Dorr she watched her hold it carefully in her hand, turning it in her fingers while she stared at the disk in silent contemplation.

"You realize," Dorr said softly, "there's a chance... a good chance, that none of our men are still alive."

"Paul's alive," Sharla said with conviction.

"I know Quentin is, too," Ruth chimed in bravely.

"I've known Scott for, well, for a long time. He's a strong man, stubborn and pig headed at times. I want to believe he'll survive this and anything else anyone throws at him. But I also have to be a realist. There are people who want to bring down both governments of the United States. They've killed once, maybe twice. And they'll kill again. Scott, Paul, Quentin, even the three of us if they think we'll get in their way. This *is* a federal matter. I want you to come with me. I can offer you protection—"

"There is another visitor requesting entrance to this apartment," the security unit interrupted.

"Who is it, Security?" Ruth asked, while Dorr slipped the disk into her waist pouch and looked at Ruth with concern.

"Claudia Morales, a resident of the lower Roosevelt Quadrant—"

"She's my roommate," Sharla told the IHSU. Dorr relaxed visibly and Ruth let a smile erase the worry on her face.

"Let her in," Ruth instructed. As she walked toward the door it slid back to reveal a terrified young woman surrounded by three heavily armed men. Ruth gasped audibly as the first of the men, Shank, pushed her inside.

"Sharla, I'm sorry. They came—"

"That's her," Shank gestured, sending one of the other two men toward Sharla.

"You've got something that doesn't belong to you," the man said. "Where is it?"

"I don't know what you're—"

"I said, *where is it!*" the man yelled, slapping Sharla across the face. "We saw you two playing with it here the other night with your boyfriends. Where's the file? Where'd you put it? Tell me or I'll—"

"It's here," Dorr said, removing her waist pouch. She handed it to the man who rifled through it. He took out the disk, examined it briefly and tossed it to the other man still standing by the door.

"Yeah, this is it. Just like the Beta Light showed."

"You have a Beta Light file of here, last night?" Ruth's mouth dropped.

"All right, let's go," Shank gestured toward the door. "All of you."

"You have what you came for," Dorr said defiantly. "These women can't do you any harm. They don't know anything. Let them go. I'm the only one—"

Shank laughed sarcastically, cutting her off with a wave of his pistol. "Save your breath. That one's Thorndyke's companion, the other is with Cottle. They've been helping them from the start. You're *all* coming with us."

"Where are you taking us?" Ruth demanded. "Where's Quentin and Paul Thorndyke? What have you done with them? I demand to know."

"You're not in much of a position to demand anything," the big man laughed.

"Think so?" Sharla said, eyeing the gun trained at her mid section. "You shoot that thing off in here and every security unit in this complex will shut down tighter than The District jail. Then you can explain to the DPO why you're kidnapping four women, one of whom is the Secretary of State of the U.S.E.!"

"She's right, Shank," the man by the door nodded.

Shank looked at Sharla with steely eyes, mulling the thought over in his mind, then holstered his weapon and grinned broadly.

"Never liked these old cartridge firers anyway. Make a lot of noise and mess. But a body's just as dead if I snap its neck, so what do you say we all just take a nice, friendly little walk? Pete, you take the disk and get back to the staging area. Frank and I will escort these ladies to a place where they'll be nice and safe and out of the way."

"Right, Shank," the man said before vanishing down the hallway.

"Ladies, we're going to walk out of here nice and relaxed. If you give me any trouble, I'm not gonna think twice about breaking your pretty little necks."

As if to punctuate his remark Shank drove his fist through the Vid-link control panel sending a small shower of sparks cascading across the floor. The monitor whined mournfully, then sputtered to a noiseless stop.

"Unit Security here," a hollow voice came from overhead. "There has been damage to the Video Link terminal. I will initiate a request for repair. Have a pleasant evening."

"If we're all ready now?" Shank smiled evilly.

"Shank, that your name?" Sharla asked defiantly.

"You like to talk a lot. Your boyfriend, he liked to talk a lot too, only he isn't talking a lot now."

"You know where Paul is?" Sharla became animated. "Where is he? What happened to him?"

"He's gone on a little trip. A real permanent one."

"You bastard! If you've hurt him—"

"He's not dead," Shank laughed. "Might as well be, for all the good it'll do him. He broke into the Transmission Center and took an unauthorized jump. Mr. Held, he don't like people messing with his equipment. Maybe, if you're real good—real nice to me, I'll ask someone to bring him back."

"Held!" Dorr exclaimed. "He's behind this. Yes, it all fits together."

"I didn't say nothing about Held," Shank blustered. "You shut up, all of you."

"You said you'd help me... bring back Paul—" Sharla's voice was low and soft "—if I... didn't give you any trouble."

149

"That's only part of it." Shank's attention was suddenly diverted to the beautiful young woman whose entire demeanor had completely changed. He smiled lustfully at Sharla who swallowed hard and averted his stare, only to let her eyes return to his and nod weakly.

"Oh, Sharla, no," Ruth sobbed.

"Think you can handle these other three?" Shank asked the other man.

"This is not a good idea, Shank."

"Don't tell me how to do my job! I got you what you wanted, now I'm gonna have a little fun."

"This isn't about abusing power," the man said. "It's about the future of our country."

"Listen," Shank barely hid his irritation. "I don't give a rat's ass about your little conspiracy. They bounced me from the DPO, and because of this I'm gonna get my job back—with interest! We'll see how that shitheel DelVecchio likes it when I throw *his* ass on the street! In two days I'll be running the show."

"This isn't going to work," Dorr said flatly. "If I could piece enough of this together, others will, too. You'll be stopped."

"Shut this bitch up, or I'll pop her right now!" Shank drew his gun and pointed it at Ruth, Claudia, and Dorr. "Frank's already left with the disk. If I shoot you now it won't stop anything, just get me thrown in jail until Monday. Then I'll be out, and you'll still be dead."

"Do what he says," Sharla pleaded. "Go with him, all of you. Don't make any trouble. I'll be all right. I've got to do this, for Paul."

"By the time we're finished," Shank laughed brutally. "You'll be calling out another name in your sleep."

Tears flooded her eyes as Claudia embraced Sharla emotionally, whispering into her girlfriend's ear. "I'm so sorry, Sharla. I never should have brought them here. I was so scared, they said they'd kill me."

"It's all right, Claudia," Sharla forced a smile. "Go now. I'll be all right."

As the other man, weapon in hand, ushered Ruth, Dorr, and Claudia from the room, Ruth glanced back at Sharla, their eyes locking silently. Sharla nodded and Ruth returned a thin smile, hoping to give her friend the only support she could at that moment. Dorr, her eyes fixed on the exit way, allowed herself to be herded behind Ruth. Her mind raced with options, none of them practical, knowing there was no way to escape.

Finally the door sealed, and Shank and Sharla were alone. The big man put his weapon on the table and entered a code into a five number digital band on the butt of the pistol.

"This thing's useless until I remove the safety, so don't go getting any ideas."

"You'll bring Paul back if I do what you say?"

"What do you want with that scrawny bag of brains?" Shank grunted. "Yeah, I'll bring him back, if you make it worth my while."

"Then I'll give you something you won't forget," she said softly. She unfastened the top of her blouse and slowly pulled it off. Shank's eyes widened with delight when her perfect breasts fell under his gaze.

"Yeah, do it like that."

Her eyes burrowing into his, Sharla approached the smirking man, tugging at the clasp that held her pants to her waist. Shank swaggered with a sinister gait and let his arms relax and defenses drop. He began to pull at his own shirt, his greedy smile broadening into a lustful grin.

"You and me, we're going to have a night to remember," he oozed. Dropping his shirt to the floor he took Sharla by the waist and pulled her close against his body. She lifted her arms around his neck and stroked his hair with the tips of her fingers while embracing him tenderly.

"Would you really have snapped my neck?" she asked.

"In a heartbeat!" he laughed.

"Then, I guess I can live with myself."

"What?" Shank frowned.

He pulled back slightly to stare at her, not understanding the remark. She returned his gaze for a moment, and then with lightening quick speed slammed the heel of her palm against the fleshy cartilage of his throat. Shank gasped in shock when he heard an audible snap, fighting for breath which became even more difficult once Sharla slipped behind him and locked one arm around his neck, forcing the crook of her arm against his windpipe and grabbing her wrist with her opposite hand. Flailing wildly, he tried to shake her loose, but she leveraged her weight against his body, making it impossible to break her hold.

Thrashing about the room, they knocked over furniture and smashed into walls; Shank's frantic movements growing weaker by the second. Even still, the force of one body slam into a corner of a doorway was powerful enough to crack one of Sharla's ribs and almost throw her off. But she held tight, almost blacking out herself while she redoubled the pressure to keep his windpipe closed.

Orange sparkles blurred Shank's vision, and he felt his legs grow weak. The look on his face, captured in a hallway mirror, was an indescribable mixture of shock and horror—the unmistakable look of a man who knew with certainty he was going to die. He made one final, desperate attempt to break her hold, but by now the lack of oxygen to his brain had dulled his reactions and he collapsed to his knees. Sharla maintained her hold until his eyes rolled up into his head and he sputtered one last dying cough before collapsing into a heap.

Exhausted, she rolled off his body as it hit the floor with a thud. Fighting for her own breath, she lay there in the deathly silence until, slowly recovering her strength, she was finally able to raise herself weakly. She stood over the lifeless corpse, wincing at the pain from a fractured rib while she rubbed the circulation back into her arms.

"Sammy the Bull Gravano killed Tony Mutolo the same way," she said to the empty room. "I saw how he did it. He felt no remorse. I'll have to live with this the rest of my life."

She continued to stare at the body on the floor while she dressed, her face an expressionless mask. Opening the door she headed into the hall, speaking to herself again with quiet determination.

"I said I'd come for you, Paul. And I will. I only hope it isn't too late."

"ALL THE KING'S MEN"
Saturday, September 28, 2416 AD
01:37 HOURS

What shall it profit a man if he shall gain
the whole world, and lose his own soul?
                                    -Mark 8:36

The clang of a heavy metal door moving on its skids snapped Quentin awake. Silhouetted against a bright backdrop of light, he made out the image of a heavily armed guard leading three women into the room.

"Quentin!" Ruth's voice cut through the damp, heavy air. She rushed to embrace him, crying tears of joy as they were reunited. "Oh, Quentin, I thought you were dead."

"Scott?" Dorr gasped. She focused on the bandaged, unconscious man half-hidden by the shadows. "Oh, dear God."

Hollock moaned softly, responding to her gentle touch when she swept back his hair and tried to give him whatever comfort she could. The sound of the massive door locking into place momentarily froze the three frightened women, who looked around the room in wonder.

"Where are we?" Claudia whispered.

"An old military communications center," Quentin answered, "almost a mile beneath the surface. Left over from the twenty-first century."

"We need to get him some medical attention!" Dorr interrupted, looking at Quentin with fear in her eyes.

"I've tried. They just ignore me. I've done everything I could for him. I don't know if it's enough."

"What happened to Paul?" Ruth asked.

"Some of Held's men caught us in the jump. They left him in stasis, like Jim Robenalt, only he doesn't know what's happened to him. God, he must be terrified." Glancing toward the three women, he

153

squinted at them through the semi-darkness. "Where's Sharla? Does she know you're missing? Maybe she'll figure out something to do. Maybe she'll take the disk to the authorities."

"Oh, Quentin," Ruth began to cry. "It's too terrible to talk about. These are evil men."

"I'm sorry I got you involved in this, Ruth," Quentin held her tightly.

"I'd rather be here with you, my darling. If anything is going to happen—"

"They're not going to hurt us. They would have killed us already if they wanted to. This is all about some kind of plot to overthrow the governments. Held is behind it. There are others too, but from what I've heard he seems to be calling the shots. Whatever happens, it's going to be soon. Then we'll be let out, after there's nothing we can do about it."

"You don't know these men," Dorr said. "Even if they succeed, they can't afford to let us tell what we know. We're only here because they don't want any more deaths showing up before their coup. If the coup fails, we'll probably be left here to die. If it succeeds, they'll come back for us to tie up any loose ends. Either way, it's doubtful we're going to get out of here alive."

"If you don't mind my asking," Quentin frowned. "Who are you? Both of you?"

"I'm Claudia. Sharla's roommate."

"Lillian Dorr."

"The Secretary of State?"

"Yes."

"How did you—"

"—get involved in this? I've known Scott for a number of years. I came to him about certain rumors and suspicions."

"So the government knows about this!" Quentin exclaimed. "This is great! They'll be looking for you."

"No," Dorr sighed, stroking Hollock's forehead. "They don't have any idea of the magnitude of this. I won't be missed until this evening when the President arrives in The District. It will raise some concerns, maybe even increase his security detail, but it won't do anything to prevent what's going to happen. There hasn't been a serious attempt against the government of either country in two hundred years. No one's thinking about anything more sinister than a few political protesters at the Resurfacing Ceremony."

"Then we're... really going to die," Claudia choked back her tears.

"Don't think about it," Ruth tried to comfort the distraught young woman. "We need to focus on here, now. What can we do to help that poor man?"

"Ruth's right," Quentin nodded. "Ms. Secretary, ma'am—"

"We're going to be together for a while," Dorr smiled reflexively. "Please call me Lillian."

"All right, er, Lillian. I've been tearing up old sheets I found in that supply closet to change his bandages. They're old, but still relatively clean. There's no medicine, but I think we're still better off trying to keep his wounds clean. You'll find fresh water in that pouch over there, some food rations too. The stuff is real old but still preserved. I think they made it out of real food, not synthetics like we have now. Go easy on the first bite or two, all of you. It's very rich."

Claudia helped Dorr sift through the supply cabinet in search of linen while Ruth folded herself into Quentin's arms, closing her eyes, and reassuring herself with the gentleness of touch.

"If we are going to die," she whispered, "I'm glad I'm here, with you."

"We're not going to die," Quentin said flatly. Casting his eyes around the room, he seemed to be searching its shadows. "There's something I didn't tell the others."

"What?"

"Shhh, I don't know if these rooms are monitored for sound. You'll see in about two hours, if I'm right."

"What Quentin? What is it?"

"All I can say is, we're not the only one's down here."

02:05 HOURS

Binding her ribs with an elastic cloth, Sharla rested against her desk in the dimly lit cubicle. Except for a single light illuminating the common area, everything in Archival Records was cast in deep, dark shadows. The makeshift bandage, nothing more than an old shawl she scavenged from an adjoining cubicle, did little to alleviate the throbbing pain that shortened her breath and made any movement difficult. Still, it helped clear her head enough to think clearly while she activated the monitor on her desk and began to search through the jump schedule for the Transmission Center.

"Good morning, Ms. Russell," a disembodied voice returned once her station was fully powered. "You're here rather early this Saturday."

"Damn," she winced, holding her side and taking a slow breath. "Computer, run a status check on Transmission Center activity. What time is the next scheduled jump?"

"O-nine thirty hours, Saturday, September 28, 2416."

"This morning?"

"The target site is Miller's Crossing, February 22, 2035, 12:17 p.m. Pre-launch protocol will begin at 06:00 hours."

"That doesn't leave me much time. Assess site security."

"Site security has been increased to Level 9. All civilian entrance and egress ports prior to the start of launch preparations at 06:00 hours this morning require full authorization and verification from Director Held."

"Even Hollock's code won't get me past that!" Sharla sank back in her chair. "But, maybe there's another way in. Computer, give me a list of Archival Records personnel who will be on duty for this morning's launch."

"Processing."

Sharla watched a dozen names scroll across her screen. She entered a command into her terminal and pulled back, waiting for the system to respond.

"Personnel roster amended. Sharla Russell has been added to Archival Records support."

"Now give me Transmission Center access at that time as a member of the on-site Archival support staff," she instructed, entering her own code to verify the change.

"Access confirmed."

"Good." Once again she leaned back in her chair, closing her eyes and taking another long, slow breath. "I don't know what good it will do me, but when they open the center up tomorrow, I'll be there."

Sitting in the shadows, knowing she couldn't return to her own apartment, Sharla wondered if anyone from Held's team had discovered Shank's body. And if they had, whether they were looking for her.

"Do you wish further information?" the computer prodded.

"No. Nothing more."

"Very well. Returning system to standby."

"I don't know how, but I'll bring you back, Paul," she said quietly to herself as her monitor flickered out, plunging the room into absolute darkness. "Just be there for me."

03:29 HOURS

"What's that noise?" Claudia gasped, righting herself with a start.

The others snapped awake when the sound repeated itself somewhere on the other side of the room.

"I heard it, too," Ruth stood, peering into the darkness.

"Kind of a scratching noise," Dorr squinted, her eyes focused on a section of wall a few feet away.

"Shhh, quiet," Quentin hushed. "Don't make any noise."

Wide-eyed in wonder, the three women listened to the scratching grow louder. Through the dim light of the makeshift cell they could see screws in a wall panel slowly turn, their corkscrew movement pushing them out farther until one-by-one they dropped to the floor, then bounced on the tile and rolled in an arc before coming to a stop.

"W-what is it," Claudia could barely form the words as two hairy palms took hold of the panel and lifted it up and out, then set it against the wall at an angle. Beady red eyes that seemed to glow in the dark stared back from the deep black shadows of the ventilation port.

"A friend," Quentin soothed.

From the interior of the shaft a hairy little beast—his face like a ferret, his body the size and shape of a chimpanzee—grinned broadly at Quentin who approached the opening and lowered himself to a squatting position. Claudia gasped and stepped back involuntarily when his yellowed, pointed teeth caught the light as he pushed his head through the opening. Her sudden movement frightened the strange-looking creature, sending him back into the shaft.

"No, wait—please!" Quentin cried. "Come back."

"Them scare me a lot," a squeaky voice returned from the depths.

"It's all right," Quentin said. "They won't hurt you."

157

Slowly, as if testing the limits of his courage, the hairy little man reappeared at the head of the ventilation shaft. Quentin extended his hand and the creature took it tentatively, allowing himself to be guided into the room. He stood slightly stooped, his arms hanging at his sides, relaxed but ready, and squinted at the three women.

"What are them?"

"Friends of mine."

"No. What sex them are?"

"Women."

"Ah, women," the creature seemed pleased. Claudia cast a worried look in Ruth's direction.

"This is Mike," Quentin introduced the strange little man, who seemed more relaxed while he approached a still uneasy Claudia. He stood directly in front of her, tilting his head backward and sniffing audibly. "He came here a few hours after I was locked in the room. There's a network of tunnels that run everywhere to parts of the Subterranean that haven't been explored."

"Mike?" Ruth puzzled.

"You be his woman?" Mike bounced to within a half step of Ruth, nose pointed upward and sniffing while he scanned her with his eyes.

"Yes."

"Her I like. Her —" he turned toward Claudia "—I don't. "

"You're a lower dweller," Dorr said. Her fear was replaced with intense curiosity as she studied the hairy little creature. "I've heard about such things, but I never thought they existed."

"Not a thing," Mike reacted sharply. "A man, like him."

"Yes, of course," Dorr apologized. "I didn't mean any disrespect. Mike, are there others like you around?"

"Others, but not like me. Some big, some small. Some bald, some lots of hair. Lots ugly. Not many pretty, like me."

"Yes, you are a very striking figure," Dorr smiled, not sure whether she was speaking to a child or an adult.

The little man waddled over to the cot where Hollock was lying. He ran his hand over the unconscious man's face and hair, then lifted it to his mouth and licked the scent from his palm. Grimacing, he turned his head and spat theatrically on the floor before reaching into a ratty-looking pouch and pulling out a sticky black substance.

"Him real sick. Gonna die soon. I bring 'em this." He placed the tar-like residue in Dorr's hand, spinning on his heels and waddling back toward the vent. "Feed 'em all. Do it now."

Dorr appeared confused at first, but with Quentin's urging placed the bitter substance between Hollock's lips and eased it inside his mouth.

"What is this?" she asked Mike as Hollock stirred slightly.

"Cures a bad stomach."

"It isn't his stomach—"

"—an all else that ails a body."

"I don't know if it will help him, Ms. Dorr, er, Lillian," Quentin said. "But he's right. He's not going to make it if we just let him lie there and do nothing."

"Thank you, Michael," Dorr smiled and fed the remaining bit to Hollock. The little man looked pleased and hopped back to the shaft.

"Time to go. All's coming, follow."

"You mean, there's a way out?" Claudia asked.

"Same way as in, only back-ards."

"Where will this take us Quentin?" Ruth looked up into the shaft.

"I don't know, but I think we can use it to get back to the surface."

"Time's wasting," Mike squeaked. "Yer comin' or not?"

"You go, all of you," Dorr insisted. "Scott can't move. I'm staying here with him."

"No, we need you, Lillian," Quentin said. "You can get to the President, let him know what's happening. You have to come with us."

"I won't leave Scott, he's badly hurt and still unconscious. He can't be left alone."

"He's right," Ruth said to Dorr. "You and Claudia go with Quentin. I'll stay back and watch over him."

"Ruth, no!" Quentin reacted in shock.

"You're wasting time, Quentin," Ruth said. "Leave now, before someone comes in and discovers what's happening."

"Ruth, I can't leave you—"

"We can't leave Director Hollock alone. You're right. Lillian has to go with you. Claudia didn't ask to be part of this. She doesn't even understand what's going on. She shouldn't be asked to stay."

"Then I'll stay," Quentin said. "Mike can lead you three—"

"Now you're just talking nonsense," Ruth scolded softly. "You need to tell the authorities what happened, give them the proof they need to act without the disk. I'm the logical one to remain behind. I'll be all right. Now go."

"I don't like this," Quentin mumbled.

"A lotta talk," Mike groaned impatiently. "Yer comin' or not?"

"Quentin," Dorr touched his arm. "Come."

With a tender kiss, Ruth pushed the hesitant young man away, kneeling at Hollock's side to tend to his wounds while the others assembled at the ventilation port.

"We've a long way a go," Mike said, bracing his arms to the side of the shaft and scrambling up the long, narrow conduit leading to a higher level. Quentin helped Claudia into the ventilation tunnel, followed by Dorr who glanced back at Hollock still lying unconscious on the cot before boosting herself up the dirty, moldy shaft. It was Quentin's turn next. He remained at the opening, not moving. Ruth smiled and whispered reassuringly.

"Don't worry about me, Quentin. I'll be all right."

"I love you, Ruth."

"Come back to me, safe, when it's all over."

"I will. And when I do, I'm going to marry you. We'll never be apart again."

"You're not leaving me, Quentin. No matter where you are, whatever separates us, we'll always be together."

Pulling himself into the vent, Quentin allowed his eyes to linger on Ruth's face. She smiled encouragingly, then turned away to dab the sweat from Hollock's brow with a folded up cloth.

Quentin looked up into the dank, smelly shaft crusted with centuries of mildew and corrosion. He braced his arms against its sides, fitting his shoe into one of the toeholds running up its side, and pulled himself toward a small pinpoint of light several hundred feet above him.

At the top of the shaft was an open area the size of a large room. It looked as if it held some of the refrigeration and re-circulation equipment that pushed the air through the tunnels, cleansing and purifying it along the way. The machinery was old and rusting, its gears clattering noisily and other moving parts in need of lubrication, but appeared to be in working order.

"This is amazing," Quentin marveled, emerging at the top of the ventilation shaft and standing to admire the surroundings. Running his fingers across the steel casing of a nearby machine, he let his touch linger respectfully before pulling his hand slowly away. "This stuff was built to last a long time, but three and a half centuries *without* maintenance! I can hardly believe it."

"We fix 'um up all right," Mike poked his head through a gap in one of the devices. "Can't breathe without 'um."

"You repair these machines?" Dorr was surprised.

"This 'un, an lots more."

Dancing around the room, the little man began identifying each piece of equipment and telling what part he played in keeping it running. Dorr and Quentin smiled and glanced his way, talking quietly among themselves while Claudia, more out of fear than curiosity, provided a rapt audience for his continuous commentary.

"It's incredible when you think about it," Dorr spoke in a low voice. "A self-contained society cut off from the rest of us, living here in total isolation using over three hundred year old technology to survive. It boggles the mind."

"Lets just hope the natives are friendly," Quentin replied.

"You think there might be a problem?"

"I don't know. Remember, we're the outsiders here. For whatever reason, these people have shunned contact with the sub-surface world. I'm not sure how happy they're going to be to find out they've been 'discovered.'"

"But I thought you said Michael sought you out?"

"He did. But I'm not sure he's all there, if you catch my meaning."

"Yes, I know," Dorr glanced again in the little man's direction.

"This is like some kind of game to him. I heard a noise in the ventilation shaft about an hour after I was locked in and I coaxed him out. It took some doing but he saw Hollock—er, the Director—and he's a real sympathetic little fellow. From what I was able to gather, he'd been into the communications center a lot of times before Held's men took it over. He left and brought us back some medi-packs scavenged from another area of the complex, but the drugs were too old to be of any use. He said he was coming back again with 'something better,' and then you arrived."

"Well, he kept his word."

"Yes. I'm sure he doesn't mean us any harm, but down deep I think he thinks this is some kind of elaborate hide and seek game we're playing with Held's men."

"What exactly is he, do you think?"

"I don't know, really," Quentin sighed. "He is pretty odd. Maybe he is what he says. A man. Human. I'm not sure I have any other explanation. I've never seen anything like him, not here or in any hologram we've brought back from the past."

"There's been speculation about what living at these depths for generation after generation would do to the body's chromosomal makeup," Dorr thought aloud. "I knew there was a possibility that there might still be people alive down here, but quite frankly I never gave serious thought about what the lower dwellers would look like. I'd always assumed they'd be essentially like us, just different socially."

"Well, 'different' is a word that comes to mind."

"He helped us escape, and that's good. If we can get him to lead us to the surface that's all we'll ask of him. Whatever—whoever—else lives down here, we can bypass them and leave them alone."

"My thoughts exactly."

"—An that 'un scrubs the air clean 'an pretty," Mike sang, returning to where Quentin and Dorr were standing. Almost immediately, he moved toward a closed door on the opposite side of the room. "Time's a wastin.' "

His hands grasped a big wheeled handle, and he gave it a spin it like an ancient submariner opening an airlock. The creaking door popped open. Stepping into a dimly lit corridor, he motioned for the others to follow.

"That-a-way," he pointed, directing the group toward a juncture of two tunnels a short distance away.

"Where are we going?" Claudia asked, stepping through the portal and looking around nervously.

"Meet more friends."

"We need to get to our people," Quentin explained gently. "It's important that we get there right away."

"No!" the little man snapped. "You gotta see the boss. I told 'un 'bout you. They said I gotta bring you first."

"I don't like the way this sounds," Dorr whispered.

"We don't seem to have much of a choice," Quentin smiled thinly.

Both of them watched with some amusement as Mike grasped Claudia's hand and began to lead her down the corridor, half-dragging the nervous young woman, who cast fleeting glances back their way while the little man gleefully pulled her along.

"I think we'd better hurry," Quentin said, closing the distance between them.

04:40 HOURS

Ambling down the hallway, Mike led the small group toward an open spaced grotto appearing in the rock. The tile floor of the ancient corridor was soon replaced with a weathered stone walkway smoothed down by centuries of foot traffic. Creeping, reed-like vines clung to the rock walls while green moss covered the in between spaces. The air was thick with moisture, and the sound of a flowing brook could be heard a short distance away—the exit point of an underground aquifer that flowed through the natural cavern. Overhead a raft of artificial lights illuminated the space, casting deep shadows in the folds and crevices of the stone, but otherwise providing enough light to make out the full dimensions of the area.

"You 'kin eat that," Mike pointed to the green growths coating the rock.

"You mean, like food?" Claudia grimaced.

"An some'll cure you, too, if you got a sickness."

"Any idea where we are?" Dorr whispered to Quentin.

"My guess is an underground fissure. They probably built the tunnel system around it, making use of the natural space. Hear that sound? It's flowing water. There's probably a hydroponic garden nearby."

"Almost there," Mike squeaked.

The group traversed the cavern and came to another door. Mike banged on it loudly, then stepped back to wait for it to open. Slowly, its rusty hinges squealing, the massive barrier swung wide and an overpowering smell rushed out to meet them.

"My God," Claudia covered her mouth and gasped.

"What... is that?" Dorr choked.

The smell, a mixture of plant life, cooking odors, and human stench, was unlike anything the three had ever encountered in their pristine world of synthetic foods and elaborate systems of personal hygiene. Mike buzzed with delight and tilted his nose upward as he took in the conflicting aromas.

"I'm going to be sick," Claudia whimpered.

"Not now, Claudia," Quentin took her arm.

Surrounding them were dozens of shadowy figures—different heights, sizes and body shapes—emerging from a long row of twenty-first century storage units that had been converted into living quarters. As each one stepped into the lighted hallway, their faces could clearly be seen. The shock was almost overwhelming as hideously deformed bodies carrying grotesque-looking heads stared back curiously at them.

"Smile," Dorr said through clenched teeth, nodding politely to a tall, gangly looking being. She couldn't be sure if the hairless, squashed-face, slack-jawed thing in a ratty-looking tunic was male or female, but she could see in its eyes that their appearance was just as frightening to them as they were to the inhabitants of the subterranean world.

"Who are they?" Claudia gasped, casting her eyes about warily. Several in the crowd seemed to be mothers holding small children tightly to their sides as if to protect them from the 'bizarre' looking, other-world creatures who had invaded their domain.

"They're descended from the first inhabitants of the underground," Dorr answered quietly. "When the ash drove our ancestors from the surface, the people came here first—to the lowest levels of The District where this complex already existed. The idea was to stay here while the sub-surface tunnels were completed, but a small group decided not to leave. They stayed where they were, and our society gradually lost contact with them. We thought the last of them died out a hundred years ago."

"What made them turn into freaks?"

"Not freaks—genetic mutations. Something about living clustered together so far beneath the surface probably caused the genetic makeup of the children born into this world to change. I think the old nuclear power system probably had something to do with it, too. They stored the radioactive waste down here from the atomic generators that powered their equipment. You can see what centuries of exposure to all these elements have done to the human body."

By now dozens, if not several hundred of the strange-looking creatures had poured out from every nook and cranny in the underground complex. Following Mike's lead, Quentin and the others were led to a large central area resembling an auditorium where a buzz of overlapping conversation hung in the air. Seated on the stage were three cloaked and hooded figures, their hands and faces visible but nothing else. One was a rotund, pie-faced man with grotesquely inflated cheeks and jowls that flapped like a turkey's neck. Next to him were two females, one almost normal-looking except for her wide, unblinking eyes, the other a slender, dwarf-like waif that at first looked like a child, but as the three drew closer they could see her weathered, heavily wrinkled skin.

The crowd, abuzz with curiosity, parted to open a path while Mike steered the group toward the stage. He stopped at the rim of a high wooden platform in need of repair and, with a single leap, hopped up onto the stage like the monkey man he resembled.

"Friends," he called out unctuously, sweeping his hand outward.

The middle female rose from her seat and walked to the edge of the stage. She looked down at the strangers.

"Why do you come?" she questioned in a voice that was not friendly.

"We mean you no harm. We only want to return to our people," Dorr explained.

"No, you come to stay. Take our space, steal our homes."

"That isn't us," Dorr said. "Some people from our depth, they use this place to hide. They brought us here against our will."

"How many of you are there?" Quentin asked, glancing around. By now the auditorium was jammed to overflowing. He could see two, perhaps three hundred people, with hundreds more peering in from the outside.

"Many," the woman answered. "And now, we will be few."

"I give you my word, as a representative of my government," Dorr said forcefully, "that no injury will come to any of your people if you help us return to our home."

"Your word, yes," the man on the stage spoke in flawless English.

Dorr nodded respectfully and took a step forward.

"My name is Lillian Dorr."

"I am Joseph, First Counsel of the Triumvirate. Once we were like you, but time has erased all connection between us."

"No, it doesn't have to be that way."

"Look at us. I can see it in your eyes. You find us hideous, deformed."

"No, that isn't true, I—" Dorr stammered.

"We know we are deformed, so we hide. But we also know the body is but a vessel. A man's soul is found in his heart and mind."

"I believe that, too," Dorr said quietly. "Despite whatever differences seem to exist, the gulf is not so great between our people that it can not be bridged."

"Words again," Joseph sighed.

"No—truths. We lived together once, shared a common heritage. Our values arise from the same foundation. Nothing separates us but surface differences that don't matter. We *can* exist together, in peace."

"How can there be peace, Lillian Dorr, when your own people still make war?"

Joseph looked out at the crowd, their somber expressions a silent affirmation of his concern. Mike, his head jerking from side-to-side, appeared nervous and confused by the turn of the conversation while Dorr, unsure how to respond, sought Joseph's eyes as she struggled to find the right words.

"Some among us have done terrible things, and they will be punished for their transgressions. But not everyone in my world is like that. Most are decent, compassionate people. Like you, we only want to survive, to have a future."

"I believe what you say," Joseph replied. "But, I know if we let you go, others will come and our world will forever change."

"Yes," Dorr answered. "It will change. Both our societies will change."

"And with it will come evil ways."

"'New ways,'" she gently corrected. "The future is what we make of it. It will only be evil if we choose to make it so."

"We must talk further among ourselves," Joseph said as he and the other two turned to leave the stage. "There is much we need to consider. Until then, you will be taken to a place to rest and replenish your needs."

"One of our group is badly injured," Dorr said, almost pleading. "We need to get him medical help soon, or he'll die."

"We know of his plight, and have done all for him that we can."

"But—"

"Do your people still believe in God, Lillian Dorr?"

"Yes," she answered solemnly.

"Then pray that He gives us all wisdom enough to make the right decision."

"W-what are they going to do to us?" Claudia hugged Quentin tightly as the three of them were escorted out of the auditorium.

"I don't know," Quentin replied grimly. "But whatever it is, I hope they decide quick."

06:09 HOURS

Pulled out of a pain-filled sleep, the cancer that ate at his body now even invading his dreams, Charles Emory sat up slowly in his sweat-drenched bed and raised his trembling hands to his face.

The images that filled his slumber were frightening and terrible. No theme, no single vision survived into the waking state, yet he would arise with a deep, dark sense of foreboding that shook him to his very soul. Snippets of action, fragments of conversation, the fleeting glimpse of faces he had to struggle to remember would combine into a menagerie of terrifying memories never settling enough to be sorted out and dealt with, but always there to torment his conscious hours.

With each sleep, the dreams grew more hideous than the night before. He would console himself only with the simple thought that one day, soon, this terrible ordeal would be over, and he would be free forever from these demons of the night

"Bad night, doc?" a voice called through the haze, startling him.

"Who—what?"

"You were screaming a few minutes ago," Harmon Bright said in a matter-of-fact voice. "I almost woke you, but then you sat up. You were yelling some pretty scary stuff."

"How did you get in here?" Emory rasped, raising himself shakily from the bed. Bright remained in his chair, facing Emory with a smug look.

"Your security protocol's a joke. Took me thirty seconds to override the command codes."

"Why are you here, Bright?" Emory said as he slipped into a robe. Sweat still dotted his brow while he smoothed back his matted hair.

"We can't afford any mistakes."

"Mistakes? What mistakes?"

"We found Shank's body in that Parker woman's apartment. He was holding Thorndyke's companion, and she's missing. She's probably on her way to the authorities right now."

"I'm not worried," Emory said after a long pause. "She has no evidence. What does she have to tell?"

"She's not stupid. If she understands what's possible, she can figure out what we intend to do with it."

"Let her say anything she wants," Emory replied blandly. "We have the disk. Cottle is the only one who really understands the physics behind it, and he's being held below, with Hollock. As for Thorndyke... well, he's no threat to any of us. All she has is a fantastic story no one will believe, until it doesn't matter."

"I don't like loose ends."

"It appears there is little you can do about it, unless you are somehow able to find this woman and detain her."

"She's not the only loose end."

"Oh," Emory cast a wary glance at Bright.

"Your girlfriend's coming apart. You had to twist her arm to do the jump to that Parker woman's apartment. I think she's about ready to lose it. She's becoming a danger to us."

"Don't you DARE do anything to harm Margaret!"

"Easy doc, easy," Bright stood, enjoying Emory's reaction. "Who said anything about harming anyone?"

"You are a brilliant mathematician, Mr. Bright," Emory said in a controlled voice. "A truly gifted man. We could not have come this far without you. But you are also a deeply troubled man. I knew it from the first moment I took you into my realm. I thought your brilliance would overshadow your faults, perhaps even compensate for your lack of basic human compassion. I thought, by working with you, I could help you grow—help you realize your full potential as a constructive

168

member of our society. But I was wrong. A mind as great as yours can still remain as shallow and devoid of human understanding as even the most flawed person among us."

"Your opinion of me means absolutely nothing," Bright laughed theatrically. "I've had to put up with your platitudes and misplaced sentimentality for the last three years. You've never had my interest at heart, not for a minute. You used me, just as I used you to get what I wanted. Well, in another twenty-four hours it will all be over. Held will be running the show, and I'm going to settle a few more scores I've collected along the way."

"You're forgetting who will be President," Emory said. "There will be no retribution against personal enemies in my Administration."

"You!" Bright smirked. "By the looks of you, you haven't got a month left. Then Held will step in and take total control."

"What makes you think Abraham Held will give you free reign to do whatever you please?" Emory's voice dripped with contempt.

"You still don't get it, do you Emory? Held hates me—more than you do right now, more than you've ever hated anybody in your life! But to stay in power, he needs me. There are other enemies to be silenced, other conspiracies to be revealed, and he can't do that without my process. No one knows the final sequencing but me. I'm the only one who can create the new Beta Light images."

"You're a fool, Bright. You've given us enough already to understand how the process works. It's only a matter of time before others figure out the missing steps."

"Yes," Bright chuckled. "But time is a precious commodity. How long do you think it would take? A month? Two? Six months? What if he needs the process earlier? And even if he can wait, first Held would have to share the secret with others, others he might not be able to trust as completely as me. No, Held isn't going to turn on me, he knows who I am—what I am. And he'll give me whatever I want to keep me happy... and quiet. You're the fool, Emory, not me."

"Perhaps I am," Emory said softly, looking at his reflection in a mirror. "I made my pact with the devil, but not for personal aggrandizement—for the good of this nation. If you, or Held, abuse the power you're given, the people will rise up against you."

"Believe what you want, doc. But keep Zhow under wraps. I won't

169

see this all come crashing down because of her, I warn you."

Bright strode from the room, not bothering to look back as the door opened and he stepped into the hallway. Emory sat wearily on the edge of his chair. After a few moments of deep thought he touched a sensor pad to activate the Vid-Link.

"Get me Margaret Zhow, Lincoln Quadrant 22396."

"That Vid-Link has been placed on restricted access."

"Override, on my command."

"That apartment security unit is no longer accepting your commands," the Vid-Link replied. "Do you wish to place another call?"

"No," Emory said, his sad eyes staring back from the mirror. "There's nothing more to say."

10:45 HOURS

"Two minutes to main core ignite," a ground tech called over the com link.

A cascade of humms and whines rose from a half-dozen monitoring stations now alive with purpose as view screens snapped on and recording equipment was engaged. The bustle of the room, already intense, was racheted up another notch in anticipation of a return jump to Miller's Crossing.

"Hell of a way to spend a Saturday," another tech mumbled, watching the spiral warp indicator rise while the transmitter core built toward critical.

"The big boys upstairs want something to show to Drees and Echeverria," his companion grunted. "I heard they made some of those poor slugs at B.E.T.A. pull a 24 hour shift to get ready for the jump."

"Nothing that couldn't wait 'til Monday! Ash won't be any worse, air won't get any dirtier, but we'll miss all the partying for the Resurfacing Ceremony. You know they opened up the Time Pavilion to the general public, even added new shows at the Theater? And we're stuck down here—on a Saturday—missing everything!"

"And this is just the first of *five* jumps they've scheduled today. We'll be lucky to find out where Gardner and Somerall take a leak with this little preparation. The chances of bringing back anything useful are zero to none-at-all."

"All right, ladies and gentlemen," Jerry Greene's voice boomed over the communications channel. "We've got enough power for a spiral warp. Mark time 9:33 am, 23 seconds. Transfer command to the Launch Director, and prepare for final countdown."

The tall, red-suited figure, senior jumper Calvin Cates, was already in position, his equipment activated and final pre-jump tests completed. Greene shunted the control line to an unusually distracted Abraham Held, who shifted impatiently while he waited for the dynamos to create a sub-vortex in preparation for the jump.

"Miss sitting in the big chair?" Dan Gleason joked as he leaned over Greene's console, nodding toward the Launch Director's station a short distance away.

"Once was enough, thank you!" Greene smiled. "Still, it was an experience."

"Held looks a little, I don't know, not himself today."

"Oh, I don't know." Green sighed. "There's a lot riding on these jumps. Both Presidents have asked for a formal briefing on the Miller's Crossing jump. Held wanted to wait until later, when they had something substantive to show, but The District Council overruled him. So here we are today, trying to get something real before five o'clock. Needless to say, the boss is not too pleased."

"Is that why he boycotted the jump the other day?"

"I don't think he boycotted it, Dan," Greene replied uncomfortably. "Held's a pain in the ass at times, but he's not *crazy*. He won't subvert a direct Council order. Not if he wants to keep his post, anyway. They can't remove him, only Drees and Echeverria can with their Senates' approval, but they can start the ball rolling. The last thing Atlanta or Phoenix wants is to get at odds with The District Council. The federal governments may supply the funding—but The Machine *is* here. And Mr. Held, if anything, is a good politician. He couldn't have survived as long if he wasn't. There's no way he's going to pick a fight the week two Presidents are scheduled to be in town. So, he'll hold his temper and do what he's told, and save his complaint for another day."

"So, where was he? Kind of odd, still, don't you think, that he didn't show up—and didn't tell anyone he wasn't coming?"

"Yeah, well," Greene's eyes drifted toward Held. "Whatever it was, I'm sure the man had his reasons. And it won't do our careers any

171

good to sit around and speculate about it."

"I hear you," Gleason straightened, smiling reflexively.

The room crackled with a bluish-white hue as the energy vortex rose up from the bowels of the core and swallowed the jumper, dragging him into the spiral. Within seconds the noise stopped and the room returned to normal. All eyes now focused on the dozens of screens blanketing the complex as the first images of the jump in progress began to return.

"If we guessed right," Robenalt said, watching the panel on Greene's station, "the signal should be coming through about now. If it works."

The holographic images from an hour before went through their standard routine, monitoring the jump to the twenty-first century as Robenalt and Thorndyke walked through the complex. It was slightly disorienting to watch the ebb and flow of the jump just as it was an hour earlier, waiting to see if their own actions would have any success. At exactly 9:45 am Robenalt had used the jury-rigged pulse band to send a reverse signal back to the Transmission Center, hoping that one of the technicians observing the jump would notice the errant signal. Contained within it was a message from him and Thorndyke with most of the information they had collected, and revealing Thorndyke's location so he could be retrieved.

"There, look. Greene's panel!" Thorndyke shouted.

A small blip interrupted the data stream from the Miller's Crossing jump. It was slight and intermittent, barely noticeable unless someone was looking directly at it.

"We've got about fifteen minutes for someone to notice," Robenalt said grimly. "There's not enough power left in the wrist bands to give it another try."

"Come on, Greene," Thorndyke coached. "Look at your console."

To both of their horror, Greene stood up and turned his back to the screen, continuing his conversation with Gleason, only now talking about mundane things to pass the time until Cates was fully oriented and ready to begin his search.

"Look, Jerry, look!" Thorndyke found himself screaming. "Turn around, damnit!"

"The signal will show up on other screens," Robenalt said in a calm voice.

"Greene's console was our best bet. You know that! The backup power shunts are routed through him. It'll be a miracle if anyone else notices something off on their screen."

Fighting to control a stabbing pain that seemed momentarily to immobilize him, Robenalt closed his eyes. Opening them slowly, he tightened his mouth in a grimace. Thorndyke watched sadly while whole sections of his friend's body phased out, then fought to reappear.

"It's getting worse, Paul. I don't think I have much longer."

"This isn't fair, Jim. If I get out of here, it'll be because of you. Back at the Institute, you were always there for me, and there's nothing I can do to help you."

"Are you serious?" Robenalt smiled grimly. "You put your own life at risk to come here to save me. You, Quentin... how can I ever thank you? Someone will see the signal. You'll get out of here and tell the world everything it needs to know. That will be my satisfaction."

In another section, on the opposite side of the room, a young woman happened to glance at her screen while the coded message repeated its cycle. Puzzled by the strange signal she watched her monitor, waiting for it to reappear. Within thirty seconds the mysterious distortion appeared again.

"What the—" she mumbled to herself, tapping the switch to activate her com link to the Launch Director's station. "Uh, this is Cohen, Section Four."

"Go ahead, Four," Held replied.

"I'm picking up—I don't know, is something bleeding into your jump data telemetry stream?"

"What?"

"There, I saw it again. It's a reverse pulse riding the sub-linear matrix on the jump data channel. I've never seen anything like that before."

"Yes," Held's voice grew strangely quiet. "I see it, too."

"Pattern's too regular to be a spill-over from another data stream. If I didn't know better, I'd say it was some kind of deliberate signal. Here, let me widen the band, see if there's any code riding the wave cycle. Maybe we can figure out what this is, or at least where it came from."

"Negative, Four," Held snapped. "Shut it down."

"Sir?"

"Held to all control stations," he barked into an open link. "Abort the mission. Return the jumper and shut everything down!"

"Abort the mission?" Greene spun, facing his console. "Senior Flight Controller to Launch Director. Is something wrong? My instruments don't show any—"

"Are you DEAF man, or just incompetent!" Held roared as everyone raced to obey his command. "I said shut the damn thing down, NOW! End it NOW!"

"Begin emergency retrieval—bring the jumper out now, immediately!" Greene shouted into the open link.

The hiss and crackle of a building energy spiral rocked the Transmission Center. Within seconds the convulsing, red suited jumper was lying on the edge of the platform amid a howling swirl of blue-white energy, spinning around him like an angry tornado before dissipating into the air.

"Get a medivac team down there on the double!" Greene yelled as two technicians rushed to the unconscious man, ripping off his helmet and stripping away the blazing hot suit.

"He's not breathing," one of the two yelled, ignoring the pain of his own burning flesh while the medical team rushed to the jumper's aid.

Standing at his observation booth, Abraham Held watched in stony silence as the injured man was hustled off the platform and taken from the Center. Greene's eyes locked on the dispassionate, emotionless Held, trying to understand what would possess him to initiate such a risky procedure when there was no apparent danger to anyone involved in the jump.

"Medical," Greene touched a sensor, bringing him into contact with the emergency team now on its way to the hospital. "Give me a report on the jumper's condition."

"Spencer, here," a voice returned. "We've got bad burns and respiratory distress. He's in deep shock... I don't think he's going to make it."

"Keep me informed," Greene said, ending the transmission.

"All right, everyone," Held spoke over the open link. "We're through for the day. Close it down and go home."

"Well," Thorndyke hung his head as the holographic images began to shut their equipment down, the dull buzz of quiet, but intense, overlapping conversation hanging in the air. "Now we know why nothing happened. It's over."

"Don't give up hope, Paul," Robenalt said softly. "You'll need to be strong to get through the next few days. Have faith. You still have good people looking out for you. Just like I did."

"I want to find Sharla," Thorndyke said, watching the room settle into quiet. "I want to be with her... near her, until it's my time, too."

"From what I've seen," Robenalt smiled bravely, "she's quite a girl."

"The best. I knew she was right for me the moment I saw her. I only wish, well—"

"Don't give up, Paul," he touched Thorndyke's shoulder. "It's not over yet."

12:02 HOURS

As the last technician filed out of the Transmission Center, Sharla emerged from hiding.

Her arrival six hours earlier as part of Archival Records's ground support team had gone unnoticed among the normal confusion and controlled chaos of every impending launch. Heading to a monitoring station, she quietly slipped away just as the energy spiral was building to secrete herself inside a storage compartment at the end of a long bank of monitors. It was common to have anywhere from five to seven Archival Records support staff present at every launch to take custody of the real-time images being fed back from the jump, so her presence at the launch site, then absence from her monitoring station, would not immediately be noticed. But she also knew that every ingress into the Transmission Center was recorded in the security system's on-line files. It was only a matter of time before someone on Held's team would discover she had been there. All she needed was twenty minutes alone to locate Thorndyke's time strata and attempt to retrieve him. Then it wouldn't matter what Held's men knew. As the day began, it looked as if she wouldn't have a chance to get to The Machine, but the unexpected abort and abrupt shutdown of all operations gave her a window of opportunity that she was determined to take advantage of.

In the semi-darkness of the powered-down room Sharla picked her way along rows of idle equipment looking for a console that would give her access to the main computer bank. She didn't want to risk using Held's personal control center for fear that any unauthorized effort to activate his equipment would trigger extra security measures. Instead, she sought out the Senior Flight Controller's station, knowing that Jerry Greene's back up and other redundant controls would give her all the access she needed.

"Computer, give me a level 2 systems config," Sharla spoke to the machine. She stood back while the control console lit up and began to shunt power to other areas of the center. "Good, now run file system diagnostic on all jumps within the last thirty-six hours."

"Processing," a voice returned. "I have the information you requested."

"Display it on the central monitor."

As the launch time and coordinates flashed across the screen, Sharla hugged her bandaged ribs and leaned forward to study the information.

"This isn't a complete file" she grunted.

"All authorized jumps have been displayed."

"I want all jumps—any use of the Machine since 12:00 hours yesterday."

"Your request requires a Level 10 authorization."

"Level 10! That's not standard protocol. That information is—"

"Security protocol has been changed," the computer replied officiously. "Your request now requires a Level 10 authorization."

"There's got to be another way to get the information," Sharla's eyes narrowed. "Computer, access all files, but route the request through the central server in Archival Records. Compare power usage to the authorized jump log. Show me any discrepancies."

"Processing. Discrepancy recorded at 12:19 hours, Friday, September 27."

"That's Paul's jump!" she reacted excitedly. "Where is the file record on this jump?"

"There is no completed file on this jump. The vortex was closed at 12:32 hours, but the jumper did not return."

"All right, what were the jump coordinates at the time the vortex was closed?"

"That information is restricted," the computer replied in the same officious tone.

"This is a file maintenance request," Sharla continued. "A jump took place at 12:19 hours on Friday, September 27. The subroutine processor would have automatically started a backup file the moment the energy vortex was engaged. If the jump was not terminated according to standard shutdown procedures, the file will remain open in the central server's redundant level memory path. Access the index and catalogue function—"

"What are you doing here?" Jerry Greene said, startling Sharla, who spun around to face the expressionless man standing in the entrance way to his command post.

"I was, uh, accessing file maintenance to, er, clean up some data from the jump, sir," she mumbled, thinking quickly. "My terminal is down for repair."

Greene stared at her for a long moment before letting his eyes drift to the data matrix displayed on his computer. Sharla's throat tightened while he studied the screen, his face still not betraying his thoughts.

"You'll never get the information you're looking for through file maintenance."

Greene stared again at the fidgeting woman who shifted nervously on her feet, refusing to look him in the eye. He remained in the doorway a few steps away, blocking her only exit from the room.

"I'm sorry, Mr. Greene," Sharla's heart raced, her hands now clammy with sweat. "I shouldn't have used your office. I'll go now."

She started to leave, but Greene wouldn't move. Certain she would have to fight her way out, her muscles tensed and her hands, still at her side, began to curl into tight, menacing fists.

"That was a clever idea, going through the subroutine processor," Greene said, walking forward to sit at his console. "But you'd have been shut out of the backup files, too." He looked at her with stone-faced curiosity. "What's so important about yesterday's jumps? Why are you *really* here?"

"I have to go," Sharla started for the door.

"You won't find what you're looking for if you do," he called, stopping her. She turned to stare at him, unsure what to do. "Don't worry," Greene laughed self-consciously. "I'm not here for Abraham

Held. I'm trying to get to the bottom of this, too... whatever this is. I know there was an unauthorized jump yesterday. In fact, there have been dozens over the last year, none more than a few minutes in duration. All traces have been buried in the power records of previous or succeeding jumps."

"If you've known about the jumps—"

"Knowing they happened is one thing. *Why* they happened is another. The only thing I know is that those records couldn't have been altered without Abraham's direct knowledge—and involvement. I want to know what you know about this."

"I don't know if I can trust you," Sharla said carefully.

Greene took a deep sigh and his shoulders visibly sagged. "Please, Miss. I don't even know your name—"

"Sharla."

"Please, Sharla, I need your help. I found out something was going on three months ago when I was preparing for a jump that would stretch our energy limits to the max. We were going to send someone farther back than we ever had before, and I needed to make sure every subsystem and power relay was in perfect working order. That's when I noticed the anomaly, or what I thought was an anomaly. When I looked harder, I found more, all bundled with the power records of other jumps to mask their presence. I didn't want to think Abraham was using the Machine for personal gain, so I kept my suspicions to myself until I could find out what was really happening. But today he almost killed a man by aborting that jump. Whatever he's hiding, I can no longer stand by and keep my silence. I need to know why the jumps were made, and I think you can tell me. Help me, and I'll help you find whatever you're looking for."

"Held's found a way to manipulate Beta Light images," Sharla spoke after a long moment of contemplation. "Make them show things that didn't really happen."

"What? That's not possible."

"I've seen it done. Others have, too. Paul made a jump back to Benjamin Mitchell's murder to prove Jim Robenalt's innocence, but Held's men discovered him and left him in stasis. It's been twenty-four hours. I've got to bring him back before any more time passes."

"Paul? Paul Thorndyke?"

"Yes."

"You're Sharla Russell. Yes, I thought your name was familiar. The other day Paul insisted on leaving the building through Archival Records. Is that why he was really here on Monday? To check things out, not just to witness the Haley jump? Do others in B.E.T.A. know about this?"

"I'll let Paul answer that himself," Sharla said in an even voice, "—when you bring him back."

"Computer," Greene commanded, entering his personal authorization code into the control panel. "Display coordinates of jump file zero delta 42-23A." Instantly the jump coordinates flashed on the screen. Greene examined them for a moment, then turned toward Sharla with a puzzled look. "I thought you said he went back to the time of Mitchell's murder?"

"He did."

"He's not there." Greene punched in another set of numbers. "From the looks of this, he's been sent to the same time strata as the man who was sentenced in the killing."

"What?"

"There was a secondary transfer that took him from the Mitchell murder to the time where he is now."

"Is Paul all right?" Sharla worried, bending over the screen.

"I can't tell from this what condition he's in," Greene said, punching in another command.

"We've got to bring him back!"

"I think you're right, Sharla," Greene said, activating the return sequencing process. "Maybe we need to ask Paul himself what's going on."

12:27 HOURS

The panel on his sleeve began to light, sending a coded signal to Thorndyke that an energy spiral was building and within minutes he would be returned to the Transmission Center.

"Well, it looks like someone noticed," Robenalt smiled, standing in the holographic image of the Transmission Center while the last few technicians went about powering down the equipment. "You've got about ninety seconds before they bring you back."

"Jim, I—"

"Don't, Paul. Please. I can feel things slipping away. Don't worry about me. I don't have much longer, anyway."

"I'll tell them about you! We can bring you back, too!"

"I can't return," Robenalt's voice was a whisper. "You know it, yourself. Even if my body could survive the return trip, I sealed my fate when I removed my helmet. I'd die the moment my atoms began to reconfigure into flesh and blood. It's better this way, Paul. You'll tell the authorities what really happened. Held and Emory will be stopped, and my name will be cleared."

"I'll stop them. They won't succeed."

"I'm counting on that," he grinned as the pattern on Thorndyke's sleeve grew more active. "Get ready, Paul. You're supposed to feel a hollow sensation first, then a bit of vertigo as everything goes blank for a second. The next thing you'll see is the vortex collapsing on the other side, and you'll be home."

"I'll never forget you, Jim," Thorndyke pulled him into a crushing hug.

"You came back for me, Paul. You're a true friend."

Thorndyke looked at his hands, now sparkling with light, and watched his arms and legs begin to dissolve. Robenalt stepped back to witness his friend's entire body start to disappear, fighting the pain which stabbed at his stomach as parts of his own torso also faded.

"Goodbye, Jim," the words came sluggish and garbled as the rest of Thorndyke's body vanished.

"Goodbye... friend."

Whole sections of his own body were now missing. Robenalt turned the palm of his hands over and looked at them, wiggling his fingers and watching the clearly defined edges of his gloves break apart and throw out ember-like streams of material. He felt the weakness in his legs increase until it was almost impossible to stand, but he was determined to remain upright and face his fate with courage.

While the last of the technicians closed out their work and powered down the ambient light in the Transmission Center, Robenalt watched a solitary figure slip out from behind a closed door and steal herself into the shadows. He smiled knowing what the next hour would bring, rejoicing in the reunion of his friend with the woman he loved, the woman who had saved him.

Then, as a creeping numbness swept through his body and began to fog his brain, Jim Robenalt released his hold on life—and faded into nothing.

12:29 HOURS

Through the eye of a swirling tornado, Thorndyke could make out the image of two people standing at the end of the short, elevated gangway leading to the central core. He could feel the heat of his molecules reforming, the tingly warmth radiating out through the pores in his skin and drenching him in instant sweat. A burning sting stabbed his flesh when the outer layer of his jump suit came into contact with the surrounding air, but before the searing heat could pass through his protective clothing and blister his skin, the blast of an almost invisible spray of moisture cooled his suit instantly. Evaporating in a dissipating sizzle it left small flakes of carbon clinging to his garment that made him look like a nineteenth century coal miner returning to the surface from a hard day's work.

As his feet grew more solid, supporting real weight, the whirlwind around him quickly subsided. The front of his helmet was blackened and pitted from the energy required to return him after a full day in stasis, but he could still make out the faces of two figures—one a man, the other a woman—waiting apprehensively for the turmoil to clear. He took off his helmet and with a wide, satisfying grin, dropped it to the platform, barely able to take a step forward before Sharla rushed the remaining distance to crush him in her embrace.

"Oh, you're all right, you're all right," she cried, kissing his mouth and running her hands through his sweat-soaked hair.

"Careful," Thorndyke rasped, bolstering himself in her grip. "I'm still a little... unsteady."

"You're lucky to be alive, Paul," Greene said while Sharla helped him to the floor.

"I'm so weak," he stumbled. Sharla tightened her grip around his waist to keep him from falling.

"Your muscles will recover in another minute or two. It's the prolonged effects of the transmission process. Your body's chemicals are all there, but they need to realign. Your circulatory and lymphatic systems will help make the adjustments. Normally it only takes a few moments."

"Held's... behind the false data file," Thorndyke said, fighting to speak. "I saw a lot. We... I... know what happening. Most of it. There's still... some pieces—"

"Don't try to talk, Paul," Sharla put her fingers to his lips. "We know a lot of it, too. As soon as you get your strength, we'll go to the authorities."

"I'm afraid none of you will be going anywhere," Held's voice boomed across the empty room.

The door to the Transmission Center snapped opened and Held entered, flanked by Harmon Bright and two other men, one of them Brian Russack. Bright carried a mid-twenty-first century cartridge-firing weapon, its red laser light locked onto multiple targets, while the other man rushed to a bank of monitoring equipment.

"Brian," Thorndyke shook his head sadly.

"I neglected to override your security clearance," Held spoke to Greene while he closed the distance between them with long, purposeful strides. "An oversight on my part, but fortunately the computer was programmed to alert me if any inquiries were made into certain restricted files."

"Abraham, what is all of this? What are you doing?"

"You are a great disappointment to me, Jerry," Held said as he stopped in front of Greene.

"I supported you, Abraham, when others questioned your judgment. I defended you when they attacked your policies, your methods—and your morals. I did this because I believed in who you were, what you were doing. I thought you were a visionary who couldn't be judged like other, ordinary men. I thought you were a great man."

"I am a great man."

"No," Greene's words were slow and measured. "I watched you almost kill a jumper today. For what? To protect your secrets? Is human life of so little value to you, Abraham?"

"I'd intended to place you in a position of great responsibility as soon as the transition was complete," Held was cool, emotionless. "I can see now that was a mistake, too."

"Only one came back," Held's man called out as he lifted his head from the console.

"Retrieve Robenalt's jump matrix and transfer him to a new set of coordinates, then delete all records of the change in the main file and subroutine processor. I don't want him found."

"Where should I send him?"

"Pick a date and time, or choose something at random!" Held snapped. "I don't care, just make sure he's lost—for good!"

"I don't know why you're doing this," Greene reacted forcefully, "but I can't let you destroy any more lives."

"Let me?" Held's face transformed with an evil smile. "You're in no position to be dictating terms."

"Stop this insanity, whatever it is. This isn't right. Whatever you're trying to accomplish—"

"The planet is dying!" Held erupted. "The governments do nothing to stop the ash. They bicker and argue over petty, meaningless distractions while the world chokes on its own vomit. Only a strong leader, with the vision and presence to command the respect of the nation—to unite its resources under a common purpose—can save us from the destruction we've brought upon ourselves."

"You, Abraham?"

"No, not me. Charles Emory will become President of a reunited nation."

"Emory?" Greene laughed sarcastically. "That frail old man? How convenient. And when he succumbs to the ravages of his disease?"

"I will serve if I am called upon to do so."

"I thought I knew you better than this," Greene turned his back on the man that, to him, had almost been a father.

"Thorndyke's been watching everything," Bright said, gesturing with his gun. "No telling what he's seen."

"I've seen enough," Thorndyke said. "And I can piece it all together. Not only me, but others too."

"Like your lady friend here?" Bright snorted, gesturing toward Sharla. "It was nice of you to find us, Ms. Russell. We'd been looking all night for you. You want to tell him about your 'other friends' now, or let him go on dreaming for a while?"

"Paul, they took Ruth, and Claudia... and the Secretary of State."

"The disk—" Thorndyke's mouth went dry.

183

"You mean this?" Bright laughed, holding the dime-sized holodisk between his thumb and forefinger. "That was a nice bit of work figuring things out, but it's not going do you any good." He snapped the disk with a flick of his hand, cracking the outer shell. "It's useless now, like all of you High-Types."

Thorndyke surged forward, blind rage overwhelming him. Greene grabbed his shoulders and pulled him back while Bright, never once reacting to the threat, looked on with amusement.

"Keep your friend under control," Held warned Greene icily. "This young man here has no hesitation about taking human life."

"You killed Mitchell!" Thorndyke shouted while Greene continued to restrain him.

"And Sherwood," Bright grinned. "You know, I thought it would be harder than it was. The holograms show it, but you just watch. There's no sensation. I thought there would be more feeling when you actually do it." He made a point of tapping a switch on his weapon that triggered a rising, high-pitched whine. "But there isn't, really. Now I know why it was so easy in the past to kill someone."

"I didn't sign on for this," Russack moved from the background, staring at Bright. "Put them underground with the others. You don't need to kill them."

"You'll do as you're told," Held barked.

Russack stared into the angry man's face, their eyes locking for a moment before his tight lips twitched and he looked away. Wordlessly, he stepped back and kept his eyes averted.

"Mr. Held," the man at the console called. "I've got a problem here. The matrix's degraded. I can't get a lock on Robenalt."

"Are you certain you have the proper coordinates?"

"Yes, sir, but it's like he's not there."

"Well," Held took a breath, his escaping sigh like a snake's hiss. "It seems we now know the limits of tolerance for the human body in stasis."

"We've got another problem, sir," the man said nervously.

"What?"

"Someone's re-routing data from the main computer bank."

"Lock out access to the file!"

"I can't, sir. It's not responding to my command."

"That's impossible," Held stormed to the console. "No one has the authority to override my code."

Held's face tensed as the terminal screen showed a massive download of main system files. He slapped in several commands attempting to stop the outflow of data, but each action had no effect.

"Only one body has higher authority than you, Abraham," Greene said quietly. "The District Council."

"Quentin!" Thorndyke grinned broadly.

"Sir, they're getting *everything,*" the technician squirmed.

"It's over, Abraham."

For a long moment Held stared at the console, not saying anything. Bright's eyes flitted between him and their prisoners, his once cocky facade beginning to crack. Nervously, he tightened his grip on his weapon as Held drew a long breath and returned Greene's stare.

"Let them go," he said, speaking to Bright.

"What? Just give up—like that?"

"The Council knows everything. There's no point going on."

"No!" Bright yelled, his weapon still trained on Thorndyke and the others. "They don't know *anything!* Just bits and pieces, facts without context. The only ones who can put it all together are standing right here."

"It's finished, Bright. Can't you see that? Don't be a fool."

"*You* call *me* a fool? If you let me take care of things before, none of this would be happening now! I've listened to you long enough, Held!"

"What are you going to do?" Held asked. "Kill them—and everyone else in this room? It's over. We failed."

The whine of the weapon completing its charge was the only response Bright gave, the venom in his eyes locking on to Thorndyke, Sharla, and Greene. Thorndyke moved to position himself between Bright and Sharla, but she slipped her hand quietly through his arm and pulled him gently aside.

"Whatever happens, it happens to us together," she whispered while the rotating lights on the gun barrel brightened and locked, ready to fire.

"I said that's enough!" Held yelled. He grabbed the stock of the short, stubby rifle and moved to confront Bright. "Disarm your weapon. I won't let—"

The scream of the firearm discharging melded with Held's own death wail as the barrel erupted in searing red light, eviscerating him almost instantaneously. The smoking, glowing corpse crumpled to the floor at Bright's feet as Russack and the other man turned and fled the room. Spinning, Bright aimed his weapon at them and looked as if he was about to fire, but his body suddenly grew stiff. While the two dashed into the relative safety of the outside corridor, he lowered the still glowing barrel, then turned and looked at Thorndyke, a cocky, sardonic smile returning to his lips.

"What's he going to do?" Sharla asked, tightening her grip on Thorndyke's arm.

"You think you've won," Bright muttered. "But you haven't. I beat you, all of you. I've done something no one else had the brains *or guts* to do. I shaped this world, not Held, not Emory, not you! Only God—and Harmon Bright—can change the fabric of time and create their own reality! I won't answer for that to my inferiors. Only God can judge me."

"Come on," Greene whispered, urging Thorndyke and Sharla toward the door. "Get out of here, now!"

With a quick, steady gait the three made their way toward the exit. They could hear the whine of the weapon again charging to maximum power but dared not turn around. As they pushed through the door they heard the shriek of the gun discharge, then Bright gasp loudly. The heavy weapon dropped to the floor and his own body fell in a crumpled heap next to Held.

Instantly the room returned to silence as if nothing had ever happened.

"RETURN TO THE SURFACE"
Sunday, September 29, 2416 AD
13:15 HOURS

How the past perishes
is how the future becomes.
-Alfred North Whitehead

Slowly, like small animals afraid to peek their heads above the entrance to their underground burrows, people made their way back to the surface.

A generation of men and women who had never seen the sun except as part of a holographic image stared skyward while they strolled along black-topped roadways or stepped onto freshly planted grass struggling to take hold in a sterile, nutrient-deprived soil. Above them, small, tornado-like gusts of wind blew thick deposits of ash from the crest of the dome to allow fleeting glimpses of the brilliant, yellow-white orb shining overhead. But for the most part, only diffuse light managed to filter though, casting dull shadows across patches of green and brown dotting the open-air Mall to make it seem as if the city was simply blanketed by an overcast sky.

As the swarm of people steadily grew, the city slowly came alive. Everywhere subsurface dwellers wandered the streets, peering into the ancient structures like tourists on a foreign holiday. The buildings—some still showing signs of damage; the outer facades of most restored—spoke to the grandeur of an earlier time when man still populated the surface of the planet. Now more myth than fact, Washington D.C. was a modern day Troy; a city of the dead resurrected from the ash to showcase a world that once was and would never be again.

"Guess we can think about opening this window now," Scott Hollock chuckled, gazing out onto the Mall from his upper level office.

Bandaged and confined to a body conforming wheel chair whose cell-regenerating circuitry helped speed the healing process, he steered the unwieldy device to the hermetically sealed window behind his desk to join Lillian Dorr already standing there.

"I never thought I'd live to see this day," Dorr said as she glanced down at the growing throng meandering through the streets.

"For a moment, I didn't either," Hollock winked, cupping her hand in his.

"You're a lucky man, Scott," President Drees said from the opposite end of the room, watching them together. "In more ways than one."

"I know that, sir."

"Wish I'd listened to you earlier, Lillian," Drees sighed. "We might have avoided a lot of the bloodshed these past few days. Henry Sherwood, even Abraham Held, not to mention the others who died on both sides of this battle. Life's too precious a thing to waste, even when the person's a misguided fool."

"What happens now, Mr. President?" Dorr asked hesitantly.

"The Federal police have arrested Emory and Zhow. Most of the other conspirators have been rounded up too by now, I imagine. We'll use The Machine to identify whoever we missed. I'm satisfied there's no more threat."

"Have you told President Echeverria?"

"No," Drees said. "And I don't intend to. We'll explain Held's death as the act of a deranged man, that Bright fellow. And your accident as an unfortunate coincidence of timing, coming so close to Held's death and Henry Sherwood's... heart attack."

"Do you really think Echeverria will believe that?"

"No. But he's a practical man. Whatever the truth is, he knows the public needs a plausible explanation, and that's what we're going to give them. If there's no outcry, and I don't believe there will be, his questions will end there. The important thing is to keep the time viewing complex running without interruption. It's our most important national treasure."

"Forgive me, sir," Hollock said. "But how can you keep something like this under wraps? The trials—"

"There's not going to be any trials. Emory is a dying man. He'll be kept under house arrest—too sick to receive visitors—until his situation resolves itself."

"What about Margaret Zhow?"

"A brilliant woman, by all accounts I hear, but a conspirator and accomplice to murder. She and the others will be resettled in the West in Montana. There's an abandoned military facility there that's still capable of supporting life. They'll be given provisions and enough technology to make a go at it, but they'll never rejoin society again. Even the U.S. West won't know they're there. It's totally isolated."

"It all sounds so barbaric," Dorr shuddered.

"No more barbaric than what they had in mind for President Echeverria and myself, Lillian." Drees walked to a statue of an armless woman mounted on a pedestal in Hollock's office, her porcelain skin as delicate and smooth as it was three thousand years ago when she was carved out of stone by an unknown artisan. He let his hands trail across the cold, hard surface of the stone. "That man Robenalt, I understand he couldn't be recovered."

"Yes."

"The boy's a hero, but no one will ever know."

"That isn't right," Hollock said.

"I know it isn't, but there's no other way. Someday, maybe, when we're all dead and gone, the truth will come out. But it can't now. There's too much at stake. If the people can't trust our technology, there's nothing left for them to believe in."

"They still have God."

"I understand your position, Scott," Drees replied sympathetically. "But that's the way it has to be. No one's going to know what really happened."

"You can't keep Bright's discovery secret, Mr. President," Hollock pressed firmly, but respectfully. "Sooner or later someone will discover the same principles he did. The genie's already out of the bottle."

"I don't have any intention of hiding Bright's invention. In a few months our scientists will announce the discovery of a new mathematical theorem that can manipulate Beta Light images. We'll use the announcement to create a new section in the Entertainment Department to produce theater holograms and interactive programs that everyone will recognize as altered images. Think of it as the next step in Beta Light evolution. We're going to demystify and de-politicize this thing before some other crazy gets an idea to do what Held and Emory tried to do. And I want you, Scott, to take personal charge of this new operation and oversee the development of this resource."

"I'm sorry, sir, I can't. As soon as I've healed and can turn over the management of this agency, I'm leaving B.E.T.A."

"—They're here, Mr. Director," Robert's image appeared on the view screen on Hollock's desk, interrupting the conversation.

"Send them in," Hollock instructed.

"Hold off a moment," Drees said gently, turning to Hollock. "I need you Scott. Your country needs you. You can't walk away now, not at this time in our history. Lillian, maybe you can talk some sense into him."

"I'm afraid I agree with him, Mr. President," she smiled, squeezing Hollock's hand.

"I've spent my entire professional life working with The Machine," Hollock explained. "I'm proud of my accomplishments, but somewhere along the way we've lost our vision as a society. I think it's time we began looking to the future for our answers, instead of into the past."

"Eloquent words, my friend," Drees said with genuine feeling. "But The Machine still remains our best hope—our only hope—for our survival as a race."

"No, sir." Hollock's words were soft but direct. "It's become a crutch. Our real chance still lies here, with the present. I never really understood that until I went deep below. There's a culture, a society down there that has something for us to learn, I think. I want to be part of the effort that opens the Subterranean to further discovery. And I want to do it in a controlled way, so we respect them for what they are, and not exploit them as a curiosity. Those people saved my life, I owe it to them."

"Well, I'm enough of a politician to know when the vote's not there," Drees smiled. "I admire your principles, Scott. It will take a strong man to keep the Subterranean from falling victim to our lesser instincts. I'll appoint you chief liaison, or ambassador, or something as soon as I get back to Atlanta. You know," he chuckled as the thought struck him. "You'll be working for the State Department if you accept the appointment. That means this pretty lady here will be your boss."

"Looks like we're destined to be together, one way or another," Hollock grinned.

"Okay then, it's settled." Drees reactivated the monitor. "Young man, you can send them in now."

The door opened and Thorndyke, Quentin, Sharla, and Ruth stepped into the cavernous office. Both Ruth and Sharla were visibly startled at the unexpected sight of the President of the United States East. Thorndyke and Quentin traded nervous glances while Drees extended his hand.

"It's an honor to meet you four," he said. "Our country owes each of you a debt of gratitude we can never repay."

Crossing the room, Dorr embraced Sharla and Ruth like two old friends while Drees continued to pump away at Thorndyke's hand.

"The real hero is Jim Robenalt," Thorndyke replied modestly. "He showed us the way. And gave his own life to save all of us."

"Yes," Drees said, placing his palm on the young man's shoulder in a fatherly embrace. "Our country owes him a special debt, too. And in time that debt will be paid. But I asked you four to come here for another reason. This new technology, falsifying Beta Light images, it can be a terrible weapon in the wrong hands. Right now other than Jerry Greene, who has more than proven his loyalty to this nation, the only people who know the full truth of what happened these last few days are standing here in this room. It's a terrible burden we have to bear."

"Burden, sir?" Quentin repeated.

"That truth must remain with the eight of us. No one must ever know what Held and Emory attempted to do."

"But, that means—" Thorndyke said, confused.

"Yes. One day your friend's name will be cleared. But for the foreseeable future this last week never happened. I know this is a tough thing to swallow, but the security of our country is at stake. There are going to be significant changes in the coming months, changes that will go the heart of the very way we organize ourselves as a society. I've already made arrangements to submit legislation to both national legislatures that will ultimately consolidate the management of the Time Machine under one authority. It's ironic, isn't it," Drees said with a self-effacing laugh. "What Abraham Held wanted most of all will eventually come about. He's the catalyst for the greatest change of our time. One strong leader will control our most valuable resource, answerable only to himself, and God."

"That person will become the most powerful man in the country," Thorndyke said. "Both countries. The world."

"Yes, he will. But there's no other way to insure that another petty demagog doesn't come along and try to usurp power for his own ends."

"Where will you find a man you can place that kind of trust in?" Quentin asked blankly.

"I thought we had that man here," Drees nodded toward Hollock. "But some things are beyond even my ability to persuade. That man will come to us, over time. The changes I spoke of will come about gradually, and as they do the person will prove himself worthy of the task. Until that time, we need to rely on the talents of the five people we can trust the most, you four and Mr. Greene, to help guide this transition."

"Us?" Sharla swallowed hard.

"I can't think of any one better to entrust this to," Drees said. "You've more than proven yourselves equal to the task."

"I–I don't know what—"

"—to say? We'll figure out the titles for each of you later, but I want you four to help our two governments control this monster before it controls us."

"Maybe we should just dismantle it, sir," Sharla offered hesitantly. "Be done with it now, once and for all."

"Perhaps we will one day, Ms. Russell. But not today. No, my offer still stands. Are you up to the challenge, each of you?"

"No," Ruth replied softly. "I'm not. This isn't where my destiny lies. I'll be there for Quentin and Paul, and Sharla, but if you'll excuse me please, I'm not suited for what you have in mind."

"I beg to differ, young lady. But I hear the sincerity in your voice. I won't force you to do anything you don't want to do. I need to know how you other three feel."

"I'd be honored," Quentin said. "I'll do whatever you ask—as long as I can still spend time in the field. That's where I really belong."

"I'm just an Archivist," Sharla hesitated. "I'll do whatever you need me to, but to be perfectly honest, what you're asking scares me to death."

"I expected no less a response," Drees laughed good-naturedly. "Which more than confirms my judgment in placing this confidence in you. And you, Mr. Thorndyke. What is your answer?"

"I made Jim Robenalt a promise," Thorndyke said thoughtfully. "If you really intend to entrust us with the kind of responsibility you suggest, I'll use it one day to keep that promise."

"Yes," Drees let the word slip out slowly. "I know you will. And perhaps one day you will have the authority to act on your intentions. I want you to know I respect your devotion to your friend. And to the truth. But I need to know if you can also put a nation's larger interests ahead of your own personal desires. The world is never black and white, and neither is the truth of things. It's a terrible thing to say, but that is the real truth."

"I don't know," Thorndyke replied after a long pause. "I can't give you an answer now."

"Then you'll give me an answer when you can. In the meantime, you still work for B.E.T.A., and if I'm not mistaken the Director will have a continuing need for your talents, particularly during his time of recovery. Have I overstated the case, Mr. Hollock?"

"Not at all," he smiled.

"Good. I'm already late for the start of the Resurfacing festivities. My old friend Jorge Echeverria has no doubt taken advantage of this lapse and is well into delivering *my* speech too. If I'm to salvage any political capital from this sordid affair, I must take my leave now. Lillian, I'll understand if your duties require your presence elsewhere. I'm sure you've had your fill of state dinners—and my oratorical excesses—and could use the respite as well."

"Thank you, Mr. President," her lips curled in a gracious smile.

"Please think about what I said," Drees called as he moved toward the exit.

He addressed the comments to everyone, but focused his gaze on Thorndyke, who shifted uncomfortably as the door opened and the President of the United States East was swallowed up in a phalanx of security officers waiting for him on the other side.

15:05 HOURS

Over four hundred thousand people, almost the entire population of The District, stood on the Mall separating the old Capital building from the Washington Monument, listening to President Drees and President Echeverria speak to the assembled crowd.

Except for the partially destroyed Capitol building which served as their backdrop, and the absence of tall, lush green trees framing the hill upon which it stood, it could have been a scene straight out of the Beta Light archives. However, instead of an inauguration speech to install a new government, the words were about man's triumphal return to the surface of a planet, which, through his own ignorance and greed, he had poisoned and made uninhabitable. For many it was the first glimmer of hope in an otherwise endless drumbeat of depressing news about their personal and collective futures, and the crowd listened in rapt attention while Drees spoke to them of a new beginning for themselves and their planet.

At the rear of the crowd, connected but apart from the happenings around them, Thorndyke, Sharla, Ruth, and Quentin watched the two presidents on a large view screen erected for the ceremony. As they listened to the words, Quentin turned to his friend and spoke softly, drawing Sharla's attention as well.

"I know how you feel about Jim, but he wouldn't want you to throw your career away because some politician didn't have the guts to tell the people the truth about what happened. It wouldn't be the first time something like that was kept from the public."

"You think that's what it's all about, Quentin?" Thorndyke asked. "My career?"

"You know me better than that, Paul. But there's more for you to do at B.E.T.A., or whatever the new organization will look like. You have a chance to make a real difference. You can't do it if you're on the outside."

"I don't know," Thorndyke let his shoulders sag. "All this—it isn't what I thought I'd be doing with my life. A week ago I was a GS3, wet behind the ears. I still am. Now I'm chatting with the President of the United States East, who's asking me to be part of a team that's going to run The Machine. Everything's happening too fast. I'm not prepared."

"Who is?" Quentin chuckled. "That's what life's all about. You roll with the punches. You know, Paul, things could be a lot worse. This is a hell of an opportunity we've been given, all of us."

"What do you think?" Thorndyke turned to Sharla.

"I think you should do what you think is right. Whatever that is, I'll support you—and be with you, if you want."

"I want," he smiled, pulling her into his arms and kissing her sweetly.

"Isn't anybody going to ask my opinion?" Ruth chided, joining the conversation.

"Yes, Ruth. I'd love to hear what you think."

"Well, you may not like it."

"So much the better," Thorndyke said sincerely.

"You did the best you could for Jim," she began. "No one may ever know what he did, but that doesn't lessen the importance of it. You put your life at risk to save him, and almost lost it doing so. No one besides us may ever know that, but it doesn't cheapen what you did. The true measure of a person isn't in what you, or I, or anyone else thinks of them, it's in what they do with their life. For whatever reason the world will never know about Jim Robenalt's sacrifice. None of us can change that. But I think it would be a terrible shame to compound one injustice with another."

The words of the podium speaker echoed off the backdrop of buildings as the crowd continued to listen to the speech, but their meaning was lost on a silent, contemplative Paul Thorndyke, who let Ruth's thoughts stir around inside his mind. Finally, he placed his hands gently on her shoulders and bowed to kiss her lovingly on the forehead.

"I admire your wisdom, Ruth," he said with genuine affection. "Quentin, you've got a heck of a woman here."

"Glad you think so," Quentin smiled as her circled his arm around her waist. "Ruth and I want you to stand with us at our wedding next Saturday."

"You're getting married!"

"Yes," Ruth opened her arms to embrace Thorndyke, who lifted her up off the grass.

"Of course! I'd be honored! A wedding, that's fantastic!"

"And we'd like you to stand with us, too, Sharla," Quentin said.

"Me? I—" Sharla was speechless. "I don't know what to say."

"Say yes."

"Yes, of course I will!"

"One day we'll both return the favor," Ruth giggled as her feet once again touched the ground, drawing a blush from Sharla, who traded fleeting glances with Thorndyke.

"That obvious?" Thorndyke smiled.

"From the first time I saw you together."

The ceremony on the Capital steps ended with a flourish of holographic fireworks exploding in the sky, the overcast grey of the midday sun not taking away from its splendor. As the crowd began to break up into smaller clusters, Ruth and Quentin bid farewell and wandered away, leaving Thorndyke and Sharla alone to talk. They strolled the Mall, hand in hand, drinking in the sights and smells of the wonderful new world.

"You know," Thorndyke finally broke the silence. "You are the best thing to ever happen to me."

"I know," she teased.

"I'm serious. What Ruth said, about us—I've only known you for a week, not even. But I know she's right, here, in my heart. I love you, Sharla. You're the most wonderful woman I've ever met."

"Are you proposing to me, Mr. Thorndyke?"

"No, well yes. I think I am."

"You're not sure?"

"Well, no. I've never done anything like this before."

"Well I should hope not!" her eyes widened.

"No, I mean—I don't know what I mean."

"I'll make it easy for you then. I accept."

"You do?"

"Of course. Did you think I'd say no? I may not have known you very long, Mr. Thorndyke, but you've already given me a lifetime's worth of experiences."

Sweeping her into his arms, Thorndyke kissed her long and passionately. An amused couple stepped around them while they continued, oblivious to anyone but themselves.

"Why do you keep calling me that?" he said when the kiss finally ended.

"What?"

"'Mr. Thorndyke.'"

"Because you are a man who deserves and commands respect, and I want you always to know that I know that."

"Really?" he grinned like a little boy. He folded her into his arm while they continued to walk toward the Capital building decked out in red, white and blue bunting. "You know," he said, pulling her closer, "you are a very complicated lady. But definitely worth the challenge."

18:23 HOURS

Far below the surface, in the dank and squalid confines of the Subterranean, another crowd assembled. The misshapen, hideous cousins of humanity collected in their central area to discuss the changes they knew would come once the subsurface dwellers returned to their domain. Would they be treated as long-lost fellow brethren returning to the community of man, or grotesquely deformed freaks to be pushed out, even exterminated, to make way for the adventurers and exploiters they knew were sure to follow? A rallying cry had been taken up against their leaders who had helped the three intruders return to their own kind, and bring with them knowledge of their existence and a certainty that others of their race would soon return.

"I say to you," Joseph, the acknowledged head of the ruling triumvirate, spoke over shouts of discontent, "that we are not animals, we are men. And as men we have the responsibility to care for our fellow creatures, however different from ourselves they may be."

"Will they care for us?" a voice shouted. "Will they show us the same compassion?"

"We know their kind," a shrunken husk of a woman waved a mildew-coated book. "Read them from the books they left. They kill and take."

"Much has changed in both our worlds since the great calamity sent us all into the earth," Joseph soothed. "I, too, have read the words, and seen the pictures. Those who killed and took were our ancestors, too. We share their blood. Why, then, can they not share our souls? Would you judge a man only by the way he looks?"

"Will you give your life, Joseph, and the lives of your family, to know the truth?"

His eyes heavy with emotion, Joseph looked into the faces of hundreds of people now serenely quiet, waiting to hear the elder respond.

"All of you are my family, as much as my own blood. For hundreds of years we have lived apart by our own choice. It is time to bury our fears, push aside our doubts and embrace the future. God brought these people to our world. It is a sign from Heaven that our isolation must end."

"I say we fight to protect our land and our people!" another person shouted. Murmurs of approval swept through the crowd as mothers clutched their young children close to their bodies and older men and women raised homemade weapons aloft.

"Then we will all die," Joseph said sadly. The crowd instantly quieted. "We cannot turn back the sands of time. Others will come, and we must learn to adapt or we shall perish—all at once in battle, or slowly with the passage of time. But perish we shall."

The crowd began to disband, breaking up into smaller groups. The din of conversation hung heavy in the air as each citizen of the Subterranean struggled with the options they had been presented.

"I fear we may have unleashed a cataclysm of unparalleled destruction upon this land and our people," another of the elders said to Joseph, glancing out over the crowd. "Perhaps we should not have acted with such haste in permitting the three intruders to leave."

"You know, as well as I, that the separation has been both a blessing and curse. To survive as a race we must end our isolation or forever lose our capacity to rejoin our fellow men."

"Yes, Joseph," the man said sadly. "But when they learn, truly, what we have become, do you believe they will still be willing to accept *us?*"

"SHADOWS IN THE LIGHT"
Thursday, June 2, 2417 AD
22:14 HOURS

The means prepare the end,
and the end is what the
means have made it.
-John Morley

The last time viewing jump of the day had been running into one snag after the other, and Elizabeth Ramsland, the fiery, forty-year-old Jump Master, was growing more and more impatient. She paced among the crew of technicians, who frantically tried to ready both the jumper and the equipment. Finally, she stopped and clapped her hands.

"Come on people! We are running out of time! Where's Raikhel?"

A wiry, dark haired man with a ruggedly handsome face stepped out of a cluster of technicians. Ten years Ramsland's junior, Tobias Raikhel towered over the woman whose withering stare could bring him, and anyone else, to a paralyzing stop. "Here Elizabeth!"

"Where are we?" Ramsland sighed, her fatigue showing.

"We're almost at go," Raikhel said with a reassuring smile. "We'll make it."

"I just hope I do," she replied. "Once our jumper is suited up we're supposed to go to minimal support—just three of us to man the controls. Delaney doesn't want to waste any more resources on a 'Theater run' than he has to, the miserable son of a bitch. That means every thing has to be buttoned up and extra tight. No mistakes, no errors."

"I understand."

"Any problems I need to know about?"

"No, just a minor concern, that's all."

"What concern?" Ramsland said, fixing him with a piercing glare.

"Our jumper tonight is Johnny Crandall. He's not the best jumper we could have, but the only one I could get."

"This is the graveyard shift, Tobias," Ramsland exhaled irritatedly. "It where they put the worthless jumps—and the worthless people. We take what we get and make it work. That's how we get back in the mainstream and out of this shit-hole of a jump slot. Until Delaney upgrades my performance for Greene's review, I'm stuck here—and you along with me. So it's not going to do us any good to complain. Now, what's your real concern?"

"He screwed up his last jump," Raikhel explained. "Right in a crucial moment he decided to adjust the record settings on his jump and left his support team with a scrambled signal that couldn't be corrected. The whole jump was wasted."

"All right. Keep a close eye on him and make sure he doesn't do anything wrong. Like it matters," Ramsland muttered loudly to herself. "I'm a god-damned research scientist. I should be investigating the socio-political dynamics of eighteenth century pre-industrial America, not babysitting some action adventure jump that's purely for entertainment." Turning again to Raikhel, she narrowed her eyes and spoke deliberately. "This is our ticket out of here and back into something useful, so let's get this damned show on the road! Chicago 1927! The Sammy Fratianno hit!"

Tobias Raikhel nodded sheepishly and hurried off to check on the status of the impending jump. Ramsland turned to face into a young man who had been watching her with rapt attention.

"Who are you?" she hissed as the startled man took a step backwards

"I'm Andy Keaton," he said, swallowing hard. "I'm here... for the jump. I was asked to report."

"Another screw-up," she grunted, locking her eyes on to his. "What did you do to get yourself assigned to me?"

"Er, nothing ma'am, that I know of. I, er, I'm just out of school. The Time Research Institute. Last Thursday."

"Perfect. Have you ever teched a jump before?"

"I've read about it."

"This is great," Ramsland rolled her eyes.

"What, er, do you want me to do?"

"Other than get out of my way?" the older woman snapped. "Find my assistant, Tobias Raikhel. He'll assign you something useful."

"Yes ma'am," Keaton bowed and backed away. "Thank you. ma'am."

"Standby!" a loudspeaker boomed. "Jumper take your position!"

Elizabeth Ramsland hurried to speak one last time to the suited jumper. Johnny Crandall saw her coming and smiled a greeting through his clear glass helmet.

"You ready, Johnny?" she asked, real concern in her voice.

"Yes ma'am!" his cheerful voice sounded from inside the suit. "I am a go!"

"Good," she sighed. "Let's review. This is a mob hit. We think it's a grudge thing between Fratianno and Capone. I want you to focus on Fratianno. Get as close to him as makes a good shot. The newspaper reports from that era said he was approached by a single man, who said something, then pulled a pistol, and shot him. Then three machine gunners entered and sweep the room. It should be fairly dramatic, even if it isn't historically significant. The gangsters will leave the restaurant, you stay put and wait for the police. They arrive quickly. Get a shot of the police work. Audiences love the aftermath."

"Will do," Johnny shouted through the glass plate.

High up in the insulated control room Tobias Raikhel placed Andy Keaton at one of the main power consoles.

"I'm glad you could make it," Raikhel said, clapping a friendly hand on Keaton's shoulder.

"This is all really fantastic," Keaton gushed. "I can't believe I'm here."

"I asked for you to be assigned to this jump," Raikhel smiled, watching Keaton's face. "My people tell me you were a bright student and one not afraid to ask the troubling questions. I value that."

"Thank you, Sir."

"Tobias—we don't stand on formality here, except maybe for Dr. Ramsland. She's a very ambitious woman who's managed to anger a few important people, so she's been assigned to the graveyard shift until things quiet down. My fate, unfortunately, is linked to hers. I've been a member of her team for the last five years, and where she goes, well, so do I—at least until I am able to establish a following of my own. Tell me, Andy, what are your goals?"

"Well, I want to go as high as I can."

"Admirable," Raikhel smiled. "Are you willing to take chances to get there?"

"Pardon me?" Keaton searched his eyes for meaning.

"Are you willing to stick your neck out to discover things that will not only push the technology ahead, but will propel you into one of the leaders of this science?"

"Well, sure," Keaton stammered.

"You know this time viewing process is commanding more and more of our limited resources. It has captivated the public, and you know what they say? Capture the people's minds and imagination and you'll own the world. You want to own the world, Andy?"

"Well, I'd like to do something that would help save it. If I could."

"You most definitely can!" Raikhel edged closer, whispering. "What I want you to do, Andy, is this. When our jumper is in the midst of action, you will over-power the jump according to these pre-set designates." He fit a small disk into an open slot and the settings on Keaton's console immediately reset.

"But, we could hurt him by doing that!" Keaton exclaimed, looking at the figures.

"Nonsense. His suit will protect him from any additional energy surge."

"But won't Dr. Ramsland object?"

"Elizabeth has asked me to keep a close eye on Mr. Crandall. She'll think we're compensating for some error he's made, so she won't interfere."

"But when I—if I, overpower the jump, it will destabilize the Beta Light strata," Keaton said, squirming in his seat. "Won't that automatically terminate the jump?"

"That," Raikhel said seriously. "Is what I intend to find out. You understand about the anomaly, don't you Mr. Keaton?"

"Yes, of course. Certain jumps in the past have triggered a massive power surge that forces us to retrieve the jumper immediately. The energy demands to keep him in that Beta Light strata simply cannot be sustained."

"Correct. And while all this is happening, before the jumper is returned to the Transmission Center, he experiences a disorientation that makes him believe that he is *actually interacting* with the holographic images around him. Since the power surge blocks out any further return to the Beta Light strata, it can never be visited again—and we can never determine the truth of what happened. But I believe there is much more to this phenomenon than has been explained so far."

"These numbers you want me to push. They'll force an anomaly to open, won't they?"

"You are as perceptive as your reputation, Mr. Keaton," Raikhel flattered. "Yes. I intend to see if I can create an anomaly, and by modulating the energy flow once it is achieved, sustain it. We will then see where that anomaly will take us."

"An interactive breach in time?" Keaton thought aloud. "I've heard the theory, but... that's not possible."

"Perhaps," Raikhel smiled. "But if there was the slightest chance that we could go back in time—really go back and set the world right, would you take that chance?"

"Does Dr. Ramsland understand what you plan to do?"

"Elizabeth is a politician. A very bad one. No, she would not approve of my little experiment, so I haven't troubled her with my decision. But you, Andy, you can appreciate the magnitude of what I offer. For humanity, and for us, both. I cannot do this without your assistance. Will you join me, Andy, and forever change the world in which we live?"

"Yes," Keaton said with conviction.

"Good man!" Raikhel gushed, slapping the young man's shoulder. "Tonight, we make history!"

Raikhel strode away from the console as the remaining technicians filed out of the complex, leaving only him, Ramsland, Johnny Crandall, and Andy Keaton alone in the control room. As the dynamos began to whine, Keaton watched his own hand on the power bar shake uncontrollably. He felt as if he'd been charged with energy himself.

* * *

Sammy Fratianno and two other *made men,* Duke Ansaratti and Mickey Marinusco, had just ordered their food when a young, well-dressed man entered the restaurant. The man looked at the few scatted tables and booths filled with customers and went right to where Fratianno's was sitting. Duke made a move for his handgun, but Fratianno stopped him.

"I know this kid," Fratianno said. Smiling toward the young man he spoke cheerfully. "Geno! How's your father?"

"Hello, Mr. Fratianno," Geno replied with a smile. "Papa's fine, thanks."

"You wanna eat? Pull up a chair!" Fratianno gestured to the empty chair at his table.

"No, thanks. I already ate," he said, unbuttoning his coat. "I gotta deliver you something from Mr. Capone. Okay?"

"Sure kid," Fratianno looked around the table and winked good naturedly. "What's Big Al want me to have? Money, I hope!"

"Naw, sorry," Geno said softly. Withdrawing a heavy .45 automatic pistol, he took aim and fired a shot into Fratianno's chest. The large man's body bucked under the heavy caliber bullet, but he didn't fall, watching in shocked amazement as Geno fired again, this time into the forehead of Duke Ansaratti—emptying his braincase against the restaurant wall.

Screaming and chaos erupted in the restaurant as customers started toward the door but were stopped by three burly men with Thompson sub-machine guns. Mickey Maranusco had just withdrawn his nickel-plated .45 revolver when the machine-guns sprayed the area. Geno stood just outside of the field of fire and watched the slugs eat the tables and chairs like a buzz saw. Blood and flesh leapt from Mickey's body as it was propelled backward away from the table. Fratianno was almost cut in two by the vicious fire that slammed him into the wall, still sitting in his chair.

The machine gunner on the right, Salvatore Valentino, saw the strange flicker of light first. Seemingly out of nowhere a ghostly form began to take shape, congealing into arms and legs as it appeared out of a billowing cloud, crackling energy and throwing off daggers of flame from a bright red suit. The gunfire abruptly stopped when Johnny Crandall, confused and disoriented, popped into view, as solid and real as the people around him.

"What the hell?" Sal shouted, depressing the trigger and emptying what was left of his 50 round drum clip into the red suited man. Crandall jerked about, more sparks flying as the others also emptied their pieces into the strangely-dressed figure. The firing stopped, and he fell with a clank while the four gangsters approached the mortally wounded man now leaking blood that mingled with the other slain mobsters.

"Looks like Rocket Man or something," Sal whispered in awe.

"Where the hell he come from?" another added.

"Get the hell outta here," Geno yelled, waving his pistol toward the door. "We did what we came here for!"

"Yeah," Sal said as the others headed for the exit. "Wait a minute."

He stooped to examine the blinking jump pack strapped to the dead man's chest. Withdrawing a folding knife he began cutting the straps that held the pack to his suit.

* * *

Elizabeth Ramsland screamed at the monitor as Tobias Raikhel watched, mouth open, in stunned silence. "What—how?" she stammered. "This can't be happening! Those are only images! They're not real!"

"Who is that talking?" Sal spun around, facing a hazy white mist that seemed to drift through the restaurant.

"We've done it," Raikhel could barely speak the words. "We've opened a bridge to the still living past."

"Oh, my God!" Ramsland gasped when the view screen showed four uniformed officers entering the restaurant with their pistols drawn. Sal swung his machine gun around as the four opened fire directly at him.

Shots flew wildly around the restaurant, a few zipping through the open vortex and shattering an overhead monitor directly behind Ramsland's head. An explosion of electrical sparks cascaded onto the floor like the dying embers of a fireworks display, sending everyone ducking for cover.

"Shut the power down," Ramsland screamed.

More fire erupted from the center of the ball-shaped room, seeming to appear out of nowhere. Raikhel drew his finger across his throat in

205

a quick motion, signaling Keaton to terminate the jump, but before he could another spray of gunfire ricocheted off the main control console and cut Elizabeth Ramsland down. She gasped in startled disbelief, clutching her throat and collapsing onto the floor. Keaton rushed to help the stricken woman only to be felled by another staccato burst of fire that sent Raikhel diving to the floor again.

As sounds of the fierce battle raged through the room, Raikhel crawled on his stomach over to the control console. Another bullet barely missed his head when it slammed into the equipment bay behind him. Hiding behind the console he waited until the sound of gun play had stopped, then reached up to throw the switch and close the vortex.

The severed jump pack immediately returned, and history instantly changed as the room returned to quiet. Shakily, Raikhel stood to survey the damage to the Transmission Center, gasping in shock when he spotted the two lifeless figures lying on the floor.

"W-what happened?" he bent to check the pulse of Ramsland and Keaton. Their blood splattered bodies were testament enough to the fatal injuries each one suffered, and he rose to his feet shaking uncontrollably. Spotting the bullet-dented jump pack on the long narrow platform leading to the core of the time viewing machine, he raced over and picked it up. Turning it over in his hands, he stared at the blinking black box in puzzled confusion. "Where's our jumper? Who's...our jumper? I don't remember us sending anyone. What's going on here?" Quickly accessing the jump data file from a still functioning console he stared at the readout in wide-eyed confusion. "There's no record of any jumper? We sent a jump pack back—but there is no jumper, that doesn't make sense. Wait, these straps have been cut. And its casing is damaged. Maybe there's something in the jump pack that will explain this."

Raikhel hooked the box up to a telemetry port and downloaded the information. On a nearby screen the image of a police shoot out could clearly be seen. The firing stopped and the police stood over the dead bodies of several gangsters—and a curious looking man in a bright red suit with a clear glass helmet over his head.

"What is this?" Corporal Terrence O'Rourk said with a puzzled frown, bending over Johnny Crandall's body.

"Some guy in a home made space suit?" Sergeant Peter King shook his head. "What is he, nuts walking around in this thing?"

"How we gonna explain this, Sarge?" O'Rourk asked. "The police killing some retard in a mob shoot-out?"

"We didn't kill no one, O'Rourk. This guy was fried by Capone's men. Take his body to the morgue—and be sure that ballistics says so. If no one claims the body in twenty-four hours, write him up for a pauper's burial. The guy's probably demented and living in the skids, he's not gonna be missed. Just the same, keep this quiet. I don't want any trouble with the captain over this."

"What's that box there?" O'Rourk said, noticing the jump pack lying next to Sal's lifeless body. He started to reach for it but the picture began to fade. The last thing Raikhel saw was the startled look on the policeman's face as the vortex closed and the jump pack returned to the future.

"There's no record of any jumper," Raikhel repeated. "But *someone* was there. Oh my God," he said as the realization struck him. "I did it! It worked! We opened an interactive breach in time! When we closed the vortex, history instantly changed. We won't have any memory of the things affected by it. There's no jumper because he doesn't exist! He died before he was born! That's why there's no memory of him."

"Are you all right?" a breathless voice called as the first emergency response worker rushed into the room. "Alarm bells are going off all over the place! What happened?" Seeing Ramsland and Keaton lying on the floor in a spreading pool of blood the man gasped audibly and looked as if he was about to faint.

"There's been an accident," Raikhel said, tapping a switch on the jump pack and erasing the images from its memory.

"Get a doctor here stat," the man called to a woman staring at the bodies in shock. "Are you all right, sir?"

"Yes, yes I'm fine," Raikhel answered. "Everything is perfectly fine."

Sitting in a chair amid the chaos of the still sparking monitors and smoking equipment, Raikel watched the unfolding action with a strange, serene look on his face.

"I think he's in shock," one of the emergency workers said to the other, glancing in his direction.

"Get him to a doctor, and call Mr. Greene. He's gonna want to see what's happened to his control room."

Friday, June 17, 2417 AD
11:00 HOURS

"I have the report for you here, Mr. Greene," Sandra Baker, a pretty young secretary said as she handed the square yellow disk to the T.I.M.E. Launch Director who slipped it into a reader.

Paul Thorndyke and Klief Steffeson, the late Henry Sherwood's chief engineer and now interim-head of P.A.S.T., sat around the oval shaped table with Jerry Greene, serving as a three member a board of inquiry into the explosion and deaths at the Transmission Center two weeks earlier. Even though Scott Hollock had fully recovered from his injuries, Thorndyke found himself representing the Director of B.E.T.A. at an increasing number of official occasions while Hollock transitioned out of his day-to-day responsibilities. The gossip and jealous speculation that followed his meteoric rise on Hollock's personal staff had long since subsided and, although many years the junior of the people he interacted with, he was treated with great admiration and respect. Whatever the reason Hollock had for picking him out of virtual obscurity to act as his de facto second in command, Thorndyke, with his fine mind and quick wit, had more than proven his worth, validating the decision.

"Autopsies confirm that Elizabeth Ramsland and Andrew Keaton were killed by projectile-firing devices from the early twentieth century," Greene read from his screen. "The chief suspect in these deaths was Tobias Raikhel, who was the third member of the jump support team and assistant to Dr. Ramsland. However, after exhaustive review, there is no evidence to connect Dr. Raikhel to the discharge of any twentieth century weapon. He was subjected to a rigorous series of forensic tests, and there was no residue of gunpowder on his skin or other DNA evidence linking him to the incident."

"An accomplice, perhaps?" Thorndyke speculated.

"The Transmission Center was sealed during the jump, and security protocol recorded no other entry or exit at the time in question. The entire complex was searched for a weapon or additional person who could have fired the shots. Nothing, and no one, was found.

Unfortunately, all recordings from the jump and the flight room video were erased by malfunctioning equipment from one of the projectile hits. An energy spike blotted out all Beta Light images in that strata, so we may never know the truth of what happened. The police have closed the investigation."

"What was Raikhel's explanation for what happened?" Thorndyke asked.

"He say Dr. Ramsland was conducting an unauthorized experiment, attempting to open an interactive breach in time," Greene read from another section of the report. "He says that a jump pack was used to test the theory, and a time portal to 1927 was temporarily opened. Gunfire from a mob assassination they were viewing killed Ramsland and the other technician working on the jump."

"An interactive breach in time?" Steffeson repeated incredulously.

"Raikhel has petitioned the management committee overseeing the time viewing process for permission to replicate Ramsland's experiment, under controlled conditions."

"He wants to try this again?" Thorndyke blinked. "How do we know it won't damage The Machine?"

"The jump was overpowered by one hundred and twenty percent," Greene replied. "Power levels were dangerously high, but Klief's team went over it with a fine toothed comb, isn't that right Klief? There wasn't any internal damage to The Machine's circuitry."

"All systems check out," Steffeson confirmed.

"So, as long as there's no intrinsic danger to the time viewing mechanism, we have the option to proceed if we want. I'm just putting that option on the table."

"Are you saying you're in favor of Raikhel's request?" Thorndyke asked Greene.

"We know from the power records the basic outline of what happened, and we can replicate it again if we want. However, whatever occurred was not completely stable, so we'd need to fine tune the energy matrix to keep the vortex from fluctuating once a bridge to the past is open. That's the real challenge."

"Tobias Raikhel hasn't been entirely forthcoming with this commission," Steffeson grunted. "I move we table his request. I don't know what his true motives are, but I don't accept the premise that he just wants to investigate a new scientific phenomenon."

"Even if he hasn't been completely honest with us Klief, you have to admit *something* did happen in that room," Greene said. "Something quite extraordinary. It's a simple enough matter to try it again with adequate protections for those conducting the jump."

"Time travel?" Steffeson chuckled. "Really? If Henry was still alive, you'd know what he'd say—most of it unprintable."

"Looks like you're the deciding vote, Paul," Greene turned to his friend. All eyes focused on Thorndyke, who set his jaw and spoke softly.

"I don't know what really happened in that room either," Thorndyke said. "We may never know. The only thing we *do* know for certain is that two people died. Even if Tobias Raikhel is correct and an interactive breach in time was opened, what right do we have to play God and attempt to re-write human history? We've sought too many of our answers in the past. It's time now to turn our efforts forward and carve out a better future from what we have, rather than keep looking backwards. Use the Machine as it was intended, as a research tool and instrument of knowledge, not as a substitute for living with the consequences of our own actions."

"Well, that settles the matter," Greene said without rancor. "The request is denied."

"What about Raikhel?" Steffeson asked.

"From what I've seen of his record," Thorndyke answered, "Dr. Raikhel is a brilliant man and can continue to make his contribution to society. But I don't think he should ever be permitted unsupervised access to the Transmission Center again. I believe he was more directly involved in the events of June 2nd than he has admitted."

"I concur," Steffeson said.

"Well," Greene exhaled, looking around the room. "I think we're all in agreement. Miss Baker, finalize the minutes and distribute the report. This board of inquiry is officially closed."

19:29 HOURS

In another part of The District, Tobias Raikhel sat in a small, secluded room, receiving the news that his request was denied and his privileges at the Transmission Center were permanently curtailed.

There would be no more unfettered access to the one device that would prove his theory beyond all doubt and reveal to the world the undisputed truth of his genius.

"So Thorndyke thinks he can keep me from The Machine," he said to himself. "I proved that the past can be entered and changed—and the future with it. This is the greatest discovery of all mankind, and no one will keep me from the recognition I deserve. It was a mistake to give Ramsland any credit for my discovery. I should have kept it for myself. Well, that's a mistake I won't repeat again—ever. The world will know about Tobias Raikhel, and what he can do."

Lights dimmed in the already darkened room as Tobias Raikhel began to plan his next date with destiny.

* * *